R4

The Love Spoon

The Love Spoon.

Pamela Kavanagh

ROBERT HALE · LONDON

Typeset in 11/16 pt Galliard
Printed and bound in Great Britain by
Biddles Limited, King's Lynn, Norfolk

One

∽

Mary Sutton came out of the house into the cobbled yard and paused a moment, looking about her. It was early March, mild for the time of year, and already the buds were fat on the chestnut trees that marked the entrance to the premises. A sign with TOBIAS SUTTON – COACH-MAKER emblazoned across it in bold black letters swung gently in the breeze.

Mary's heart swelled with pride as it did every time she saw it. All of her fourteen years had echoed to the hammer and clatter of the men in the workshop as they fashioned the carts and carriages of her father's trade. Come Easter when she left school he had promised she could help with the books, recording the sales and accounts in the big old ledgers kept for that purpose. She had a good head for figures and a neat hand at penning – otherwise she would never have been allowed near.

'Mary? Come on, maid. Stop day-dreaming and give us a hand with this trap, will you?' came her father's blustery voice from the barn where a brand-new governess cart, yet unvarnished, stood waiting to be hitched to the pony.

About to obey, her attention was caught by a figure approaching up the road. She screwed her eyes, trying to make out who he was. Aston Cross was a place where everyone knew everybody and a stranger was as rare as a swallow in winter.

And this was a stranger.

He came trudging along, a tall figure, dark-haired and eyed, bearded, youngish ... clearly footsore. Even at a distance something about him suggested he had been living rough. Closer, the fact was all too obvious. His clothes were travel-stained and crumpled, his boots thick with mud from the unmade roads. Over his shoulder he carried his belongings done up in a large bundle.

Reaching the gates he glanced briefly at the sign, lowered the bundle thankfully to the ground and directed Mary a brief smile. 'Good-day, miss. Is the boss about?'

His voice was not local. Everyone Mary knew spoke either with the slow sweet drawl of the Shropshire Marches or the lilt of the Welsh valleys. This man's speech was broader, more resonant. Curious, she stared up into his ruggedly handsome face, noting the firm mouth and steady brown gaze. He in turn saw a small figure, slightly plump, with glossy golden-brown hair falling in ringlets about a rosy face and blue eyes that had deepened visibly with interest.

'Yes,' she replied. 'Tobias Sutton is my father. Are you looking for work?'

'Depends.' He picked up the bundle. 'If you wouldn't mind showing the way?'

Clearly he was not prepared to take her into his confidence. Undaunted, Mary led him across the yard, her dove-grey skirts and starched white petticoats swishing with every step. Reaching the barn, she called to Tobias. 'Father. This ... gentleman wants to speak with you.'

He emerged from the depths of the building, a big man, broad-shouldered, his frowst of greying hair and huge bushy beard with side whiskers framing a strong face. 'Tobias Sutton?' The stranger wasted no time. 'Kester Hayes from Blackwood in the Midlands. I'm looking for work. Someone directed me here.'

'Oh aye?' Tobias regarded the man through shrewd hazel eyes. He always prided himself on being able to sum up a fellow's character at first glance and he did so now. A man with a past, he thought. Well, that was nothing new. Honest seeming. And the direct brown gaze was reassuring. 'What's your trade?'

'Smelter,' Kester said. 'Or was. Had a job in the ironworks, but I'm not a townsman by birth. Something more rural would suit better. I can do smithying – wrought-iron work, repairs ... shoe a horse if I'm pushed. And I've some experience in carpentry. Bit of a Jack-of-all-trades.'

'I see.' Tobias Sutton sucked in his cheeks reflectively. 'All I can offer at present is sweeper-up. 'Tain't much of a position for a skilled man but if you want it, it's yours.'

There was the briefest hesitation, then, 'Fine, I'll take it,' Kester said.

They shook hands on the deal. A firm handshake, Tobias noted. 'Show your worth, and we can maybe upgrade you to the bench,' he heard himself say. 'You got any place to stop?'

'Not yet.'

'We don't generally put up men on the premises, the wife's got enough on with the house and children. But I daresay there'll be no objection if you bed down in the hayloft for now. Just till you get sorted with lodgings. Meals taken out of your wages of course.'

'Fine. Thanks.'

Mary, who had stood taking in the proceedings, gave a little cough. Tobias smiled fondly at his daughter. 'This is our Mary,' he said to his new employee. 'My right-hand man, is Mary. If you want to know anything about the trade, this is the one to ask!'

She giggled, glinting an impish glance. 'Right-hand *woman*, you mean, Father! Will I fetch the pony now?'

'Aye, do that, maid. You can take the trap out on its trial run if you like. Just through the village, mind. Don't want it getting too muddied up afore the varnish goes on. Right then, young fellow, best introduce you to the men. Like as not they'll show you the ropes.'

Musingly Mary watched them go. Taking on an extra man when they were already fully staffed was something out of the ordinary for the yard. Her father must have been smitten by the stranger. She could understand it; despite the down-trodden appearance and a certain unhappiness in the droop of his shoulders and tight set of the mouth, there was something wholly likeable and trustworthy about Kester Hayes.

She left the barn and headed for the deep-littered yard where the horses spent their winter days. Three of them browsed there, nosing the hay she had put for them earlier. Her father's bay cob raised his head and whinnied a greeting. The chestnut gelding used in the bigger vehicles carried on with the important business of eating. Brownie, the bay trap pony, knew instinctively that his services were required and laid back his ears wickedly and swung his quarters.

'Stop that, Brownie.' Mary cornered him neatly, slipped the halter over his head and led him to the barn. Harnessed up, she backed him between the shafts of the governess cart, slid the tugs into place, fixed the traces and looped the reins over the rein guard. 'Stand!' she bid the pony, and going to the rear of the trap she opened the small door and clambered in. Taking up the reins, she clicked her tongue and sent the pony forward, the iron-rimmed wheels rumbling noisily over the uneven cobblestones of the yard. Soon they were trotting briskly along the road, the March breeze lifting the pony's mane and setting Mary's bright curls dancing.

In the workshop Kester was coming to terms with his new surroundings. The building was large and airy, lit all the way round with square windows. Sawdust and shavings lay thickly underfoot and the air was redolent of wood, varnish and tar.

Six men were employed at Sutton's yard. At the far end of the workshop, ankle deep in litter, Dan Turvey and his son Alfred were planing a set of shafts. Dan Turvey ran a roughened palm lovingly along the silken white surface of the length of wood between the cramps. 'Best ash, this,' he said to Alfred. 'Plenty of whip in it.'

Josh Millet was the wheelwright. He sat absorbed at his bench beneath a window, brows drawn together in concentration as he shaved the felloes or segments for the wheel rim with a newly-sharpened adze. Then there were brothers Chas and Wallace Pilkington, body-makers, who could turn out anything from a functional hay-wain to the smartest high-wheeled gig, and had never yet been known to use a measure for the task.

'Know your wood, do you?' Wallace enquired bluffly.

Kester indicated the half-finished body of a two-wheeled butcher's cart, set up on trestles in the middle of the floor. 'Decent bit of oak there.'

'Aye, we generally use oak for the framework of the body,' the craftsman said. 'Elm for the side panels and floor. Ash is a springy wood. We use it for the out-rails because they have to take a lot of strain. Same for the shafts. Mester Tobias generally buys his timber raw, you can sell the bark for tanning that way. We got a fair few butts of oak and elm ready for the sawpit. The ash the mester gets ready seasoned from the woodyard at Much Wenlock. Then he stores it a while longer. You can't be too careful with wood. Use it green, and you're in trouble.'

'Who does the iron-work?' Kester wanted to know.

'Smith from Aston Cross,' Wallace Pilkington said. 'Interested in smithying, are you?'

'It was my previous trade. Well, in part. Did a stint with a cabinet maker's before that.'

'Oh aye?' Wallace grinned, showing more gaps than teeth. 'Small wonder you know your wood, man!'

Roland Marks, a long streak of a man with a face as brown and wrinkled as old leather, was responsible for the carriage painting and chamfering. A boy, known to all as Chips, ran errands and did the odd-jobs about the yard and house.

Kester was handed a broom. 'Better get sweeping.'

At midday work stopped for half an hour. The men ate their noonpiece – bread, cheese and an onion, swilled down with cold tea. Kester had no food with him. He was gratefully surprised when Mary slipped him a meat pasty and a half-loaf of bread.

'Guessed you might be hungry. I know I would be, having walked half the night, and then had to put in a day's work as well!'

It was the best meal that had passed his lips for many a long day, and Kester savoured every delicious mouthful right down to the final crumb.

'Mother! Father! Everybody!' Mary cried, her cheeks flushed with excitement. 'I've been chosen for May Queen! I'm to wear a white gown with frills. And either a blue sash or pink.'

'Blue to match your eyes,' her brother Ned established. At fifteen Ned was sturdy and blunt-featured, a younger version of his sire. Alice, thirteen, had a narrow face and a prim nature. Ten-year-old Violet was as timid as her name implied, the home-bird of the family. Another boy born between the two girls had died in infancy.

'Sixteen, May Queen,' chimed Tobias, laughing mightily at his own clumsy attempt at verse. Proudly he ruffled Mary's curls. 'We'll have to find Your Majesty a decent carriage. We can't have the coach-maker's lass riding on a farm float. May Queen, our Mary! Well I never!'

'Well done, child,' Mary's mother Lilian said evenly. 'Just don't let it go to your head.'

'May Queen! She's talked herself into it,' Alice put in with a sniff. 'I heard you at chapel, our Mary. Sucking up to the folk on the village committee.'

'Didn't then,' Mary said lightly.

'Of course Mary didn't.' Violet gave her shy smile. 'I'm glad for you, Mary. Will I help make your gown?'

Violet was a promising needlewoman and since sewing was not Mary's strong point she jumped at the offer. 'Oh, would you, Violet? Three weeks to go. We must get the stuff and make a start. Alice can stitch the petticoats. Three, with lace trimming I think.'

'Fine feathers!' Alice retorted. 'You can make your own dress, Mary Hoity Toity Sutton! *I've* got better use for my time.'

'Such as?' Mary rounded impatiently on her sister. 'Who was it helped stitch your boring old Sunday School skirt when you started helping with the little ones? Me, in case you'd forgotten. So you can return the favour. You can!'

'Girls, girls!' their mother said. She smoothed her apron over her dark-grey skirts and turned her pale, homely face admonishingly on Mary. 'Mary, you forget yourself. Don't ever let me hear you speaking like that again. Go and take Kester his rations. He's working on the cottage.'

Her tone and steely gaze brooked no argument. Mary clamped her lips on the retort she was about to make and reached obediently for the basket of food on the kitchen table. 'Very well Mother.'

'Alice, you can make a start on the potatoes for supper. Violet dear, would you mind seeing to the fowl and collecting the eggs. It's usually done by now, but I don't seem to have had a minute today.'

'Oh but—' Violet began in panicked protest.

'I'll do it, Mother,' Ned offered good-naturedly. 'You know Violet, not fond of hens. Come on, Vi. You can bring in the cows, make a start on the milking....'

Lilian sighed. Beamsters was a big house and the demands of her family were many. She took pride in keeping the place spotless and was renowned for her batches of crusty loaves and crisp golden pies, savoury and sweet. Happily, as the girls grew older, they were taking over many of the chores. The younger ones scrubbed the kitchen and dairy floors and shook out the many rugs. Lilian saw to the dusting and polishing of her precious furniture and beeswaxing the wooden floors to a lethal finish. She burned herbs in the rooms to sweeten the air and made constant war with spiders and invading mice.

Every Thursday she entertained members of the Fellowship from chapel. Her best Minton willow pattern was brought out for these occasions, and the set of silver cutlery which had been a wedding gift.

Ned also was proving a willing hand, especially with the animals. They had two house cows and a mixed flock of hens. In the orchard Tobias kept four skeps of bees. Long before the coach-yard was established, bees were kept at Beamsters. It was rumoured that this was how the old house was named – Bee Masters. To be honest Lilian was wary of the bees. In summer she lived in fear of a swarm, and was always on the lookout for the buzzing black cloud swirling over the orchard trees.

Mary was her other bane. Never an easy child with her quixotic moods and defiant stare, she had, Lilian admitted, a lot of charm as well. She liked to sing and dance and was never happier than when playing to an audience. Intelligent, with the promise of beauty later, Lilian was hard put to keep their eldest daughter under control.

'You shouldn't encourage her, Tobias,' she said now, the children having all gone their various ways. 'You always have given in to her and it does no good. She can twist you round her little finger.'

'Ah, leave it be, Lilian love,' Tobias replied easily. Mary was his favourite. They all knew it, though he did his level best to conceal the fact. 'A bit of high spirits in a maid does no harm. A grand sight she'll be as May Queen. A sight for sore eyes!'

Mary was heading along the track through greening hazel copses, the basket over her arm. Trust Mother to put a damper on her good news, she grumbled to herself. It was always the same, nothing else mattered but the Fellowship. She was bored with chapel, three times every Sunday and Sunday School as well! She was bored with helping around the house, all that washing and cleaning. Scrub scrub scrub! If it wasn't for the business and helping Father with the office side, she would scream with the monotony of it all.

And even here she was only unpaid help, a small voice prompted, adding salt to a recently acquired wound. When she had suggested that Tobias put her name on the books and paid her a wage – anything, however moderate – he had just laughed and said all in good time. Mary bristled at the memory. Given the chance she could run the yard. She could!

At least Kester never treated her like a child. She wouldn't mention the May Queen, keep it as a surprise. His face rose in her mind and his quiet strength settled around her like balm. Impulsively she smiled and quickened her step.

In the two years since Kester had been with the yard he had certainly proved his worth, and the cottage in the wood was how Tobias showed his appreciation. More and more the carriage-maker found himself relying upon the talented stranger from beyond the Marches. The men liked him. It was Kester who was elected spokesman in the event of any minor disagreement. Also his experiences of life – those he cared to talk about – made him a sparky drinking companion in the taproom of the *Plough*.

As she neared the cottage Mary could hear the sound of

hammering and Kester's clear tenor voice, singing as he worked. Not a hymn, which were the only songs her strict Methodist upbringing permitted her to know, but a folk song, sweet and musical.

> *Oh the summer time is come,*
> *And the leaves are sweetly blooming,*
> *And the wild mountain thyme,*
> *Grows around the blooming heather,*
> *Will you go, lassie, go …*

She came to the cottage and paused at the gate. It was a one-up one-down place, nestling in the trees, and in a sorry state of disrepair when Kester had first claimed it earlier in the year. Already he had made a vegetable patch and cleared the small orchard of nettle and dock. The stone pigsty at the bottom of the garden held a half-grown Blackspot gilt and several White Leghorn chickens pecked busily under the apple trees. Occupied with the house, Kester as yet had no plans for the patch of weedy land that went with the cottage. He had removed the sagging thatch of the roof and was now balanced on a ladder, replacing the rotted rafters. Abruptly his singing stopped.

'Mary! How long have you been there?'

'Wouldn't you like to know?' she said, eyes twinkling, her earlier grievances now shelved. She held up the basket. 'Mother sent this. Butter from the dairy, a loaf of new bread and some bacon. Honey as well. She spoils you, Kester.'

He came clambering down the ladder. He looked a different man from when he had first arrived. Fitter, more content. His face was still lean but his colour was healthy and his dark hair and beard were neatly trimmed. He took the basket from her.

'Two pots of honey?'

'One's for Widow Goodyear. I'm calling on the way back.'

Widow Goodyear was once the village midwife, amongst other skills. Now retired, she still managed, with the help of a lad, the Goodyear farmstead close to the river.

Mary said, 'Mother never fusses over the other staff. You're a favourite with her.'

'Happen Lilian takes pity on waifs and strays.'

Mary cocked her head. 'Is that how you consider yourself, a waif and stray? Goodness! Where *did* you live before, Kester?'

'Told you. The Midlands. Place called Blackwood.'

'I meant the house you lived in. Haven't you any family? Brothers or sisters. Everyone has family.'

'Oh, do they now? You're mighty well informed for a young miss.'

Mary heaved a sigh. Kester never would be drawn into telling her about his past. She switched her attention to the cottage. 'It's coming on a treat.'

'Only because the gaffer sent this load of roofing timber. I'd never have been able to afford it yet otherwise. He said it was going begging.'

'True. Those oak trusses have been in the store-house for years, Father was probably glad to be rid. Did you know he's ordered a wagon-load of reeds? I heard him telling Mother that as he's getting the cottage fixed up for free, he may as good provide the materials. D'you know how to thatch, Kester?'

'Just the plain thatching, nothing fancy.'

'Is there anything you don't know?'

'Plenty, I dare say.'

'That song you were singing. It was lovely. Will you teach it me? Oh please do, Kester.'

He looked into her eyes and saw their colour deepen with longing. 'Wild Mountain Thyme?' he said. 'Don't see why not. It's a bonnie song. You coming in? Warm evening, best put this butter away first in the well-hatch before it runs away … and I've something to show you.'

Indoors too showed evidence of renovation. When scraping the walls a whole section of the plaster had fallen out. Kester had renewed the lot while he was about it and the smooth new surface gleamed dully.

'I'm leaving the white-washing for another time. Best get on with the roof while the weather holds,' he said.

Mary looked up through the rafters into the evening sky, where a flight of ducks were winging homewards. 'D'you lie here and look at the stars?' she said. 'Do you stare at the moon?'

'No, generally I sleep,' Kester replied with dry humour. He went to the rough-hewn table he had knocked together from odd bits of timber and from a drawer took out a small object. 'Look what I found hidden in the wall. Pretty thing, eh?'

Mary took it wonderingly. 'Why, it's a spoon.'

He laughed. 'So it is! Not a kitchen spoon. More decorative, an ornament perhaps. Look at the handle. Grand bit of carving. Someone sat here on winter nights and worked at it. Must be quite old. Haven't a clue why it was stashed away in the wall.'

She fingered the carved handle with its two hearts and vines entwined. Some long-ago message spoke to her. 'Oh, may I have it, Kester,' she whispered. 'Please?'

''Course you can. It's yours anyway – or your father's. This is his cottage.'

'Thank you.' Dimpling, she put the spoon in the basket and sat down on the single stool. 'Now teach me the song.'

The April day was thickening to dusk when she left. She walked swiftly, singing the song to herself, committing the words to memory. Poignant words, evocative, stirring feelings in her she could not begin to understand.

I will build my love a bower
By yon pure crystal fountain.
And round it I will bind
All the flowers of the mountain
Will you go, lassie, go.

Suddenly she remembered the extra pot of honey. It was more than her life was worth to return home without having delivered it! Instead of taking the road to Beamsters, Mary climbed a stile, sped across a meadow damp with dew and arrived breathless at the door of the farmstead.

Her knock was answered by a spare, white-haired, fresh-faced woman in a dark gown and working hessian apron. Behind her a pile of feathers and row of dressed birds bore witness to the preparation for tomorrow's market. 'Why Mary. There's lovely to see you, *cariad*.' Widow Goodyear accepted the gift of honey with a smile and ushered Mary into the kitchen. 'Want a cup of tea? Better make it quick. It's coming dusk, your mam will be getting anxious.'

The Welshwoman moved briskly, her fingers deft with teapot and cups. Mary sat down at the table and took the carved wooden spoon out of her basket. 'What's this then?' the widow said, bringing the tea to the table.

'It's a sort of spoon … I think.'

It was dim in the room and she drew the candle closer to inspect the item. 'Why, it's a lovespoon. We had a collection of these back home when I was a girl. Lovely, they were.'

She paused, her face suddenly remote in the flickering light. Gossip had it that she was fey and could see into the future. Mary knew her purely as a true confidante and a gifted teller of stories.

'But what is it?' Mary asked impatiently. 'What does the lovespoon stand for?'

'It's a sort of promise. Where I come from in the valleys, when a boy likes a girl well enough to want to wed her, he takes a piece of wood – cherry or yew – and carves his hopes into it, see. This one has two hearts bound together with vine. A vine stands for the future. For children and the continuation of life.'

'And the hearts?'

'What do you think? For love, of course.'

Mary's heart skipped a beat. And Kester gave the spoon to *her*. He'd said he didn't know its meaning, but then you never quite knew whether Kester was teasing or not.

Widow Goodyear was studying the spoon, twisting it this way and that. 'Some have names carved on to them and the date of a marriage. Not this one. There are many different symbols. A sailor might carve an anchor or rope and cable. A farmer a sheaf of corn. A keyhole stands for home and a cross, faith.'

Mary pulled a comical face. 'Mother would go for that. On second thoughts perhaps not. I don't think she'd hold with lovespoons.'

The Welsh woman smiled. 'Then you'd best keep it hidden, *cariad*. Clean it up a bit first. Lucky girl, to be given a lovespoon – I wonder who it was?'

'That'd be telling!' Mary said mischievously. She dropped a kiss on the woman's soft cheek and said she must go. 'I'll come again soon. Do you like shortbread? Mother made a batch just today. I'll bring some.'

Reaching home, light from the porch lantern spilled out over the yard and the air flickered with bats' wings. Before going indoors Mary tossed some hay to the horses and watered them. She fastened the door to the pigsty, which Violet had omitted to do, and checked that the hen-cote was secure against marauding foxes.

'There you are,' said her mother when she finally stepped indoors. 'Supper's ready. Look at your hands. Go and wash them. What have you been doing all this while?'

'Seeing to the animals,' Mary replied glibly. Well, it was true …

in part. Then guilt smote her and she added, 'I nearly forgot Widow Goodyear, then stayed longer than I intended. She was glad of the honey. I promised her some shortbread. Don't mind taking it if you like. Save you the bother. I know you don't like walking across the fields.'

'Only when the path is muddy. But it's thoughtful of you, thank you Mary. Was Kester pleased with what you took?'

'Very. He said thank you. He's almost done the rafters. Just the tarring to do, then it's ready for thatching.'

Her sisters and brother were already seated at the table. Their faces glowed healthily in the light of the lamp and flare of the fire. 'Where's Father?'

'Locking up the workshop. Roland stayed late to finish varnishing the governess trap,' Lilian replied. She looked up from dishing out mutton broth thick with vegetables and herbs. 'Mary – now where are you going?'

'To get a handkerchief. Won't be long.' Mary slipped up the uncarpeted back-stair. In her room she took the lovespoon from her pocket and hid it under the pillow. Already dreams were weaving a magical web about her. She loved him, and Kester loved her, she knew it. In her mind's eye she saw them both at the altar, he in dark worsted, herself a vision in bridal white. Her sisters as bridesmaids ... At this point the dream fractured. Not by any stretch of the imagination could she picture Alice in shell pink or cornflour blue. Yellow would highlight her sallow complexion, mauve bleach it. Mary skipped the wedding and went on to plan the home she and Kester would make, together.

'Here she comes! Here's our Mary! Don't she look a picture?'

Tobias clapped his big beefy hands together and beamed broadly as the procession rolled by. Headed by the May Queen in her froth of white, a veil over her gleaming curls and posy of honeysuckle and larkspur in hand, the flower-decked carriage and floats rumbled along the village street.

Like everyone, the Sutton family wore their Sunday best. Ned eased the too-tight collar from his neck and curled his toes in his best boots, which were a shade too small. Violet smiled quietly, slight and insignificant in her gown and cape of pale blue, straw bonnet over her straight mouse-brown hair. Alice wore grey. A starchy miss, Tobias thought, and felt a pang of guilt. Why was it his second daughter was so unlovable?

Lilian was her neat self, dark-grey gown immaculate, collar and cuffs a pristine white, her soft-brown hair parted in the middle and tucked demurely away under her bonnet.

Following the vehicles were the mummers and the morris dancers. Their clogs clattered over the hard surface of the road and a dog ran out barking to nip at the leader's heels. Overhead the sky was blue and the sun shone. It was a perfect day for the May Celebrations.

In the meadow earmarked for the event, stalls and booths were set up. As ever Lilian was in charge of the cake stall. She had been up since five, icing the fancies and spreading jam in the sponges. By eleven the stall was cleared of goods, leaving her free to roam the ground with her family. Ned tried a hand on the coconut-shy and failed every time. Violet spent the three shining pennies her father had slipped her on a bunch of ribbons and a silk bookmark.

Alice, to everyone's surprise, won the jackpot in the Roll-a-Penny and treated everyone to tea in the big tent with her winnings. They watched the terrier racing and marvelled at the jugglers. All around, the crowd pushed and swayed and laughter echoed on the breeze. Everyone enjoyed a day off and folk were set to make the most of it.

Soon it was time for the Queen to be crowned. A hush fell on the crowd as Mary removed her veil and the garland of lilies was placed on her head.

'My Mary!' Tobias took his kerchief from his pocket and blew his nose loudly. The toast was given and the crowd clapped and cheered, and Mary was driven round the arena in her flowery carriage, the horses prancing and tossing their long manes, beribboned tails swishing.

Presently there was a variety show of local talent. Dancing, reciting, playing an instrument. A crude stage had been erected in the shade of the trees and the audience gathered round, applauding each stumbling performer heartily. When a song was requested it was Mary who obliged. Standing straight and confident in her pretty white gown, she sang the song Kester had taught her. She sang unaccompanied, her voice rising pure and clear above the spellbound heads of the crowd.

> *If my true love he won't come,*
> *Then I'll surely find another*
> *To pluck wild mountain thyme*
> *All around the blooming heather.*
> *Will you go, lassie, go ...*

Kester was standing at the rear, half a head taller than anyone else. As she sang the final note she caught his gaze and her heart fluttered wildly.

The clapping went on and on and there wasn't a dry eye on the floor. 'Making an exhibition of herself!' Lilian tutted, then had to add, 'but she sang the song without a fault. I wonder where she learnt it?'

'Doesn't matter,' her husband said, his shining florid face wreathed in smiles. 'She's done us proud, our Mary has. Listen to that applause.' At his side young Ned joined in exuberantly, Alice with slightly less enthusiasm and Violet with eyes filled with awe at her talented sister.

Evening fell. Judd the fiddler struck up with his twinkling bow and pulled the dancers out on to the floor. For once Tobias ignored his wife's protests and led her in a jig, huffing and sweating, his face redder than ever with exertion.

Mary danced until her feet in their soft white slippers ached and throbbed. Her lips smiled, but her eyes searched the crowd for Kester. Where was he? She had seen him just before, she was sure.

All at once she spied him. 'I'm sorry, d'you mind if I sit this one out?' she asked her partner, a hefty lad who had trodden twice on her toes. Like quicksilver she was off, pushing through the crowd to where Kester stood on the edge of the gathering, drinking a tankard of small ale.

'Kester Hayes,' Mary said, waggling a finger in mock reproof. 'I've been looking for you. Don't you dance?'

She came towards him, hips swaying, her mouth curved in a smile, deep-blue eyes vivid and steady. Kester swallowed. In that moment he had a glimpse of the woman she was to become. 'No peace for the wicked,' he said, draining his tankard and putting it down. 'Seems a fellow can't even have a quiet drink! Right then, miss. You say you want to dance?'

A waltz had just struck up and sweeping her into his arms he twirled her on to the floor. They completed the dance and went into a lively reel, heel and toe, dip and twirl, after which both fled breathless from the floor.

'Wonderful!' Mary cried, eyes shining up at him. 'You dance marvellously, Kester.'

'Only with the right partner,' he parried. He took out a kerchief and mopped his brow.

'Really? Did I do all right? We don't have much opportunity to dance at Beamsters.'

'You did perfectly. And I like the frock. Bet I'm the only one to claim two dances with the May Queen. I'm honoured.'

'Oh – Kester!' She flushed in delight, and impulsively she flung her arms around his neck and kissed him on the cheek. 'There. I do love you, Kester. Do you love me?'

'Hey now!' Horrified, Kester put her firmly from him. 'Of course I don't love you. At least, not in the sense you mean. You're still a child, Mary. Behave. People are watching.'

He left her, walking away into the dusk. Mary stared after him, her face flaming, humiliation boiling up within her. By now a throng had gathered. An argument always was good entertainment, particularly when it involved the queen of the show. 'Mary!' came her father's voice from the back. 'Mary, what is it? What's happening?'

The crowd, mostly merry with drink and sunshine, started to poke fun. 'Had a tiff, young Mary?' 'Run after him, maid. Tell him you're sorry!'

Mary spun round and fled, sobbing, across the field and over the stile, ripping her flowing white skirts on a briar. The words of the song she had sung with such feeling echoed mockingly in her head. She didn't want to find another love. She wanted Kester!

'There you are, Widow Goodyear. The list of Fellowship Meetings for the next three months, and here's a punnet of gooseberries. Nice in a tart.'

Lilian put the items down on the red chenille-covered table and smiled across at the old midwife. A fire had been lit in the front parlour in honour of the visit and Widow Goodyear served tea in the best china and a plate of Welsh cakes. Lilian took the proffered seat, glad to take the weight off her feet after the long walk across the fields. She accepted her cup of tea and sipped, eyeing her hostess over the rim of the cup. Of all her Fellowship visits, and despite their long acquaintance, Widow Goodyear was the one with whom she felt the least at ease. There was just something about her. Not that she held any truck with the talk of wise-woman nonsense. Dear me no! She stiffened her Methodist back and winced as her stays dug agonizingly into her ribs.

All the same, today the widow had that certain glint in her coal-black eyes and Lilian braced herself. Sure enough, up cropped the topic of Mary.

'She's a good girl, really,' Lilian began in defence of her wayward daughter. All week it had been the same. Snide comments, knowing tuts. Trouble, you'll have if you don't watch her, Lilian Sutton. 'Mary's young and impressionable. Everyone was in high spirits on May Day.'

She heard the worry in her voice and struggled to master it. Widow Goodyear gave a wry smile.

'Tittle-tattle, that's Aston Cross for you. Same as most places. You don't have to make excuses. Mary's a fine girl. Spirited, but you wouldn't want her cowed, would you?'

'Well no,' replied Lilian, uncertainly. 'Though I would prefer her to show a little more decorum.'

Again the smile. 'And you wish she were plainer. More like the other two girls – not that I'm calling them, mind. Fine children they are, even if they haven't got Mary's looks or vivacity. You'll never quench that. Those energies need channelling. Not easy, especially when it's not your own.'

Lilian simply gaped. Her hands shook and she put the cup and saucer down with a rattle. Widow Goodyear leaned to pour more tea comfortingly. 'Thought no-one knew, didn't you?' she went on in her soft valley tones. 'But I delivered Ned, remember? I knew he was your first. A midwife always knows. Besides, Mary's too different. A cuckoo in the nest!'

'But ... why did you never say anything?'

'None of my business, was it. She doesn't know, does she?'

'No. Tobias and I have kept it secret. We thought it best but now ...'

Her voice trailed hopelessly and Widow Goodyear gave a sympathetic cluck. 'Want to tell me about it? It won't go beyond these walls I promise.'

She made a helpless gesture with her hands. 'I was living in London at the time. My aunt had been poorly and I was sent to help out. It was a big house and she took in paying guests. Tobias was one. Oh, he was so dashing, so full of enthusiasm. From the start I liked him. He'd go off, sometimes for weeks on end. But he always kept the room on, was never late with the rent or anything.'

'He wasn't a carriage-maker then?'

'Oh no. He made props for the theatre. And he took other commissions. Anything to do with carpentry. He rented a workroom just off the square. Wasn't afraid of hard work. Funny thing, I used to think what an asset he would be at Aston Cross. My father's carriage business was very run-down by that time. It needed a man like Tobias to pull it round. And then one day he came home with this tiny motherless baby. Mary was such a pretty little thing even then, and he was so utterly helpless. My heart just went out to him.'

'So you got wed and came back to Aston Cross?'

'Well, not immediately. My aunt ailed for a while then died. The house was sold. I stayed on to sort out her affairs. Tobias was very supportive throughout. I'd been away for three years by then. No-one questioned the marriage or the baby. And I was right about the business. Tobias was exactly what was needed. My parents saw the yard thriving again before they passed on.'

'And Mary's true mother?'

'One of the performers, I never questioned Tobias too closely. Sad, a young life cut off, even though it turned out fortuitous for me. I promised Tobias to look after Mary as my own and I've tried. I've really tried …'

*

Despite an overwhelming relief at having shared the burden of years Lilian was glad to get outside in the warm sunshine and head for home. It was no good. Mention of Mary's mother brought it all back. A faceless woman. Who had she been? Was Mary like her? On the single occasion she had broached the subject Tobias had brushed it aside.

'We're wed. Happy, successful. The childer thrive. What more do you want, Lilian? Let the past go, for pity's sake!'

He had made her feel ungrateful. Besides, she always had bowed to his word. This time it was different.

Tobias was in the workshop, notebook in hand, writing up a list of supplies.

'Husband, could you spare me a moment, please?'

Tobias peered at her absently over the list. ''Course, m'dear. What is it?' Nobody looked up, but over the saw, hammer and scrape Lilian was aware of the watchful atmosphere.

'In private, I think,' she said quietly. Heaving a sigh, Tobias pocketed the book.

'Remember we've that farm cart to have finished by haysel,' he shouted over his shoulder as he followed her out. 'No shirking, or else there'll be wages docked! And you, boy. Get along and fill up the timber rack. It's half empty. And stop dribbling.'

'Yes, mester.' Chips rubbed a fist across his permanently chapped lips and fled. Around the benches shoulders were mentally shrugged; faces wore a smile. Everyone – apart from the unfortunate odd-job lad – knew the mester's bark was worse than his bite. At least, generally.

In the living room, Lilian faced her husband squarely. 'Mary's performance last week did us no favours, Tobias. I'm just back from Widow Goodyear's.' She stopped. It would not do to let Tobias know that the woman had guessed their secret.

'Garrulous old fool!' Tobias muttered. 'Criticizing Mary, was she? You'll not go there again, Lilian. Fellowship or no Fellowship, you'll not go to that house again!'

'Oh – whisht! It wasn't just that.' Lilian slumped wearily down on the couch. 'Everywhere I go people are talking. It's understandable. Mary's behaviour was disgraceful.'

'She was just over-excited.'

'That's the excuse I've been making, and much against my own judgement. Standing up and singing the way she did!'

'For pity's sake, Lilian, where's the harm? What of the Sunday School Anniversary? Childer stand up and sing and recite all the time, don't they?'

'This was different and well you know it! And then to go and throw herself at Kester. Shameful. All credit to him that he dealt with it in such a manly way …'

It was too much. Lilian found herself trembling on the brink of tears. Tobias's face softened. He came and sat on the couch beside her and patted her shoulder clumsily. 'Don't take on, now. Happen Mary's just feeling her spirits a bit. She'll calm down, you'll see.'

'You spoil her,' Lilian persisted, mastering her tears. 'You always have. And now we're paying the price. Tobias.' She paused, then blurted. 'Mary's true mother. Is she like her?'

Tobias was silent. Esther. He supposed Mary had grown up in her mother's image without him really accepting the fact. Same bright hair and blue eyes. Same verve that lifted her way above other girls. Talents, the singing and dancing that came as naturally to Mary as breathing. Esther had been like that.

'Reckon she is, just a mite. You knew the background. Esther was on the stage.'

'A music hall star!' Lilian was contemptuous.

'Ain't nothing wrong with entertainment and Esther was all set for the top …' For one blind unfortunate moment he forgot himself. 'She made it, too, by all account.'

'What?' Lilian stared at him aghast, the colour draining from her face. 'But ... you said Esther Green was dead.'

Cornered, he started to bluster and stumble. 'So what if I did! Esther *was* dead to me. And to Mary. It was over between us. Dead. Anything I said was in your interest, to protect the infant and yourself, save you both from hurt. Sometimes you've got to bend the truth a bit.'

'But you lied to me, Tobias,' Lilian said shakily.

'Only the once. I promise you. Only the once. Lilian love, think what you will of me but don't hold this against Mary. Her mother wasn't a bad lot. High spirited, yes. A laughing, lively creature. But she wasn't bad and she wasn't forward.'

Tears swam again in Lilian's pale eyes. 'Did you truly love her, Tobias?'

His broad shoulders lifted in a shrug. 'Thought I did at the time. Infatuation, more like. She was that sort of person. Pretty, fun to be with. Made you feel good ... oh, come on Lilian, I didn't mean anything. I was trying to explain.' He felt a pang of impatience. He never was much good with words.

His wife mopped a fresh flow of tears with a tiny square of cambric and raised her blotched face to his. 'Did you wed me for love, Tobias? Or was it more to give Mary a mother? I have wondered.'

'Then you should have asked. Of course I love you. You're my wife. We've built up this home together. We've a family we can be proud of. That other romance, for want of a better word, it was nothing. We were too young for one thing. Then she got pregnant. She hated it, every day of it, couldn't wait for the ordeal to be over. Get her figure back and resume her work on the stage. Even when Mary was born she never took to her. Ugly little thing, she said.'

He passed a hand wearily across his face. 'Oh, what's the use! I might as well finish now we've come this far. Truth is it wasn't just

Mary and you I was shielding. It was myself as well. I wanted her gone, may God forgive me. We were to be wed, y'see. She didn't turn up. God, the humiliation! Standing there, waiting, listening to the church clock chiming away the quarters. The urchin arriving with the note. She'd had this amazing offer. She'd be the star she always dreamed of. It would never have worked between us, she wrote. Sorry. Sorry!'

Lilian could picture it. His hurt was hers. The anguish, the bitter rejection. She slipped a forgiving hand in his.

'Esther was right, Lilian. It wouldn't have worked, not like you and me. She changed her name. Esme Greer, you must have heard of her. Went off to Paris and never looked back.'

'Not even an enquiry after her child?' Lilian shook her head helplessly. 'I don't know how she could!'

'Not all women are maternal,' Tobias said. 'Not all are as motherly as you, or as dutiful. I'm sorry you ever doubted my feelings for you, Lilian. But they go deep. Far deeper than that other. It was pure dalliance. Mind me?'

She gave a watery smile and nodded. 'Now I know it makes things easier somehow. I'll certainly change my approach with Mary. To think her own mother ... Why don't we have Mary in here and tell her the truth? Not that she was rejected, that's too cruel. But the circumstances as they stood. Everyone has a right to know their natural parentage, and blood ties can be powerful. She might have wondered at the differences between herself and her sisters.'

Tobias got up heavily and strode to the window. In the yard Mary was laughing at something the men had said. She looked young and lovely and it smote his heart to have to hurt her. But he knew that Lilian was right.

He opened the window. 'Mary. Come on inside, maid. There's something we want to tell you.'

Two

❧

'You mean I'm not who I thought I was?' Mary gasped, her face paling, blue eyes darting in shock from her father to Lilian. 'You're not my mother after all? Ned, Alice and Violet aren't my true brother and sisters?'

'Yes they are. At least, they're your half-brother and half-sisters,' Lilian corrected herself hastily. She reached out her hands in a gesture of appeal. 'Mary dear, this makes no difference to how we feel about you. How I feel. You're my daughter, the same as Alice and Violet. I brought you up from a tiny baby. I love you. I always will.'

'Of course it makes a difference!' Mary cried, tears spurting. 'It means I'm not who I thought I was. It means I've been living a lie all these years. How would you like it if someone suddenly told you your mother was someone else? Someone totally at odds to what you thought. A music hall star of all things! How would you like it?'

'Mary, enough!' her father said. 'Your mother was a grand person. Talented, beautiful.'

'And heartless! She walked out on me. Huh, a fine mother she was!'

'Not every woman is cut out for motherhood,' Tobias reasoned. 'Esther knew her potential. Just because she made the stage her career doesn't make her no good.'

'Tell *her* that!' Mary choked, flinging a hand in Lilian's direction. 'She's always been against my singing and dancing. Now we know why. She was afraid I'd go wrong, like my mother!' She dashed the tears from her cheeks. 'I hate you for lying to me! I hate both of you! Oh!'

She spun round and slammed out. She fled across the yard, dodging a hay-wain that stood awaiting collection, new paint gleaming in the bright summer sunshine. She flew past the workshop, doors open to the air, the hammer and clatter and saw of the men at work fading as she tore through the gateway and took off blindly down the lane. She ran until she could run no more and came to a gasping stop at a humpy stone bridge spanning the river. Her heart thumped in her throat and there was a stabbing stitch in her side. Mary flopped down on the low stone parapet and gulped in great lungfuls of air.

Different. She was different from the rest of her family. A misfit. Naughty little Mary who never could keep out of mischief. Deep-down she had always felt the odd one out, and now that feeling had become reality. But never in all her wildest imaginings had she considered this.

Gradually her pulse settled, and her breath came more evenly. The splash and gurgle of water gushing over brown stones invaded her senses. It had been a wet spring and the river was in full spate. Giving a final shuddering sob, she watched the sparkle of sunlight on leaping spray and tried not to think at all.

Kester came striding through the trees, bundle of firewood over his shoulder, a song on his lips. Seeing the familiar figure in the blue dress sitting on the bridge, he stopped. His first instinct was to sneak away. Everyone needed time to themselves. But something in the uncharacteristic droop of her shoulders and abstracted air made him change his mind.

'Mary?' he called, approaching. 'Nothing wrong, is there? Your mother, I thought she seemed peaky of late. All right is she?'

Mary looked up. Her face was white and tear-streaked, but at the mention of Lilian her blue eyes sparked fire. 'She isn't my mother,' she blurted. 'She's just pretending to be. They both put up a pretence. Lies and deceit all the way! Oh, Kester, I'm so unhappy I don't know what to do!'

Dropping the firewood, he went to sit beside her on the sun-warmed stone parapet. He took her cold hands in his and chaffed some life back into them, murmuring words of comfort until some of the colour returned to her cheeks and her body ceased to tremble.

'Now,' he said gently. 'What's it all about?'

She shook her head hopelessly, then her face crumpled and the whole sorry tale came tumbling into the open. 'They said my real mother was a music hall artiste, Esme Greer – at least, that's her stage name. Father knew her as Esther Green. She wouldn't marry him. She preferred the stage to looking after a baby. Then Father married Mother … I mean Lilian, and she took me on and p … pretended I was hers …'

The disclosure provoked a fresh flow of tears. In silence Kester heard her out and then drew her to him, comforting her as if she were the child he yet believed her to be. But the quivering figure in his arms was far from childlike. Against his face, her burnished brown hair was soft and honey-scented.

'Hush,' he said. 'Hush now.'

Eventually the storm of weeping subsided. She pushed his arms away. 'Better?' he asked.

Miserably she hunched her shoulders. 'Not really.'

'Listen,' he said, handing her his kerchief. 'What you've just told me must have been a huge shock. But it's hardly the end of the world, is it? You've still got two fine parents. A father who dotes on you, and Lilian who's probably the most compassionate person I've ever known. Look how readily she took you on. She would only have been a young woman then, with precious little experience of life. She acted purely by instinct. You were tiny and helpless and she loved you. Still does.'

'Huh, that's why she's so strict no doubt,' Mary said bitterly. 'It's always been the same. Getting at me, never the others. Don't do this, don't do that. She doesn't even like me to sing. Now I know why. She's afraid I'll turn out like my real mother!'

'I'm sure Lilian's very proud of you in her own way,' Kester said smoothly. 'She did her best, and that's what you must do. Great heavens, you're still Mary, aren't you? Still the cheeky miss who demanded a May-time kiss?'

She blushed. 'Don't remind me! Anyway, that was ages ago. I was just a girl.'

'And now you're an old crone I suppose?' The gentle teasing brought a glimmer of a smile. Encouraged, Kester said, 'Seriously, things could be far worse. You've got a good home, Mary. Two parents who love you, your sisters and brother. And what about your work in the yard, those account ledgers you keep up so well? Try and look on the bright side and things will shift into perspective.'

'But it won't ever be the same,' she objected. 'It won't.'

'Nothing is perfect. D'you think I'm happy with my lot? Stuck away here at Aston Cross, far from home and those I love and love me? All right, so it was my decision to strike out on my own. But it came through a chapter of events which made it impossible for me to stay. Some day I'll tell you about it, but not now. Doesn't do to dwell on the past, Mary. Better to look to the future. Take it a step at a time. Play it out if you have to. But endure, eh?'

The wide blue gaze flickered briefly. For a moment Kester imagined she was about to argue, but the words never came. Instead, 'I suppose I have no choice,' Mary said slowly. 'I suppose what you say is true – but it doesn't make it any more right,' she finished with a healthy spark of rebellion that was all her own.

Kester smiled. 'That's my girl. Another thing. Don't go being ashamed of your real mama. Esme Greer's a famous name. Went to see her myself once. It was at the Hippodrome in Sheffield. Grand theatre. Esme Greer was top of the bill.'

Interest flared. 'Oh. Was she ... do I look anything like her?'

'Quite. You're prettier I'd say. Her colouring is more russet perhaps. You've certainly inherited her flair for dancing and her lovely singing voice. Sing? She had the audience in floods of tears one minute, laughing the next. Incredible, to be able to entertain like that.'

'She abandoned me,' Mary said woodenly, the whole scenario clearly washing over her again. 'Father should have made her see sense. He should have made her marry him. You know what this makes me, don't you?'

'It makes you Mary,' he said simply. 'Who cares about anything else? Nobody else knows, or ever will. So let's leave it at that, eh?'

As she walked homewards through the summer twilight, Mary pondered on Kester's words. He was right of course. Had anyone else told her to look on the bright side she would have thought it patronising. But coming from Kester it had to be genuine. Mary straightened her back and tossed her tumbled curls from her face. She felt a changed person, just that little bit older. Not quite an old crone, she thought ruefully, but certainly more grown up.

She arrived home to chaos.

'Typical!' Alice flung at Mary as she entered the kitchen. 'You cause a load of trouble and just walk out. It was another argument I suppose. Typical!'

'Why? What has happened?' Mary glanced around. Ned was cutting himself doorsteps of bread and cheese and Violet had obviously been crying.

'It's mother,' Ned told Mary. 'She fainted after you left. Father's with her now. I went for Widow Goodyear. She's given Mother something to help her sleep.'

'But what's wrong with her?' Mary pressed.

Violet gave a snuffling sob. 'Mother looked ever so poorly. Father had to carry her upstairs.'

'And you're the cause of it, Mary!' Alice snapped. 'I heard Mother telling Father not to put the blame on you, that it wasn't your fault, but I know it is. Mother's always sticking up for you. You don't deserve it. Selfish, that's what you are. What's it all about this time, I wonder?'

'None of your business,' Mary said wearily. She gave Violet a comforting hug and sent Ned a wan smile over the girl's head. 'Sorry I wasn't here to help. Something ... something cropped up. Is Mother all right?'

'The widow said she will be,' Ned replied, chewing hungrily on a mouthful of bread. 'Mother's to stop in bed and rest for the next week or two.' He looked suddenly doubtful. 'Don't know who's going to get the meals.'

'I will,' Mary said briskly.

Alice snorted. 'Chance will be a fine thing! You'd get bored with it. You could never peel a pan of potatoes without a grumble. Er ... where are you going, Mary?'

'Up to see Mother of course, what do you think?' Mary said.

Even to Mary, it was surprising how competently she slipped into the role of housekeeper and nurse. Cleaning, cooking, washing and ironing, not to mention looking after Lilian. Suddenly there weren't enough hours in the day. If her father's shirts were not quite as snowy and starched as usual he did not complain. Violet, probably the most domesticated of the three girls, was quick to lend a hand with the pastry and cake making, and Ned, providing his meals were regular and plentiful, was not one to grumble if they were sometimes not quite up to the usual standard. Only Alice found fault, but then that was Alice.

'Dear Mary,' Lilian said, easing herself up in the big bed for Mary to plump the bolster and pillows. 'You've turned out the best of nurses. I think you've found your vocation.'

'Don't know about that,' Mary replied briskly. 'There. Now the tray. Can you manage, Mother?'

After two full weeks the title still did not come easily. Mary had to school herself to use it. But it was worth the effort to see the smile that brightened Lilian's thin face. Nothing further had been said about the circumstances of Mary's birth. Evidently her parents considered the matter closed.

Lilian surveyed the tray with its bowl of savoury-smelling broth and crisp roll of bread. Mary had picked one of her favourite yellow roses and put it in a vase.

'It's chicken broth,' Mary said. 'I made it myself. You must try and eat something, or else I'll have Widow Goodyear after me.'

Amused, her stepmother shook her head and tutted. 'You are a one!'

'Try it,' Mary chivvied, handing her the spoon. 'The bread's freshly made too. Eat up, and then there's a nice egg custard to follow. At least so I hope. Saw Ned sneaking in before. How he does guzzle! Don't know where he puts it all, he must have hollow legs or something.'

'Growing boys are all the same,' Lilian remarked, sipping. 'Mmm, nice.'

'It's your own recipe. I found it in the dresser drawer. Isn't that rose lovely? The honeysuckle's out on the hedge. The bees are working like mad, there'll be a good harvest again this year ...' Whilst keeping up a steady chatter, Mary fixed the invalid with a watchful eye. After the fainting attack Lilian had been nauseous for days. Nothing would stay down and the weight was beginning to melt from her already lean frame. Mary had done her best to concoct tasty, nourishing dishes and at last it looked as if her efforts were paying off. Today she was gratified to see a clean bowl.

'Well done. Will you try the custard now?'

Lilian nodded. 'Very well, dear. What's that?'

Mary had slipped a small flat tin on to the bedside table. 'Ginger root. Widow Goodyear said if you chewed some after eating, it would help stave off the sickness.'

She bustled off with the tray and was back directly, a dainty custard in a dish in hand. 'There you are. Now I'll make a cup of tea.'

She was astounded when Lilian shook her head. 'Not tea, Mary. I couldn't. Is there any lemonade?'

'Why yes. I did a whole quart. But you never drink anything but tea.'

'Just fancied something sharp. This custard is lovely and smooth. When I think of the way you never liked cooking. Boring, you said it was.'

'Actually, once you get interested, it's not bad,' Mary said. 'Apart from one thing.'

'What's that?'

'Having a Ned in the house. No sooner do you make something than it's gone, and you have to start all over again.'

She pulled such a comical face that Lilian went into titters of laughter.

'Well well, that's what I like to hear,' said Tobias's voice from the doorway. 'Supping up, too, I see. Soon have you back in harness, wife,' he jested. 'Won't have to put up with Mary's muddle-and-come-again for much longer.'

'Father!' Mary looked scandalised.

'You are bad, Tobias,' Lilian scolded affectionately. 'Take no notice, Mary. Go along and make that tea.'

'Tea? But you said you wanted—'

'Cup of tea will be fine,' her mother said firmly.

'Very well, tea it is.'

Smiling through her confusion, Mary left the sickroom. As soon as the door was closed behind her the smile fled. 'Dear goodness!' she murmured to herself, heading across the wide landing for the stairs. It had been the same all along. Bring me this, bring me that, and every instance had brought a change of mind. Mary had never known Lilian so contrary. Whatever her complaint was, it was trying Mary to her limits.

Still, at least she was coping. It was Kester who had given her the idea. Play it out, he had said. And that was exactly what she was doing – playing the role of nurse, or housekeeper, or cook. If she flung herself into the part and imagined she was that other person, the work came if not easily, but with a lot less hassle than if it was being done by Mary. And it was actually quite fun, she reflected, descending the final stair and turning for the kitchen.

The long summer days slipped by. Life fell into a pattern. Now that she was organised, Mary found the odd hour to slip into the office and work on the accounts, for which her father was thankful. But nothing, it seemed, was plain sailing that year. Disaster fell when Chas Pilkington slipped when carrying a load of timber and broke his arm. However, Chas's misfortune was Kester's gain. Observing the man's ability to turn a hand to most things, Tobias promptly offered Kester the joiner's job for the interim.

'Be weeks before Chas is mended, and then the arm has to get its strength back. After which there's a job as foreman going, if you're interested. Never bothered before, but business is steady and I could do with a right-hand man.'

'Thank you, sir,' Kester said. 'I'm happy to accept.'

They shook hands on the deal. 'Always got to look ahead with a business,' Tobias went on. 'Must get young Ned sorted for when he leaves school this summer end. Might apprentice him out to the timber merchant in Much Wenlock. He's a good man and will teach Ned thoroughly. Don't hold with the lad learning everything on home ground. Be good for him to break with the apron strings as well.'

Right out of the blue Tobias received a specialist order for a two-wheeled phaeton. It was the sort of work the men relished. Kester watched the care that went into selecting exactly the right timber, with the grain matching for each side panel. Only the best leather went into the upholstery, in this case a dark green, quilted with matching buttons.

The boy Chips was set to sweeping out every corner of the workshop before work on the vehicle commenced. And when it did start, the concentration in the workshop was almost tangible.

Tobias went about the yard with a smile. Business was thriving and young Mary had settled down. Lilian's health was improving, if slowly.

'She's talking about getting up for an hour in the afternoons,' he reported to Kester who daily showed his concern.

'That's good news,' Kester acknowledged.

'Mary's been a gem,' Tobias said. 'Got the house running like clockwork. Would never have believed it of her. Mary always preferred the carriage-making to the kitchen. Nowadays she just gets on with it. And the way she's looked after her mother is commendable.'

Kester just nodded. He knew precisely how Mary played her part. He had made no further reference to the day on the bridge to Mary. Neither did he indicate that he knew the situation to Tobias. Most things in life ironed themselves out given time. But by heaven, he thought as he went into the workshop, in this case there were a lot of wrinkles!

He whistled tunefully to himself as he fixed a piece of elm

between the clamps and started to plane it. Trust his first attempt at professional joinery to be something complex. A farm vehicle or a pony trap would have been less wearing on the nerves.

'Not bad,' Wallace Pilkington said when Kester had finished. 'Us'll make a skilled man of you yet.'

Kester sent him a grin. Banter was rife in the workshop and the joiner's easy attitude spoke reams. Kester had been quietly apprehensive when Tobias had offered him the position. Temporary though it was, the men could have shown a grudge. Happily none was apparent. He said, 'Got the top to make yet. Bowed, isn't it? Tricky.'

'Not when you know how,' Wallace replied. ''Tes done in sections, rather like a wheel, see. Thing is to get all the sections even. Painting's the worst job on these private vehicles. Customer's always want to see their faces in the finish. Isn't that right, Roland?'

The coach-painter looked up from the wheel he was sanding down in preparation for a second coat. 'Aye. But I've got a trick or two up my sleeve. Spot of varnish added to the black paint, plus one or two other ingredients, and you get a finish like glass.'

'Just so long as it don't smash the instant it's taken on the road,' put in Dan Turvey. Everyone laughed.

Kester looked up as the door opened and the boy Chips barged in. 'Hey you, steady!' Wallace growled. 'Almost knocked the frame off the trestle, you did.'

'No I never!' Chips said. 'I wunna nowhere near.'

At the far end of the workshop Dan Turvey frowned across the pair of shafts he was matching up. 'Less of your lip, boy!'

Chips swallowed. It would not have been the first time one of them had fetched him a warning cuff. A man's hand fell heavy, even if the blow was not aimed to harm. He rubbed a grubby fist across his dirty face and eyed the men warily. He reminded Kester of a mongrel terrier they'd had when he was not much older than

Chips. Crafty, well able to look after itself, yet pitifully anxious for a friendly word.

'Ah, leave the lad alone,' Kester said. 'Here, Chips, fetch a broom and sweep up these shavings. And when you've done that you might fill up the nail tins.'

Willingly he scuttled off. 'Doesn't do to be too easy on youngsters,' Wallace said. 'They take you for a soft touch.'

'Get away,' Kester replied lightly. 'Feel sorry for the lad. Scruffy little mutt! He looks as if a square meal wouldn't come amiss. Is he an orphanage boy or what? Where's he from?'

'End cottage on the green,' Josh Millet supplied. 'Family of lads, all with the cheek of Riley. The mester took Chips on when his dad got crippled in a ploughing accident. The mother works up at the big house. She's out all day, so the younger ones run wild. Chips will be all right once he's knocked into shape.'

There was a general growl of agreement. Kester returned to his bench. Unkindness wasn't intentional amongst the men. They just saw Chips as a scapegoat. Kester's first job had been messenger boy in a brewer's yard. He knew what the score was.

At midday he sought Chips out. 'Hey lad, you had some vitals?'

'No, mister,' came the reply.

He passed him some bread and cheese from his own lunch and watched the boy scoff it hungrily. 'Doesn't your ma put you up some snap?'

'I dunna live at home no more. 'Twere too crowded. I sleep in a barn and eat what's going. 'Tes less wear on Ma this way, an' I can give her all of my wages. Ma needs every penny she can get, see.'

'Yes, I do see. Fancy a decent roof and a meal each night? You'd have to earn it, mind.'

Chips's face brightened. 'At your place?'

'No,' Kester said, amused. 'D'you know the widow?'

'Widow Goodyear? 'Course.'

'I heard she was looking for a yard lad. Well, she's not getting any younger. You could bide there, see to the chores and still put in a shift here at the workshop. Can you milk a cow?'

''Course.'

Kester eyed the boy's tattered breeches and bare dirty feet. 'Need to spruce you up a bit. Might have a word with Mary.'

That evening Chips, unrecognisable from a dowsing under the icy pump of the yard, was handed over to Widow Goodyear. The greasy dark locks had turned out a surprising thatch of yellow and the grubby skin was fair and dusted with freckles. With his ragged garments exchanged for some much-mended but clean ones of Ned's, a pair of Ned's outgrown boots on his feet, he looked a different lad.

Kester sent the widow a wink. 'Beat him if he won't do as he's bid!'

'Oh, listen to you!' Widow Goodyear exclaimed, eyes twinkling. 'Want some supper, boy? There's rabbit pie and a rice pudding. Go wash your hands first. Hot water, mind. There's soap by the sink.'

'But I've just—'

Kester gave him a shove. Once he was out of earshot the Widow said with a probing look, 'How's Mary these days?'

'Well enough.' She knew, he thought. Sure as nails were nails she knew. They said in the village she had certain powers. Fate and fortune telling never had been Kester's creed. He believed you made your own destiny. Now he had cause to wonder. She said, 'Mary's tougher than you'd think. She'll weather the storm, you'll see.'

Mary tucked the woven shawl over Lilian's knees where she sat on the horsehair sofa in the parlour. 'Comfortable? I could fetch another pillow for your back?'

'No, I'm fine, thank you Mary. Lovely to be downstairs again. My, you have been busy. You could see your reflection in the shine on the dresser.'

Mary put a glass of water and books to hand. 'Actually, Alice did the polishing.'

'Indeed? Then I must remember to give praise where it's due!'

Their eyes met in perfect understanding. Never one to accept approval with good grace, Alice nevertheless knew her worth and expected it to be acknowledged.

'Little sour puss,' Mary couldn't help but remark.

'It's just her way,' Lilian said with customary patience. 'Oh, I meant to ask before. Is there more of that ginger root?'

'No, but I can get some later when I go into town. Is it the sickness again? Has it not gone away? Oh dear.'

'Well …' Lilian hesitated, then said confidingly, 'Mary, you've been so patient these past weeks. It can't have been easy. If I tell you something, will you promise to keep it to yourself?'

Mary stared at her. 'Of course. What is it?'

'This malady of mine. It's nothing bad, far from it. I'm pregnant Mary!' There was no mistaking the joy on Lilian's face. 'Is it not wonderful? Another babe, just when I was almost resigned to thinking that Violet would be my last.'

Mary chewed on her bottom lip. All too clearly she remembered Violet's entry into the world. Lilian closeted upstairs with the midwife. The long, long hours of waiting. Her father grim-faced and anxious. Then, finally, the urgent summons for the doctor. 'I thought you weren't supposed to have any more after Violet,' Mary said.

'Oh well, the doctor thought it might be risky. But that was then. This time Widow Goodyear has promised to keep an eye on me all the way through. There are herbs one can take for strengthening the system. Raspberry leaf tea, she recommends. I've got faith in her, so let's not worry. A new little brother or sister for you, Mary. I'm so happy I want to shout it from the rooftops.'

'Then I'm happy for you,' Mary said tactfully. 'When are you going to tell father?'

'Not yet. I shall have to choose my moment. Then all that remains is to look forward. 'Twill be a Christmastide babe. Wonderful!'

Mary was quick to agree, though in reality her heart sank. Wonderful yes, though a baby in the nursery would mean more demands on herself. After four hectic weeks, the role of dutiful daughter was beginning to pall. She didn't want to be bound to a house and an ailing mother. She wanted her freedom, and she wanted it now.

Giving the blanket a final tweak, she directed a smile at her step-mother and left the room. In the kitchen, Alice was waiting for her.

'I saw Kester hitching up the horse. Are you going to town? Can I come?' the girl asked.

'Yes, I am going shopping. And no, you cannot come. Not today, Alice.'

'Why can't I? It's Saturday, I've nothing else to do,' Alice said.

'I'm not planning to be in town long,' Mary told her sister. 'Just one or two things to pick up. While I'm gone you can read aloud to Mother if you like. She'd be pleased.'

'You'd take Violet with you. It's because it's me. You don't want me asking questions, do you, Mary? There's something going on.'

Mary made a silent bid for patience and said briskly, 'Nonsense. What did you want to come for anyway? Was there something you especially wanted? Can I get it for you?'

'No, you can't. It's something to do with Mother,' Alice persisted. 'Or is it Father? You're afraid he'll get paid help for the office. That'd put your nose out of joint! Or perhaps it's another thing. Perhaps it's something I'm not supposed to know about.'

'Tut! What ideas you do get, Alice,' Mary said, glancing up in relief as hoofbeats clattered outside on the yard. 'There's Kester now with the horse and cart. Don't forget Mother's mid-morning drink. See you later.'

She flung on her cape and bonnet and hurried out.

Alice and her prying! Alice was the very last person she wanted to get to know her secret. It would be all over the village in no time.

Her mother. What was she like? Really like? Was she still pretty enough to twirl and sing in front of an audience? A frisson of something akin to envy fluttered down Mary's spine. What an exciting life compared to hers.

It was as if thinking about her mother released the vibes. The five mile drive into town was taken at a steady trot. It was good to get away from the house and she hummed happily as the horse jogged along. Reaching the outskirts of town she slowed the animal to a walk.

They were clopping down the main street in a stream of other traffic, when she saw the playbill pasted on the ugly red brick wall of the indoor market place.

Esme Greer, the Great Music Hall Star.
Appearing at The Castle Theatre, Ludlow.

In shock and excitement Mary's hands tightened on the reins and the horse jibbed, rocking the cart. 'Hey missie, watch yerself!' someone called out. Mary scarcely heard. She craned her neck as they edged past, trying to establish the date of the performance.

It was next week, and she was there for the whole of September.

Three

❧

'Of course, I could always say I'd like a day out, Brownie,' Mary said as she brushed the pony down. 'Trouble is, Mother would fuss. She'd insist I took Alice along as chaperone and that's the last thing I want.'

She stopped grooming and gnawed her lip in thought. Somehow she had to get to Ludlow and seek out Esme Greer. She mustn't miss this heaven-sent opportunity to meet her real mother. Problem was, how to get away?

Brownie turned his head inquiringly and nuzzled her hand. 'All right, all right. Let's finish you off, then you can have your feed. Wish I could jump on your back and gallop to Ludlow. I do!'

As it happened, fate played into Mary's hands. Next day Tobias came blustering into the house in high dudgeon with the news that his accountant had moved premises.

'To Ludlow of all places. How can the likes of me spare an entire day off just to deliver a list of accounts? Pity Ned wasn't around. He could have gone for me.' Ned had started his apprenticeship with the timber merchant, and would be away from home for two long years.

Mary seized her chance. 'I'll go, Father.' Her heart thudded so loud she was afraid everyone could hear it. 'I'll take the milk train. It will get me there in good time.'

'But you can't go on your own, Mary.' Lilian's pale face puck-
ered up in concern. Her health had improved over the past month.
Slowly she was taking over the management of the house again,
although the bulk of the work still fell to Mary.

'I'll be back in time for tea, Mother – Ludlow's not that far
away! Kester can drive me to the station in the trap.'

Tobias eyed his daughter thoughtfully. 'You sure, Mary? It's only
a matter of handing over the books. Hargreaves needs to go over
the recent figures, then update his own records. You'd have to wait
for him to copy them up.'

It got better. 'I can do some shopping in the meantime.
Ludlow's far better than Market Drayton for shops.' The words
came so easily. Mary fixed her father with her deep-blue gaze and
drove her advantage home. 'I know the business figures as well as
anyone. Better than Ned would have. If there's a query I'll be able
to answer it. Of course I can cope. I'm not a child. I'll be seven-
teen next birthday remember.'

He smiled at her. 'Aye maid, so you will. All right, I'll pen
Hargreaves a line. If we make it Saturday the girls will be home to
see after your mother....'

All the way there on the slow country train which stopped at every
station to load up the milk churns and pick up passengers, Mary
rehearsed what she was going to say to Esme Greer. She had
dressed with care in her new Sunday gown of mid-blue woollen
and grey cape with banded blue trim. Her long chestnut-brown
curls were tied back with a matching ribbon. On them her poke
bonnet framed her face beguilingly. The overall effect, if not exactly
high fashion, was at least crisp and businesslike.

The quarterly account ledger, tucked in a leather satchel on the
rack above her head, gave her a sense of importance.

I'll tell her precisely what I think of her, Mary vowed fiercely as the train chugged along. No decent woman forsakes her child for the stage, no matter how strong the urge.

Fields and woods gave way to houses and streets and at last the train pulled into Ludlow station. Alighting nimbly, Mary made her way out into the town where, in a fashionable square off the main street, Hargreaves and Hargreaves, Chartered Accountants Ltd., had their smart new office. It was a matter of minutes to hand over the books and arrange a time of collection.

That done, Mary headed for the centre of town and the main issue of the visit.

Arriving at the theatre, she felt a stab of nerves. The Castle Theatre was a tall, sooty building with a flight of shallow steps leading up to the main entrance. All four doors were locked. The foyer was in darkness. A display board on the wall announced the current programme with Esme Greer's name heading the bill in big black letters. For a long moment Mary stared at her mother's name.

Quick footsteps and chattering, laughing voices alerted her to a group of girls who seemed to know where they were going. Mary ran down the steps and followed them round the side of the building. They disappeared through a back entrance marked Stage Door in peeling paint. Mary knocked, but when there was no response she opened the door and went in.

Sitting with his newspaper in a small shabby office, the doorman cast her a cursory glance. 'Better look sharp, darling. The others have already gone up,' he stated.

Blushing rosily at the familiar address, Mary flashed him what she hoped was a grateful smile and mounted the flight of stairs, her boots tapping noisily on the bare wooden treads. At the top was a long corridor with doors leading off. No sign of the girls; they must have gone into one of the rooms. Mary walked on, reading the names on the doors as she went. Walls were painted a functional brown and the passage was dimly lit. There was a smell of dust and human sweat and old greasepaint. The passageway seemed to go on forever.

She came out eventually at the stage itself. A lot of hammering and cursing was going on from two men in overalls setting up the scenery. Trees, flowers, a rustic archway. A garden scene or a park maybe. Mary stared at it in disgust. Leaves were never that green and the paste flowers were of no particular variety. And as for the archway ... it looked so flimsy that if a sparrow alighted on it the whole structure would collapse. The backcloth was quite awful too. All those garish splodges and lines. A child could have done better.

Mary shuddered. It was all so cheap, so tawdry. How could anyone have wanted this? Her mother could keep the theatre and all that went with it. She, Mary, had a better sense of what was decent and right.

Someone was approaching with a mug of tea in each hand. He nodded to Mary as he edged past, slopping tea, and delivered the drinks to the stage hands. 'There y'are. Nivver say I don't do nothing for the show.' He came back, grinning cheekily at Mary. 'You lost, lovey? Auditions, is it? You're early for them.'

'No, nothing like that,' Mary said to the call boy. 'I'm looking for Esme Greer.'

'Oh? You got an appointment?'

'Yes,' fibbed Mary.

'This way then.' He took her arm, shepherding her back along the corridor down which she had come, branching off along another even longer, darker passageway. 'Like a rabbit warren, this place. Practically born here I was and I gets lost myself at times. Singer, are you, sweetheart? Thought as much ...' The chatter stopped outside a door marked, boldly, Miss Esme Greer. He knocked, and a light voice bid them enter.

She was sitting at her dressing table, a soft-green satin peignoir thrown carelessly over her stage-costume, dusting her face with a swansdown puff and very pink face-powder.

Hardly aware of the call-boy leaving, Mary entered the room, pulled the door gently shut and just stood, staring at her mother in the mirror. Her own face was reflected there as well, a younger, rounder version of the other woman's. Deep-blue eyes met sparkly cornflour-blue ones that were heavily made-up for the dress-rehearsal. Shakily the powder-puff was returned to the bowl.

'Um … Esme Greer?' All at once the carefully-rehearsed words had flown from Mary's mind. 'I'm Mary. Mary Sutton.'

With a little cry the older woman jumped up and rushed across the room to envelop Mary in her arms. 'Mary! After all this time. My own Mary!'

It was the very last sort of greeting Mary had expected and she stood awkwardly, stiff and unresponsive in her mother's embrace. She breathed in Esme's perfume, rich, cloying, different from the lavender water she was allowed or the rose favoured by Lilian. It was delicious … exotic like the white jasmine that grew on the south wall at Beamsters. Jasmine could be a touch overwhelming. Perhaps not quite the scent for Aston Cross.

'Come, Mary …' Her mother guided her to a chair and sat down again herself, her eyes suspiciously bright. 'There. Let me look at you. Why, your eyes are the very same shade as my own mother's. A darker blue than mine, so deep they could almost be violet. Oh, if only you knew how much I've wanted to meet you. And now here you are, all grown up.'

She paused for breath and Mary said woodenly, 'You mean you actually thought of me sometimes? Gracious!'

'Well of course I did, you sweet, foolish child,' Esme responded gushingly. 'You're my one and only daughter. My own dear girl. All these years I've been wondering what were you like? Were you a naughty little poppet like I was as a child? Were you blonde, brunette or a red-head like me? I tried to trace you, but every route I took led to a blank and—'

'Maybe you should have tried harder,' Mary blurted out before she could stop herself.

Esme Greer blinked, as if she'd just been dowsed with cold water. 'But I did try. Every spare moment I made enquiries about you,' she insisted, attempting to justify herself. 'Trouble was, there aren't many spare moments to be had in this business. Every minute is taken up. If it isn't rehearsing it's performing. Or learning a new routine. Or being fitted for costumes. Then there's the socialising, the round of parties and dining out which you have to attend even though your entire being yearns for a quiet evening in. There's the travelling as well. Never in one place for more than a few weeks at a time, and so many people depending upon you. In my case my manager, my supporting cast, my public.'

'Didn't your baby need you just as much?' Mary said quietly.

Her mother's face crumpled. 'Oh, of course. But I was young and eager for life. I had talent. The chance was there, I had to grasp it. Don't you see?'

'No.'

'It was what I'd always dreamed of. Paris. An opportunity to make something of myself. I had what it took in those days. I could sing and dance all night if need be and never tire. My audience would never let me leave without three, four, half a dozen encores.'

Mary's young face hardened. 'I suppose the prospect of bringing up a little child must have seemed tedious compared with all that.' She could not get that abandoned baby out of her mind. She got up to leave. 'I'm sorry. This visit has been a mistake.' What a fussy, selfish, shallow woman her mother was. She had reached the door when she remembered her purse left on the dressing table. 'My purse, my rail ticket – oh!'

Her mother was standing rooted, tears streaming down her

rouged cheeks. 'Please, Mary love,' she begged. 'Please don't go like this.'

She held out her arms. Feeling the prickle of tears behind her own lids, Mary walked back into the room.

'You stand here. You'll get a splendid view. I'm on in one minute.'

Esme stood with Mary in the wings. The lights were on now, dazzling, amazingly hot, bringing out the brilliant colours in the scenery and turning it into a wonderland. The shoddiness, the tawdry paste and paint and false glamour, all had gone. In its place was glitter and excitement. Out there beyond the footlights the throbbing pulse of the audience was almost tangible. Mary caught her lip between her teeth and watched entranced. Her mother observed her, smiling a little.

The orchestra struck up an introduction. 'That's my cue.' Esme gave her daughter's hand a small squeeze and moved lightly on to the stage.

A tumult of clapping and whistles greeted her and in that moment Esme changed from a less-than-young woman to a mere girl. She threw back her head, smiled enchantingly and began to sing and move in time to the music. Mary felt her heart tug. This was it, the magic of the stage. She had felt it herself to a lesser degree, singing for that May-time crowd in the softness of a summer evening. She thought ... she almost understood how her mother had felt when she had to make a choice between her baby and a career.

Then again, her mother *had* been genuinely glad to see her, Mary reflected, her eyes still fixed on the dancing figure on the stage. They had talked long and hard. Esme had expressed her delight that Tobias had found his happiness with Lilian and in his work. She insisted upon knowing everything about Ned, Alice and Violet. She went into fits of laughter over Alice and called her a character. Mary had never thought of her waspish sister in that way, but mulling on it, Esme could be right. She seemed interested in Mary's everyday life, how she helped her father in the office, and she was fascinated by Mary's account of being May Queen at the fair.

But ... and it was a big but.

As Esme took her curtsy and revelled in the audience's applause, Mary reminded herself that her mother was an actress, and pretending to be what she wasn't was second nature to her. Perhaps all the attention and interest was put on, just for her daughter's benefit.

Mary glanced at the theatre clock. It was getting late and she had a train to catch ...

'Damned if I'm happy about it, Kester,' Tobias confided to the younger man. 'It only takes one disgruntled customer to damage the reputation of a business. Especially one with a name like Reginald Tythe. That phaeton's been bad news for the yard, I'm sorry to say.'

They were taking a cup of small ale together in the cobwebby little office over the barn. It was evening, the workshop closed and silent, a hazy sun setting over the misted autumnal landscape.

The phaeton into which the men had put such care and expertise stood shafts up in a corner of the yard. The gleaming body leaned drunkenly on its splintered axle. Surveying the damaged vehicle through the dusty window, Kester heaved a sigh. 'God, but the man was hopping mad! First time out and it breaks. And a promising young horse spooked into the bargain.'

Tobias grunted. 'Serve him right for using an untried animal. Anybody with a grain of horse sense would know never to put anything but an experienced beast between the shafts of a new vehicle. Any vehicle, never mind a flimsy set-up like a phaeton! No.

I'm taking no blame for a skittish horse, but the vehicle's a different matter entirely. The timber was faulty. Had to be to break like that. Wish to goodness I'd checked that load of ash for myself.'

'Wallace must have eyed it all up,' Kester pointed out. 'I'm no judge myself, haven't the experience. But it looked a quality piece of wood. I even remarked upon it. Never seen a poor batch of timber in this yard yet, come to that.'

'Nor will you, Kester. Nor will you.' Thoughtfully Tobias replenished both their cups. 'Seem to recall Chas making some comment after one of the deliveries. Got a good eye, has Chas. Sharper than his brother. It was a few days before his accident. I'm sure he mentioned a suspect flaw in the grain. Was under pressure myself at the time. Lilian took badly, and other problems up at the house besides.'

Kester drained his cup in one long thirsty gulp. 'What would Chas have done with the sub-standard timber?'

'Put it to one side to be exchanged on the next delivery. Could be that particular piece of ash was the one Chas was carrying when he tripped and fell. That would have weakened the thing further. We shall never know for sure. What's certain is that a section of faulty wood found its way into the workshop and that disaster out there in the yard is the result. It'd only take a single pothole going at speed to cause the damage.' Wearily he drank ale. 'I don't know, sometimes I think these things are planned. If a thing's meant to go wrong, it does, and no stopping it.'

Kester was alarmed to see the damson-dark flush spreading over his employer's cheekbones and the way he rubbed his big red fist over his chest, as if to ease a tension there.

'Not to worry,' Kester said in an effort to sooth. 'Thing is to get the damage put right. How about a sweetener? Offer the customer a rebate on his price. Or else suggest we throw him in another vehicle for good measure. Governess trap or something similar. Few can resist a genuine offer.'

'Too late, I've already given him his cash back. I know the type only too well. Flashy young blade out to impress. He'll do no more business with me, you mark my words. Bet you he's chuntering to his mates right now, damning the good name of my yard. Reckon we've not heard the end of this, Kester.'

Kester gestured towards the grounded vehicle. 'So what do we do with that?'

'Fix it up, put it in the auction for a quick sale. Cut our losses. Damned pesky fancy efforts. Give me a good honest farm wain or brewery cart any day.' Tobias reached again for the ale. 'Want another jar?'

'No thanks. Best be getting along. Have to meet Mary off the train before I push off home.'

The bushy brows rose in surprise. 'She's not back yet? She was catching the two o'clock from Ludlow.'

'I went, but she wasn't on it. She did mention she'd get a later train if there was a hitch in the accounts. Don't look so worried, man. Mary can look after herself.'

'Happen you're right. Better get off then. Mustn't keep her hanging about on the station. Take the big horse and four-wheeler. You'll get there in no time.'

He stood up and followed Kester to the door. 'And Kester?'

'Yes?'

'Not a word about our suspicions over the dodgy wood.'

''Course not. Sutton's is renowned for using only the best. Might look in on Chas Pilkington later, make sure he knows nothing as well. How's Lilian, by the way?'

'Better, lad. Peaky still, but on the mend, I'd say.'

They descended the stone steps and parted company, Kester to hitch up the bay, Tobias to his house.

As Tobias crossed the yard the voices of his two younger daughters rang out from the byre.

'Let me milk the cow, Alice. I can do it easily.'

'No, Violet. You'll only tip the pail again like you did yesterday. Such a waste of milk! I'll do her. You go ahead and collect the eggs.'

'Oh, must I? You know how I dislike the hens. It's the feathers. Horrid!'

'Just get on with it, you great baby. Feathers never harmed anyone.'

'I know. I just don't like them, never have. It's not fair, Ned never made me. I wish he was here now. He'd tell you what's what. He would!'

The voices grew shriller. About to bellow an admonishment, Tobias checked himself. After all, they had been working hard all day. They weren't very old to be running a house and he'd bet a pound to a penny that Alice had got everything, including her mother, soundly organised. He went round the side of the house to the byre.

At their father's step the argument ceased. Two flushed faces stared up at him warily, one sharp-featured and astonishingly mature, the other rounded and sweet. The cow lowed plaintively, anxious to unload her burden of milk.

'Want me to milk her?' Tobias offered, nodding towards the pail.

'No thank you, Father,' Alice replied. 'We can manage perfectly well, and you must be tired. Violet, if you're going to milk this animal, then do get on with it.'

Obediently the child sat herself down on the low three-legged stool, buried her cheek in the cow's warm flank and began to pump the teats rhythmically.

Tobias contemplated his youngest child in open wonder. 'Who taught you that?'

'Alice did.' The hands never stopped and the milk flowed with a satisfying hiss into the bucket. 'And I know how to make queen cakes. Alice showed me earlier. She showed me how to do subtraction sums as well. I'll get them all right in future.'

'Well well.' Tobias shifted his gaze to Alice, standing prim and neat on the strawy floor. 'Have we a budding schoolmistress in the family I wonder?'

'Quite possibly, Father,' Alice replied. 'I like teaching. It's very nice when children pick up what you are telling them. I like taking the tiny ones at Sunday School. Mary hated it, but then Mary never did have any patience with that sort of thing.'

'Is that so?' Tobias allowed himself a smile. 'Will I put in a word for you at the dame school in a year or so. You could be a student teacher there.'

Alice considered the idea. 'Yes please. That would suit me very well. I'd have my own little house like Miss Trench. I wouldn't need to get married then and have children of my own. Well, you wouldn't want them if you were teaching all day, would you? I'd make my class behave as well.'

'I bet you would, God help the poor little beggars!' Tobias said with a chuckle. Alice's face remained impassive.

'I'd better go and do the hens.'

'Aye, all right then.' Tobias fished in his waistcoat pocket and brought out two shiny sixpenny pieces. 'You've been handy little maids today for your mother. Well done Alice. Well done, Violet.'

The milking stopped as Violet took her reward. 'Oh, *thank* you, Father.'

'Thank you.' Alice actually smiled. 'I shall buy a book I've wanted. Violet will spend hers on sweets and sewing things I suppose.'

'Well, that's all right,' Tobias said.

'Yes. I never said it wasn't.' Standing on tiptoe, Alice planted her father a kiss on his whiskery cheek and then was gone. He put his hand where her soft young lips had been. Alice had never been demonstrative in her affections like Mary. Perhaps he should pay more attention to the girl. To both of them.

He ruffled Violet's hair as she bent once more to her task. Wishing all his problems were so easily solved, the carriage-maker left the byre and entered his house.

Lilian was waiting for him in the front parlour. On the polished mahogany table were her best cut-glass goblets and matching decanter filled with ginger wine – the nearest concession she would make to an alcoholic beverage.

'Hello there, are we celebrating?' Tobias put on his most jovial tone which Lilian, had she been less worked up, would have known to be contrived.

'I thought a little refreshment might be in order, Tobias. And yes, there could be something to celebrate, God willing.'

Nervously Lilian played with her handkerchief, twisting it between her hot fingers until it resembled a piece of rag rather than the crisply-laundered square of cambric she had just pulled from her pocket. She stiffened when the clatter and rattle of a vehicle sounded crossing the yard.

'Is that Kester? Did you know Mary wasn't on the afternoon train, Tobias? What ever can have made her so late?'

'Hargreaves' young assistant, if my guess is right.' Tobias poured out the home-brew and braced himself. Ginger wine was not to his taste. If Lilian wanted to try a hand at wine making, why not brew up some good rich mead with the honey from his own bees? She wouldn't of course. Mead had a barley base, and anything that smacked of strong liquor was sinful to a good Methodist.

'What do you mean, a young male assistant? Oh dear!'

'Now, now,' Tobias said soothingly, handing his wife her drink. 'Didn't mean to insinuate. How you do jump to conclusions, Lilian! What I inferred was that the youth was probably slow checking out the quarterly figures, and that's why Mary has missed her train. 'Tes no matter. Trains run every hour from Ludlow, and our Mary's not the panicking sort. She'll pass the time in a tea-room. Happen she'll bring you a trinket back. I gave her spending money.'

'You spoil her, Tobias,' Lilian remarked fondly. 'Me too.' She paused, then enquired, 'Tobias, what would you say to having an addition to the family? What would you say?'

He frowned, his mind still on his troubles. 'Addition? Another infant you mean? Weren't we told it would be dangerous after young Violet?'

He stopped and met Lilian's lucid gaze. All the symptoms of her recent indisposition which should have been significant to him at the time were suddenly brought home. His weathered cheeks paled. 'You don't mean? Lilian, you're not with child? Oh my God!'

Shakily he put the untasted wine down on the table and stood raking his fingers agitatedly through his beard. Lilian rose and came to face him. Now that the worst was over she was calm.

'Tobias, please tell me you are as overjoyed as I am myself. Please don't worry too much. I've been seeing Widow Goodyear. She has my symptoms firmly under control. There are herbs to take which will help my condition. She makes no promises, but she feels that with care and an untroubled outlook there is no reason why I should not have a reasonably trouble-free confinement. Given my age, of course.

'Oh, Tobias.' She looked up at him beseechingly. 'You are pleased, aren't you? A little babe in the nursery again. I do so love babies. They're so sweet and innocent. I cannot wait to hold him in my arms. Listen to me, it might be another lad like Ned. I know you'd favour a boy.'

'Maid or lad, makes no difference,' Tobias said gruffly. 'Of course I'm pleased. Just so long as you're all right.'

Having mastered his shock Tobias took Lilian in his arms and kissed her. Then he held her to him and rocked her gently. His face above her head in the plain white cap was troubled, the hazel eyes clouded with guilt.

More worry, and just when he could have done without it.

Kester thrust the letter which had arrived unexpectedly for him care of Sutton's Coach-Maker's back into the envelope and put it in his pocket. Word from George, and after all this time! How had his brother managed to trace him? There was the cash he'd sent on a few occasions. Most likely the package had Sutton's stamp on it. That would be it.

The kitchen was quiet, flooded with morning sunlight. The younger girls were at school and Mary had gone frisking off with polish and duster to tackle the front parlour. Full of the joys of spring at present, was Mary, Kester thought absently. Very likely it was that young apprentice at the accountant's that had put the sparkle in her eyes.

Tobias had taken Lilian in the trap to visit Widow Goodyear. They went every week, and whatever the good widow prescribed for Lilian seemed to be working. She was looking much better, colour in her cheeks at last.

The tramp of boots and rumble of voices heralded the men turning in for work. Kester had already opened up and set young Chips to fill up the nail and tack boxes in preparation for the day. He liked to be on the premises early. If time allowed, like today, there was always a cup of tea and slice of buttered bread waiting for him in the house.

He rubbed his chin reflectively. He appreciated the way they trusted him to come and go as he wished. Lilian treated him as one of the family, always had. And as far as the yard was concerned, Tobias had come to rely upon him, confiding in him as an equal instead of master and employee. The coach-maker would not be pleased at the contents of the letter ... Kester wasn't enraptured himself. He thought he had left all that behind. What a quandary to find himself in!

All the same, it was good to hear news from home. George was working again, thank God, and young Jack was growing apace. Lisbeth was well.

Kester caught his breath. Lisbeth, the soft darkness of her.

Suddenly the door burst open and Mary appeared. She was humming merrily, her face flushed, feet executing a dance as she crossed the flag-floored kitchen. 'Hey-ho, Kester, why the glum face? The sun's shining. You should be happy.'

'I am happy,' Kester said.

She dimpled. 'So am I. Guess what, Father had a note from Mr Hargreaves. He wants to do an audit on the past twelve months. He's asked if I can take in the ledgers. Father doesn't mind. He's delighted to have the task taken off his hands. Pesky bookwork, he calls it.'

'So you'll be off to town again. You're pleased about it.'

'Oh, I'm very pleased.'

'It ... er, wouldn't have anything to do with Hargreaves' young assistant?'

'What – him? Don't be silly, Kester. What on earth would I see in that lanky creature? And he's got spots! No, it's a different reason entirely. You'd never guess.' Excitement shone in her dark-blue eyes and in the rosy flush of her cheeks. 'Kester, I've seen my mother. I've seen Esme Greer. Actually talked to her and watched her on the stage. Oh, Kester, it was wonderful.'

Kester stared at her in sheer disbelief. 'Esme Greer's in Ludlow? Good God above! Mary ... you knew all along. The visit last week, you contrived it purposely to get to see her.'

'So what if I did?' Mary said defensively. 'Wouldn't you in my circumstances? She wasn't a bit how I'd imagined. She was much nicer. She gave me a pass for any performance I want. And she gave me this shawl. She said it matched my eyes exactly. Do you think it does, Kester?'

'How should I know? Men are useless at that sort of thing.'

'She said I was very pretty. Do you think I'm pretty, Kester?'

Whether she knew it or not, Kester couldn't be sure, but she was flirting again. He looked into those provocative eyes and knew he had to put a stop to it. 'It's a fetching shawl and it suits you well enough.'

'Yes, it does. Everyone thinks I bought it for myself.'

'That's a fib then.'

'No, it isn't. I never said as much. They just assumed. Alice wants one like it only in beige.' Mary giggled. 'She hasn't got a hope, this was from Paris. I'll have to find something really special to wear for Wednesday. That's when I'm due at the accountant's – what luck, it being matinee day too. I can hardly go looking like a Sunday School teacher, can I? Esme – she told me to call her that – well, she's promised me a spray of flowers for my hair. *And* chocolates. Oh, I can't wait!'

Kester heaved a sigh. 'Mary, this can only lead to trouble. Think how upset your parents would be. You'll feel guilty at deceiving them. Guilt makes an uneasy bedfellow – and I should know.'

'Don't be an old stick-in-the-mud, Kester. What harm can it do? They'll never know.'

'They will if I tell them.'

'You *wouldn't!*'

'No. It would hurt Lilian too much. You know she's not up to it.'

'Anyway, I'm going. It's all fitted together splendidly, just as if it were meant.'

Kester rubbed his face helplessly with his hand. He knew when he was beaten. So what next? One thing was certain, she was not going alone. There was nothing for it but for him to go with her.

Four

〰

The applause almost lifted the roof. Watching her mother take yet another curtsy, Mary clapped and clapped, her eyes bright and cheeks glowing. At her side, unfamiliar and amazingly debonair in his best suit and snowy shirt with the stiff collar, Kester applauded the performance with appreciative movements of his hands and a wry smile on his dark face. In the past he had been to many a music hall and it had not lost its magic.

'Wasn't it wonderful?' Mary said, beaming. 'I don't know which turn I liked best – next to Esme of course. The ventriloquist was so clever and funny. And the conjuror, the way he brought that white rabbit out of his hat! Oh, and the tap dancers. How do they keep such perfect timing?'

She sighed, incredulous, and Kester smiled into her delighted face. 'You'd better ask them if you get the chance. I'm glad you enjoyed the performance, Mary.'

Around them people were preparing to leave the auditorium, the ladies securing their hats and hooking vanity bags safely over their wrists, gentlemen checking nothing had been left behind on the seats. Mary glanced down at the frilled front of her blouse, where nestled the posy of violets Kester had bought her off the flower seller at the entrance to the theatre. Her mother had also left a floral adornment intended to be worn in her hair. Mary had never been given flowers before.

Two lots in one day! Wonderful!

Chocolate too. The Fry's Chocolate Cream Stick she had eaten lingered deliciously sweet on her tongue. Oh to be free to buy the confection if and whenever she wanted.

'Come along,' Kester said, 'if we're going to honour that invitation to go backstage, we'd better look snappy. And mind you keep the chat to a minimum. You and I have got a train to catch, remember.'

He guided her down the aisle, shuffling with the crowd towards the exit. There was the mingled smell of ladies' perfume, the pomade the men used on their hair, of human sweat and the camphor that went in the closets to protect best clothes against the moth. Behind them they left a litter of chocolate wrappers, cigar stubs and orange peel. Oranges had been a favourite amongst theatre goers for decades.

Kester retrieved his topcoat and Mary's blue woollen cape from the cloakroom. A word in the attendant's ear and they were directed through a doorway marked Private and along a corridor which brought them, eventually, to the hum of voices and Esme Greer's dressing-room.

'Mary!' smilingly Esme Greer pushed through the throng to welcome them. 'Listen everyone, this is my long-lost cousin Mary Sutton and her escort ...?' She looked inquiringly – interestedly – from Mary to Kester.

'This is Kester Hayes, Esme,' Mary said hastily. 'I told you about him, remember? Kester works for my father. Kester, this is my cousin, Esme Greer.'

He bowed, then took Esme's hand and brushed it with his lips. 'Madame Greer. Charmed to meet you.'

Mary stared at him. This was a different Kester to the one she knew. A suave, polished Kester. She felt proud to be with him.

Esme dimpled and swept him a coy glance under long lashes. 'Mr Hayes – or may I call you Kester? Such a strong, masculine name, I always think.'

He smiled. 'Kester it is.'

'And you must call me Esme.' She turned to the company. 'Wine please for my guests. Mary, do come and meet Janette and Rollo. The tap dancing couple, you know. Didn't you tell me you loved to dance yourself?'

'Why, yes.' Mary found a glass of sparkling wine put in her hand. She took a sip, spluttering a little when the bubbles went up her nose. It tasted sweet and flowery at once. Nothing like the ginger wine of Lilian's making, non-alcoholic and decidedly boring. She liked it and took another sip. 'Janette? I loved your act. How ever do you manage to keep up that perfect footwork, and so quick as well?'

One after another the performers made themselves known to her. Soon the wine was beginning to sing in her blood. Her tongue was loosened and laughter came easily. She was flattered when a male member of the troupe – she was beyond remembering names – complimented her on her milk-maid complexion and midnight-blue eyes.

Milk-maid sounded so much more poetic than country-girl, which was bucolic in the extreme!

Out of the corner of her eye she saw Kester, also enjoying himself immensely. Stage folk were so friendly and bright. They glittered and gleamed, knew how to make the most of themselves, made you feel good. If only it could always be like this, Mary thought. If only ...

'I love your escort,' whispered Esme Greer's voice in her ear. 'So handsome. And such an air of mystery!'

'Do you think so?' Mary trilled a laugh. 'He's just Kester to me, but then I suppose we've all got used to him at home.'

They broke off as the door opened to admit yet another visitor into the room. Everywhere went suddenly quiet. 'Pierre!' Esme cried, sweeping off to plant a kiss on the newcomer's cheek. He was a dapper gentleman, not tall, though his upright bearing gave him the appearance of being so. He carried a top hat and cane, and had a wonderful twirling moustache and darting black eyes.

'Mary, come and be introduced to Pierre Pascal, my agent. If it wasn't for Pierre, we wouldn't be here now. Pierre, Mary Sutton.'

Greetings were exchanged, and then Pierre Pascal – who confusingly was not French as his name implied, but then that was stage people for you – got down to the reason for his visit. 'Good news, Esme my dear. That lead part I've been angling for you?'

Esme drew a quick breath. 'The musical at the Prince of Wales theatre in London?'

'The very one. I dined with the producer the night before last. They want you, Esme. The female part is yours. Frederick Mears is to play the male lead.' He twirled his moustache in obvious glee. 'Musical plays will be all the rage in the future. The days of the music hall as we know it are numbered. Oh, it will still have its followers,' he declared to the relief of all present. 'But there's a greater interest in music now. This new play with songs shows a great deal of promise. It's by a young composer, I might add. The producer is taking a risk. That is why he wants a well-known name for the heroine. And who better than Esme Greer to draw the crowds? And Freddie Mears of course! It's all arranged, subject to the signing of contracts. Once we get this present tour over with, Esme, you'll have three week's break over Christmas in which to study the script and the musical score. Rehearsals begin in the new year. Operetta, Esme! Precisely the change of direction we've been after. Here's a chance to prove yourself an actress as well as an entertainer!'

'Oh!' Esme clapped her hands together in joy. 'Oh – how perfectly thrilling! Dearest Pierre, where would I be without you?'

Everyone started talking at once. Congratulations were spoken over and again. Esme could not keep the smile from her face. 'You've brought me luck!' she said to Mary, hugging her. 'We should have met earlier. If we'd been together something similar might have happened ages ago. A part in a brand-new musical play, and just when I had almost given up hope!'

'I don't know when I've enjoyed myself so much before!' Mary said with a happy sigh. Fields and woods went streaming by as the train clattered and rocked its way homewards. Above her head on the rack lay her leather satchel containing the ledger of accounts for the business. Mary had been so rapt by the matinee perform-ance she had nearly forgotten the true purpose of the trip to Ludlow.

'Good thing I remembered the books,' Kester chuckled. 'I can just picture Tobias's face if you'd turned up without them. He'd have had forty fits, poor man!'

Mary giggled. 'Oh, Kester, wasn't it wonderful? Esme has a beautiful voice, hasn't she? And to think she's going on to perform in musical plays. I intend to brush up my piano playing now. I let it go when Mother took ill, there simply weren't time to fit every-thing in. Did you enjoy the show?'

'Very much.'

'Thank you, thank you for taking me. And the flowers and everything.' She held the posy to her face. The violets were sadly wilting but their fragrance still clung faintly. Mary put the flowers into her reticule, alongside the floral hair adornment. She would press them as a keepsake. No-one must know about them.

'You're welcome,' Kester replied. 'Esme Greer was every bit as good as when I saw her before. Better perhaps. Her voice has matured.'

'It was at Sheffield, you said?'

He nodded. 'We all of us went. My brother George and his wife Lisbeth. Young Georgie wasn't born then.'

'You have a brother and small nephew? I didn't know. Is your brother like you?'

'To look at you mean? Not really. He's five years older. He's a big fellow. You couldn't miss him in a crowd. Lisbeth looks a wraith beside him.'

'Is she pretty?'

'Very.' Kester swallowed. He preferred not to go down that road, thank you very much. 'We were happy then, all of us. A proper family. George and I both had jobs, enough money coming in to keep us in comfort if not in luxury. Lisbeth had the house like a new pin. She was so proud of it, and of George. Then he had to get mixed up with the Chartists – the fool!'

Mary frowned. 'Chartists? You mean the people who caused those awful riots? Shocking!'

'Mmm. I'm the last person to go along with wanton destruction, but it wasn't totally without cause,' Kester pointed out reasonably. 'The working man has a right to his say, and unfortunately the Reform Act fuelled a great deal of disappointment amongst the ranks.'

'It did? I wouldn't know. All the same, mob violence and everything.' Mary shuddered. 'How dreadful. Let's not think about the past, Kester. Let's think of Esme. I did so love the song she sang. The one about the galleons in full sail. It was funny. She made the audience rock with laughter.'

'It was risqué! Naughty but nice. For heaven's sake don't start singing it around the house. Poor Lilian will have the vapours!'

Mary giggled and turned to look out of the window. Her eyes dreamed. The train was rambling and juddering through familiar farmland now. The movement was soporific and Kester's eyelids closed.

Let's not think about the past, Kester.

Easier said than done.

On the verge of sleep, George's strong dark face entered Kester's mind. He was back there in the living kitchen of the small terraced house. They had just finished supper and were sitting round the table having another mug of tea.

'There's a meeting in the back room of the Crown tonight,' George said. 'Come with us, Kester. I tell you, this is the very thing we workers need to get ourselves heard.'

Kester put down his mug with a frown. 'Wrecking and hurting? There are better ways. It's wits you need to fight with, George, not brawn. Rioting will only put Parliament's back up. It gives the wrong impression. The working man needs a better image. A bit of dignity.'

George snorted. 'Dignity! Let me get my hands round the necks of some of those toffs they call politicians, and I'll show them what dignity is!'

'George!' Lisbeth protested. 'I don't like it when you get on to this subject. It changes you. Do you have to go to the meeting? Again?'

He reached out and ruffled his wife's soft dark hair. 'Yes, sweeting, I have to go. Don't worry, George Hayes knows how to look after himself. You coming, Kester?'

He shook his head. 'Some other time. I managed to pick up a bit of seasoned oak at the manufactory today. I thought I'd take up carving again. Used to be good at it.'

They stood up. George went to the door and took his topcoat from the peg. Lisbeth cleared away the supper dishes with more clatter than was necessary. The room was bright and warm from the fire of coals burning in the grate. Kester took his tin box of tools from the dresser and went to sit by the hearth. He took a sharp little knife from the box, picked up a section of wood and studying it for a moment, started to carve.

'Well, I'll be off then,' George said.

They heard his heavy boots tramping away down the cobbled road. Having dealt with the pots, Lisbeth fetched her sewing basket and went to sit opposite Kester. The silence was friendly and relaxed. This was the fourth night in a row George had been absent. Not his sort of thing, Chartism, Kester thought. But tomorrow he might go with George, if only to get away for a while. It was getting too cosy, himself and Lisbeth and the dancing firelight …

The train hissed and trundled into the small rural halt of Aston Cross and Kester woke with a start. His first thought was George, in trouble again. He'd have to go and help out. Tobias would understand, being a family man himself.

'You were snoring,' Mary giggled.

'I wasn't. I never snore. One more remark like that, young lady, and I shan't take you out again. Careful. Wait for the train to stop before you get up. Now we can go. Here's the case with the ledger. Goodness, you'd forget your head if was loose.'

'Stop fussing, Kester. There's Chips with the pony and trap. Lovely. Half an hour and we'll be home. Come on, I want to pick out that tune on the piano. Not the one about the galleons, the ballad about the fair. That was nice too …'

Chattering brightly, Mary alighted on to the platform. Kester followed, his face sober in the late afternoon light. He hoped he had done the right thing, going with Mary. Still, it was done now. Secrets and subterfuge seemed to follow him somehow. And all he ever wanted was a quiet life!

The tinkling of the piano resounded in the drawing room. Mary had made sure the doors were closed and everyone occupied before she started playing. Lilian had gone for a nap. Alice and Violet were at school and Father was working. With luck she had a whole hour to herself.

Scales first to get her fingers supple. Then a harvest hymn, just to be on the safe side. She paused, ears straining for any movement. But the house was quiet, golden autumn sunshine streaming in through the deep sash windows. Humming the melody line of the galleon song which had so taken her fancy, she began to pick the tune out on the piano. A few tries and she had it. Mary was good at improvisation. She soon had the bass chords and started to hum along with the playing. What a pity she didn't know the words.

The hour sped by. Mary moved on to a popular medley. Sometimes the men sang snatches of songs as they worked – Josh Millet especially was a staunch music hall fan – and Mary was quick to pick up the tunes and lyrics. She sang them now to a lively accompaniment. Her voice rang out and she did not hear the door opening and her sisters entering the room.

'What a din!' said Alice. 'I thought the cats were out! Whoever showed you how to play that common stuff, our Mary?'

Mary shut the lid of the piano with a slam. 'None of your business, Alice. And popular music isn't common. Why are you such a snob?'

'Mother wouldn't be pleased if she heard you playing that stuff,' Alice persisted. 'She wouldn't!'

Violet said, 'I thought it sounded nice. Jolly, you know. You've got a lovely voice, Mary. I wish I could sing.'

'You know how to sew,' Alice said to her younger sister. 'That's far more useful than caterwauling to the piano. What a waste of time!'

Mary pulled a face. 'It isn't, not at all. Music gives pleasure. And to be able to entertain is a skill, so there!'

'Girls, girls!' Lilian said, coming into the room. 'I do wish you wouldn't squabble. You can be heard all over the house. Mary, did you put the rice pudding in the oven?'

Mary's hands flew to her face. 'Oh heavens, I quite forgot! Sorry

Mother. I suppose it's too late now for it to cook. Shall I whip up an apple sponge instead?'

'It might be as well.' Lilian sighed and shook her head as Mary escaped the room. Some things never changed. She had hoped Mary had turned over a new leaf, become more responsible, but ...

'She was playing those common pieces,' Alice said. 'Like they sing across in the workshop.'

'But it sounded much nicer,' Violet put in loyally. 'You have to admit, Alice. Mary's got a way with songs. She makes the music tell a story.'

Alice sniffed. 'Sloppy love and all that. I bet Father never went in for that sort of thing when he was courting you, Mother.'

Lilian smiled. 'He gave me a beautiful Valentine card. I still have it. It has roses and forget-me-nots painted on it and a cover of real lace. There's a verse too.'

'Oh,' said Alice.

'I hope someone sends me a Valentine when I'm older,' Violet said wistfully. 'I do.'

'I'm sure you'll have lots, my love,' her mother replied.

'I won't, nor do I want them,' Alice declared. 'Did you know Mary has a lovespoon hidden in her settle in her bedroom?'

'No, I didn't.' Lilian was startled. What had the girl been up to now? 'Perhaps it was something she picked up at a fair. Not a proper one. And anyway, you had no right to pry, Alice.'

'I wasn't prying. I was looking for that shawl you asked me to find and just came across it. And it is a proper lovespoon. It's all carved and shiny.'

Violet giggled. 'I wonder who gave it to her? Maybe it was Kester!'

'Don't be so silly,' Alice said. 'Kester's old.'

Her mother burst out laughing. 'Well, if Kester's in his dotage, I dread to think how your Father and I must appear. And me with another infant on the way. Which reminds me, Violet. The wool has arrived in the post for those baby jackets. We can make a start this evening. Cosy now the days are drawing in, sitting by the fire knitting.'

Violet nodded, pleased. Alice gave another disparaging snort. 'Myself, I would prefer to read. But I suppose we can't all be the same.'

'No,' Lilian agreed.

Later, after the two younger girls had gone to bed, Lilian ventured her concern about Mary to Tobias. 'Tobias. Alice said Mary was playing unsuitable songs on the piano. Music hall songs, I took her to mean. You know how quick Mary is to pick up a tune. Where on earth could she have heard them?'

Tobias frowned. 'In the workshop, most likely. Though I do warn the men not to get too bawdy when the lasses are about. Did you hear her playing yourself?'

'No, I did not. Apparently she's got a lovespoon in her bedroom as well.'

'What, one of those Welsh nick-nacks? Beautiful things, some of them. Great deal of skill goes into the carving of them. We once delivered a haywain to a farm over the border. They had a whole collection of spoons on the wall. Some of them dated right back to early times. Can't think what our Mary would be doing with one, though. Can't think why she plays those songs on the piano either, when she knows you wouldn't approve.'

'You could always ask her. Tactfully, of course. You know Mary. She can be touchy.'

'So can I when I'm riled! Where is she?'

'Out bedding Brownie down. He's getting old. Mary's started stabling him now the nights are growing cooler.'

'Best get it over with I reckon.' He pulled himself up out of the comfortable chair, then stood rubbing his chest with his hand. 'I don't know. As if there isn't enough mither with folks taking their custom to this new-fangled carriage-yard, without Mary adding to the bother. No Kester either. God, but I'm missing him around the place.'

'Have you had any word from him?'

'Not yet. These domestic crises can take some sorting.'

'Did you say his brother was a Chartist follower?'

'That's right. Got himself in a speck of bother once before, apparently. Got flung inside with a ruck of other trouble-makers.'

'In gaol?' Lilian drew a quavering breath. 'How dreadful! Has he any family?'

'One small boy. Wife's a bit frail, not the managing type. George, that's the brother's name, wrote to Kester asking if he'd go and look after them as before.'

'And Kester being what he is couldn't refuse. Ah well, let's hope he's soon back amongst us.'

'Amen to that. Hope Mary's not up to some sort of mischief. Lot of worry, girls.'

'It may be nothing, Tobias,' Lilian said soothingly. 'As to the matter of the yard, these things blow over. As soon as people realise that it's better to stay with what you know, they will come back to you. Farmer Benson already has had second thoughts. According to Widow Goodyear he's cancelled his order with Wilberforces and is coming here. A tumbrel cart, I think he wants. Right up your street.'

'Aye, it is that!' Tobias beamed at his wife. It was the best news he'd had in weeks!

Mary threw an armful of hay into the rack and turned to the pony. 'There you are, Brownie. Good boy.'

The pony pulled a mouthful, munching, then flicked an ear as Tobias entered the stall. 'Mary. I want a word.'

'Oh? What is it, Father? Is anything wrong?'

'Depends. What's this about playing theatre tunes on the piano?'

Mary made a face. 'Alice! What a little sneak for a sister!'

'Your mother was concerned. I won't have her worried, Mary, and her in a delicate condition.'

'I wouldn't have thought it was me giving any cause for worry. Alice is the one making all the fuss.'

'Oh, stop griping about your sister. Alice has got a good head on her shoulders. Likely she'll make a decent living for herself someday.'

'Meaning I won't?'

'That's up to you, isn't it?' Again Tobias eased his chest in agitation. 'You've not answered my question. The songs.'

Mary glowered at him mutinously. The pony took more hay and the comfortable sound of munching filled the stable.

'Mary?'

'Well, if you must know,' Mary replied awkwardly, 'I went to the theatre to see Esme Greer!'

He stared at her in disbelief. 'You what? But ... but when?'

'Wednesday. When I took in the ledgers. It was the matinee.'

'You went into one of those bawdy places, and on your own?'

'No. Kester went with me if you must know. And before you fly off the handle about him too, Father, Kester did it for your own good. He knew you'd be anxious. He knew he couldn't stop me from going and thought it best to accompany me and make sure everything was all right. Which it was.'

'Kester went ...' Tobias gasped for air. His face was livid in the chancy light of the stall. 'I'll have him out on his ear! I'll have the Law on him! Wait till he comes back and I get my hands on him! Double-dealing scoundrel, wheedling his way in here, taking my money—'

'Which was well and truly earned. Come on, Father. Where

would you be without Kester? I repeat, it wasn't him, it was me. With or without him I would have gone to meet my mother. I had to see her, don't you understand? Kester did. He stayed at my side the whole of the time and brought me safe home again. So you've nothing to reproach him for.'

Tobias gathered his scattered wits. He'd speak with Kester another time, but for now, 'You say you saw her to speak to?'

'Yes I did.'

'You took it on yourself to go and seek her out, with never a word to us, your proper family? Are you out of your mind, girl? I trusted you. Get the books to Hargreaves, have a look round town, collect the books and come back home. And what do you do? Go slinking off behind my back to see your real mother. Good God, Mary, there's more of her in you than I realised. It's just the sort of thing she would have done.'

'So what if it is?' cried Mary, stung. 'What's wrong with doing the natural thing?'

'It was the way you went about it. Behind my back. Thinking only of yourself. Good God above, you're turning out just like her. Selfish, devious and … and shallow!'

Mary's temper broke. 'Is that so? In that case I may as well go. If you don't want me, my own mother does. She says I bring her luck, d'you know that? She got the offer of a lead part in a new London production while I was there.'

'Did she now! Well, that's impressive I'm sure. All right, girl, if that's what you want. But you'll be sorry. Mark my words you will!'

It was morning, still dark. Mary flung her clothes randomly into the two holdalls by her bed. Her eyes ached from lack of sleep. She wondered did she have enough in her savings for the train fare? Trust Kester to be absent. He would have loaned her some money without a wink.

There was a light tap on the door. Mary jumped. 'Who is it?'

'Me. Mother. May I come in?'

'Of course.' Mary steeled herself. She didn't want to upset Lilian, especially now with the baby and everything. But nothing Lilian could say would change her mind. She was going on the first train she could get – once she had got this dratted packing done!

Lilian was already dressed in her plain blue morning gown, a light shawl draping her shoulders and obvious pregnancy. Her hair was drawn back under a plain white cap. Suddenly she looked the epitome of security and comfort.

'Mother, I'm—' Mary began, but Lilian forestalled her.

'Your father told me. You want to go and try your luck with your own mother. It doesn't come as a surprise. I think I've always known you'd leave us some day.'

Mary swallowed. This was not the response she had expected. 'It was Father. He said awful things.'

'He didn't mean the half of it, Tobias never does. He's got worries, Mary. The yard. Kester not being around. And I know he's anxious about me. He feels guilty. It's no use telling him how happy I am about the coming baby, he just doesn't take it on board. But this isn't helping you. What he said last night he's already regretting. Too late now of course. He'll never come up and apologise – these men and their ridiculous pride!'

'You mean, you don't mind my going?'

'Of course I mind, child. You're my first daughter, my lovely Mary. I shall miss you. But somehow I think this is for the best. You're the sort who has to experience something to be convinced.'

Mary felt a quick rush of tears. She had misjudged Lilian. Here was someone who understood. A quiet, dignified woman, God-fearing – the very opposite of her own mother who now seemed a rather unknown quantity. Was she taking too big a risk? But she had said she was going, and go she would.

'I ... I don't know what to say,' she whispered, and gave Lilian a tearful hug.

'There now. Don't say anything.' Lilian patted Mary's damp cheek and then cast a look at the mess of packing. 'Let's take all these things out and start again, shall we?'

Half an hour and the two cases stood closed and ready, the garments neatly folded inside. Lilian had raided her own wardrobe for flannel petticoats, winter coming on and she knew how chilly London could be, with the river fog and everything.

'Have you enough money?'

'I think so,' Mary replied. 'I'm sure my ... Esme Greer will help out there.'

'Wait a moment.' Lilian left the room and was back directly with two gold sovereigns and a heavy gold ring with a pearl setting. 'Those are real pearls. The ring belonged to my grandmother. It's too small for my finger but should fit yours perfectly. Take it and when you wear it think of us. Sell it if need be, it will fetch a good price.'

Mary nodded mutely and put the items in her purse. Lilian went on, 'A word of advice my grandpapa gave me. Always make sure you have enough money on you for a ticket home. Even if your venture takes you across the seas. Remember that, Mary. And remember we love you. You have a home here, always.'

The rattle and clatter of the pony cart sounded below. 'That will be Chips. I told him to drive you to the station. The bags. You'll never carry them all that way.'

'No. Thank you. Er ... there's Violet. Alice. I've not said goodbye ...' All at once her sisters were very dear to her – even Alice. And there was Ned, away doing his apprenticeship. It seemed ages since she saw Ned.

'I'll give them your love, never fear. Go now, before your father appears. Write to us, Mary. Keep in touch. Promise.'

'I will. I'll be thinking of you at Christmas. The baby and everything.'

They hugged again and then Lilian pushed her gently towards the door. 'Go now. I'll send Chips up for the luggage. Goodbye my love. May God go with you.'

The sky was lightening as the pony trap rumbled across the yard. Sitting in the passenger seat, her winter cloak heavy on her shoulders, Mary glanced back at the house where she had been raised. Beamsters sat cosily in its pretty garden, rosy-red brick damp with dew, smoke wisping from the tall chimneys. The workshop doors were still closed and shuttered against the night. From the byre the cow lowed mournfully, anxious to give up her burden of milk.

Brownie was between the shafts. The pony was her special pet. She'd say her farewells to him at the station. The other horses were in the winter yard. Someone else would feed them from now on.

'Giddup there!'

Passing between the two chestnut trees at the entrance on to the lane, Chips flicked the reins and obediently the pony sprang into a trot. In a few moments the house was gone from view.

Mary bit her lip. When would she ever see it again?

Five

❧

The cab swayed and bounced through the foggy London streets and Mary, jolted about on the passenger seat, clutched the leather handgrip and strained to see through the swirling yellowish vapour that pressed against the window.

Shapes were smudged and unreal. A building here, a hurrying pedestrian there, a street lamp glowing through the murk. The city she had so looked forward to seeing was lost to her, and she sank back on the seat with a sigh.

Winter at home was never like this, Mary thought fretfully. She could even taste the fog, foul on her tongue. And how on earth could the cabbie see to drive the horses?

Already exhausted from the long train ride south, Mary was having doubts about her new life. The stage was not all glamour – far from it. The journeying, the overnight stops and the unremitting round of rehearsal and performance had been arduous. Christmas came and went in a blur. None of it was what she was used to, and she wondered if joining forces with her mother was turning out a terrible mistake.

Beside her Esme sat with a smile on her lips. Nothing ever got Esme Greer down. 'Soon be there,' she said cheerfully, her green eyes bright beneath the brim of her feathered hat. 'Robbie will have supper pending – one of her specialities, if I know my housekeeper.'

Mary listened mutely as Esme chatted on. 'You'll adore number fifteen, Mary. We're not a large household. Just Robson, who's cook and housekeeper in one, a girl to help her and Webster, who deals with the outside work. And there's Standish, of course.'

The third member of the party sat opposite with her eyes closed. Rose Standish was Esme's personal maid and dresser. A thin unsmiling person, Standish was rarely seen without a flat iron or needle and thread in her hand. Though she affected to be sleeping, Mary was sure she heard every word that was said.

The cab slowed as a corner was taken. Esme peered around eagerly. 'I do believe we're here. Yes, Nightingale Square at last.' The horses were reined in with a loud, 'Who ... oa there!' and they all lurched to a thankful stop.

Mary gazed out incredulous. After the smoky pall of the streets, the windows of the tall double-fronted residence in the quiet South Kensington square blazed with light. How could they afford all those lamps? she thought, and remembered Esme telling her of the new gas lighting recently installed.

Clambering stiffly down from the cab, fatigue washed over her afresh. She felt oddly disorientated, as if this was happening to another person and not herself at all. Someone came to help unload the baggage, and the housekeeper was there, stout and important in her rustling black gown.

'Robbie!' Esme cried, embracing the woman. 'How marvellous to be back. Dear, foggy old London. A regular pea-souper to welcome me home!' Through her own personal fog Mary heard herself being introduced as Esme's cousin. 'From the country. Cousin Mary's come to live with us. Mary, this is Robson.'

Mary managed a smile and a mumbled greeting. Behind them Standish was in command of the packages, boxes and trunks that were being transported into the house. The cabbie was paid off and went driving away into the late-December gloom.

'In we go, Mary. Why, I vow you are swaying on your feet!' Mary's arm was firmly taken. She was ushered up the steps, past the glossy green-painted front door with its letter box of gleaming brass and lion-head door-knocker, into a spacious hallway smelling of beeswax and fresh flowers.

Being divested of her cape and bonnet, she had a confused impression of gleaming surfaces, rich brocades, paintings in gilt frames and delicate porcelain. The scent of hothouse lilies was over-powering and the lamplight dazzled. Mary closed her eyes against the glare and wished, heartily, for somewhere that did not chug, rattle or jolt to lay her head. Robson was telling her something, but for the life of her Mary could not take it in. Esme, not indifferent to the girl's unusual pallor and silence, tactfully suggested a rest before supper.

'A cup of hot milk perhaps, Robbie?'

'I'll send some up, madam,' the housekeeper said.

Mary never got round to drinking it. When the maid tapped and entered the bedroom, she found Mary curled up in the bed sound asleep. The girl withdrew, closing the door gently behind her.

Mary woke to the dawn twitter of sparrows and the distant clatter and clop of traffic. She lay wondering where she was. London! That was it, she was in London!

Getting on for six o'clock, she guessed – her customary hour for rising, though Esme never emerged before ten. Excitement tingled. Yesterday with its gruelling journey and unwelcoming fog was forgotten. She couldn't stay in bed any longer.

She got up, fumbled to light the lamp and the room sprang into brightness. Appreciatively she took in the forget-me-not-sprigged walls, the fringed rugs and dainty furniture. At the foot of the bed her trunk stood unopened. She made a move towards it, then stopped. Unpacking was for later. First there was the house to explore. Splashing her face with cold water from the jug on the marble-topped washstand, she dressed quickly in the travelling skirt and high-necked blouse of yesterday, and left the room.

Not a sound anywhere; the house still slumbered. Softly Mary crossed the landing, stole down the curved stairway and peeped into the first room. A withdrawing room, elegantly furnished in the French style, grand piano in the corner. Next was a sitting room, chintzy, intimate. A dining room, formal, with furniture of glowing mahogany. Contemplating the table, Mary was reminded of the one at Beamsters that was polished every day. Ned had once accidentally scratched the top and Kester had done a remarkable repair on the damaged surface.

Kester.

Kester and home seemed suddenly very far away.

A healthy grumbling in her stomach reminded her of the missed supper. So leaving her investigation of the house for now, Mary headed for the kitchens and something to eat.

Opening the green baize door, she stopped short. Robson, a white pinafore over her black gown, stood at a big central table slicing up rashers from a flitch of bacon. Before the range a maid was feeding the flames with billets of wood.

Both servants looked up at the intrusion. 'G ... good morning,' Mary stammered. 'I didn't think anyone was up yet. I was hungry. I thought I'd get myself some bread and butter.'

Robson sniffed. 'Breakfast is at eight, miss. I did mention that last night.'

'Oh, did you? I must have forgotten. I was a bit tired.'

'Sleeping like a babe you were when I brought your drink,' the maid piped up. 'No wonder you didn't wake for supper.'

'Best fillet of beef and an apple snow! What a waste of good food!' Robson grumbled. 'It strikes me, Dorcas, that some folk don't know when they're well off!'

She picked up the kitchen knife and deftly sliced another rasher. Mary's mouth watered.

Dorcas stood up and brushed the wood bits from her grey cambric skirts. She was small and snub-featured, with peat-brown eyes and fairish hair scraped severely back under a linen cap. 'Listen to you, Robson!' she said saucily. 'Wouldn't Miss Mary relish some of that ham fried up crisp with an egg or two? It's what you fed me when I first came here from the orphanage. Thought I'd died and gone to heaven, I did! I'd never tasted food like it!'

The housekeeper pursed her lips. 'Well … all right then. Ham and eggs it is. Dorcas, pour the girl some tea while she's waiting.' She flung Mary a glance. 'You'd better sit down, miss.'

The tea was hot and strong. Adding milk, the colour barely changed, and Mary realised with a shock it was watered down. Recalling the rich pailfuls her hands had coaxed from the cow at home, she could have told Robson a thing or two about good food! But the tea was reviving and she did full justice to the breakfast that followed.

'Thank you. That was delicious,' she said, and collecting up her dirty dishes she made for the scullery. Dorcas had gone off with ash bucket and brush to deal with the fires. Robson looked up from the breakfast tray she was preparing. 'And where do you think you're going with those?' she demanded.

'The sink,' Mary said. 'To wash the pots.'

'You'll do no such thing!' thundered the housekeeper. 'A guest washing up after herself? I've never known the like! Away with you into the morning room, miss. You can sit there until Madam comes down.'

Tight-lipped, Mary abandoned the dishes and went. What a fuss about nothing, she thought irritably.

The pleasant morning room overlooked the garden – big, she

saw, with pear trees and a vegetable plot at the bottom. A breeze had got up in the night, driving away the fog, and a hazy sun was struggling out between grey clouds. Directly beneath the window a rose bed still yielded a few late buds. The warm smell of them teased her nostrils, until she realised there were roses in the room as well. Red ones, arranged in a crystal bowl on a side table. There was a card, gilt-edged. Curious, Mary picked it up.

'To my dearest Esme, with all my love, Perry,' announced the sender in a bold, flowing hand.

Who's Perry, Mary wondered. She replaced the card and went to sit by the fire. It was newly lit and burned fitfully, giving out little heat as yet. This room too boasted a piano, an ordinary upright this time. Looking at the silk curtains and spindly chairs, Mary couldn't help comparing them with the heavy old country furniture and dark plush of Beamsters. She wondered had Lilian had her baby yet? The new little half-brother or half-sister Mary would never see. At least now she was at Nightingale Square, communication would be easier. When they had been on tour Lilian's letters had taken days to catch up with them. Some, Mary suspected, never arrived at all.

Through the open door Robson could be heard at work. Not a large household, Esme had said. It seemed gargantuan to Mary, used to a house twice this size and kept in sparkling order by their own hands.

The rattle of coal scuttles announced the return of Dorcas. 'Is that madam's tray? Will I take it up?' she asked Robson.

Here was a chance to return the favour the maid had done her. Jumping to her feet, Mary braved another visit to the kitchen. 'I'll take Cousin Esme her breakfast, shall I? Save you bothering and I've nothing else to do.'

'Very considerate of you miss, I'm sure,' said Dorcas. The housekeeper checked the fare. 'Coddled eggs, toast. Pot of chocolate. Honey. If madam wants anything more, perhaps you wouldn't mind bringing the message, miss,' she said to Mary.

'Of course not,' Mary agreed, and lifting the tray she left the kitchen.

She found Esme awake and yawning. Her auburn hair was twisted in two burnished braids for the night and her face was innocent of rouge and powder, but she was still beautiful.

'Mary. You've brought my breakfast. How sweet of you,' she said, sitting up and accepting the tray. She patted the side of the bed. 'Come and sit. Let's chat.'

Sitting down, Mary glanced around her. A pink and gold room, luxurious, cluttered. All those ornaments and pictures, she thought, feeling a stab of sympathy for Dorcas who had the dusting of them. There was a portrait of a younger Esme posing in an arbour of flowers. The likeness to Mary was unmistakable and she remarked upon it.

'Now you see why I had to pass us off as cousins. No-one would have taken us for mere acquaintances,' Esme said, pouring chocolate.

'No.' Mary bit her lip. 'Esme, I've been meaning to ask you. I don't feel easy with the deceit. Couldn't we tell the truth now? You needn't mention you and Father weren't … wed. But there's nothing wrong in our being mother and daughter.'

'There is when you have appearances to keep up.' Esme made a wry face. 'Think of my public, Mary. Esme Greer with a grown-up daughter? Tut! Besides, cousins are much more fun. Treat it as playing a part – you'll enjoy it. Now …' She broke the top of an egg and dipped into the yolk. 'My dressmaker is due later. We must get you a whole new wardrobe made up.'

'Oh, lovely,' Mary said, brightening.

'Another thing. You'll want to get out and about, and I can't be acting as chaperon all the time.'

'But I can go out on my own. I'm used to it.'

'Not here you can't. London isn't the country, you know! What if we promote the girl in the kitchen to companion?'

'Dorcas?'

'Is that her name? I wouldn't know. I leave the staffing to Robbie. She takes girls from the orphanage and trains them up. This one seems bright enough. She'll soon learn what to do. We can always get another girl for the house.'

'I like Dorcas,' Mary said impulsively. 'Better than Robson.'

Esme peeled with laughter. 'Oh, don't mind Robbie. Her bark's far worse than her bite, I do assure. That's settled then. I'll tell Robbie of the new arrangements later. Now. The dressmaker. You'll need a fashionable cape. Cherry red would suit. I never could get away with it with this hair, but with your colouring it would look rather splendid, *Cousin* Mary.'

She smiled winningly at Mary. Smiling back, Mary felt herself relax. So her mother enjoyed her company. Things were working out after all.

'You have to watch those market traders. They put the pennies on if they think you're well-to-do,' Dorcas commented.

Mary nodded. 'Same back home. I always left the pony and trap out of town. Tuppence farthing went on a score of oranges in a wink if the stall-holder saw you had your own transport!'

Laughing, Mary switched her laden basket to her other arm. The two girls had been to the fruit and vegetable market and were walking home via the Serpentine, since Mary craved fresh air and grass beneath her feet. It was cold, a hint of frost in the air, and even Dorcas's pale cheeks had a touch of colour as they tramped along. In the few days since the orphanage girl's promotion, a friendship had struck up. If Dorcas was learning how to dress her young mistress and style her hair, so was Mary adjusting to having these things done for her. They made a game of it – out of earshot of Robson.

'Better hurry,' Dorcas said. 'I forgot to mention. The dressmaker's due. Another fitting.'

Mary pulled a face. 'I can't abide that woman. Madame Babette – she isn't even French!'

'*And* she diddles the mistress,' Dorcas said. 'Puts pounds on the bills, not pennies!'

'Truly?' Mary tutted. 'Well!'

They increased their pace, hurrying over the frosted grass of Kensington Gardens, passing under Marble Arch and arriving, red-cheeked and breathless, at Nightingale Square. Entering number fifteen, Dorcas took the baskets of fruit and vegetables to the kitchen and Mary darted up the stairs.

In Esme's dressing room dress fabrics of all type and colour were spread out over the chairs. Capes and skirts had already been ordered. Today's appointment was for gowns.

'I've made my choice.' Esme seized a length of emerald green silk and swathed it around herself. 'What do you think?'

The silk shimmered and the colour brought out the vivid green of Esme's eyes. 'Perfect,' Mary said. The dressmaker was eyeing Mary's blue day gown with undisguised contempt.

'Dear me, child. We must be quick and fit you up with something. That blue woollen. So countrified!'

Mary's face flamed. How dare the woman! Lilian and Violet had spent many evenings making this dress. It was her best, the one she wore for chapel. Biting back a retort, she said instead, sugar sweet, 'I'm sure I can trust your judgement in the matter.' And vowed to get her own back, somehow.

That afternoon, the sound of a carriage turning into the square sent Mary speeding to her window. Critically her eyes roamed over the pair of matching greys and the stylish coachwork of the vehicle pulling up outside. From the carriage stepped the figure of a man; tall, elegantly clad, a slightly rakish air.

Soon afterwards Dorcas came to say that the mistress wanted her in the withdrawing room. 'It's Lord Peregrine,' she giggled. 'He's a card, that one!'

Lord Peregrine Sayle stood with his back to the fire. He was older than Mary had first thought. She liked his twinkly blue eyes and the way his sandy hair flopped over his forehead. When Esme made the introductions he came forward and lightly brushed Mary's hand with his lips. 'Call me Perry,' he said, sweeping aside in one easy gesture Mary's anxiety of how to address a member of the nobility. 'So you're Cousin Mary.'

'Yes,' she said. 'And you're the red rose gentleman!'

He chuckled. 'Red rose gentleman, eh! Oh, I like that.'

Dimpling, Mary then caught Esme's disapproving glare from where she sat on the chaise longue. She was dressed to go out and rose abruptly to her feet. 'Shall we make tracks, Perry? The exhibition opens at two, and I do so hate to be caught in the crush.'

At once Perry was attentive. 'Of course, m'dear.' Then he checked. 'But what of Cousin Mary? Can't leave her here all alone. Would you care to accompany us, Mary? It's a Millet exhibition at one of the new galleries. I'm rather taken with the pre-Raphaelites myself. What about you?'

About to reply that she had never heard of the pre-whatever-they-were, Mary opted not to show her ignorance and blurted instead, 'Oh but I can't. I've got nothing to wear!'

The blue eyes flashed with amusement. 'Nonsense, m'dear. You look charming as you are. Ring for your cape, and let us go. Mustn't keep the horses waiting too long in the cold, eh?'

The exhibition with its colourful display and bustling crowds was a revelation to Mary. Their escort was witty and attentive. Any shyness Mary felt was quickly dispersed. She chatted freely and even gave her opinion of the paintings, which Perry seemed to find hugely entertaining. Over refreshments in the tea-rooms, she pantomimed an impression of Robson – not as forbidding as she had first supposed, a great subject for mimicry.

'All you have to do is praise her cooking and you're accepted,' Mary said, helping herself to a muffin. 'Dorcas says she was petrified of Robson at first – well, after the orphanage, what do you expect? The new maid looks half scared to death at present, but Webster says it'll all change once she beds in. Did you know Webster was an ostler before he came to number fifteen? He got fed up getting nipped by the horses and chose to break his back gardening instead.'

Perry choked on his tea. Over the rim of the cup his eyes danced with laughter. 'Such a refreshing change,' Mary overheard him remark to Esme afterwards, and blushed when she realised it was herself he was referring to.

Later however, Esme rounded angrily upon Mary. 'Showing yourself up like that! If you can't talk properly in public then don't talk at all. And another thing – stop hobnobbing with the servants!'

Upset, Mary was comforted when the evening mail yielded a missive addressed in Lilian's clear hand. She took the letter up to her room to read it.

'My Dearest Daughter,' Lilian began affectionately, and continued with the usual enquiry after Mary's health and reassurance that all at Beamsters were well and happy.

'I keep in good health. Tired perhaps but that is to be expected. The new little one is biding his time. Widow Goodyear thought Christmas, and now we are into the new year and no baby yet! You should see the layette Violet and myself have prepared, Mary. Your father sends his love and says he misses you dearly. In a different way I suspect he is missing Kester too. Tobias is not as young as he was and Kester shouldered much of the work. I tell Tobias he pushes himself too hard. Kester is due back any time, I am happy to relate. Alice has gone to the cottage to light a fire and air the place. It will be damp being empty these long weeks.'

Pierced with a sudden jealously, Mary let the letter fall to her lap. The thought of Alice in Kester's home, putting a match to the fire, dusting the furniture some of which she herself chose, was more than she could bear.

Homesickness scorched through her. She thought of the din and bustle of the workshop and the easy banter of the men. She thought of summertime at Beamsters. Blown roses and honey-suckle, the waft of new hay, the droning of bees in the orchard. It was winter now and the bees would be hibernating. Father always left some honey on the comb so they had nourishment over the lean weeks.

The clatter of Perry's carriage and ring of voices penetrated her reverie. She had forgotten he and Esme were dining out tonight and the evening stretched ahead endlessly. With Esme's angry warning still rattling in her ears, she opted not to pass the time with the servants, and penning an answer to Lilian would have to wait until her mood brightened.

She trailed downstairs. In the withdrawing room a fire blazed invitingly. Mary went in and sat down at the piano. The top brimmed with framed copies of programmes from Esme's shows. Sending them a defiant glower, Mary spread her hands over the keys and started to play. It seemed ages since she had sung Wild Mountain Thyme, but her lips framed the words unbidden, and her clear voice lifted and carried as she performed the song Kester had taught her.

A peremptory rap halted her mid-verse.

Robson went to answer it. There was the murmur of voices, and the withdrawing door opened. 'Mr Max Conway,' the housekeeper announced.

He was a lean young man with bright black eyes and a head of unruly black hair. Under his arm he carried a bulging leather folder. It was raining, and raindrops glistened about his person. 'Good evening,' he said, and made a bow. 'I hope I'm not intruding. It was actually Miss Greer I came to see. I'm the composer of *Love's Rhapsody*, the show in which she is to perform. I've brought her a copy of the musical score.'

'I see. I'm sorry to have to disappoint you, but my cousin is not here at present,' Mary replied. 'Would you like to return another time? Or I'll willingly pass on a message and the music, if you'd care to leave it.'

'That might be best.' He came to put the document on the piano. 'Miss Greer will want to study the part.'

The young man seemed in no hurry to leave. 'May I offer you some refreshment?' Mary said. 'Some wine? Or would you prefer tea and some of Robson's fruit cake?'

'Pot of tea and cake is exactly what the starving composer ordered,' Max Conway accepted with a smile.

Mary summoned Dorcas and put in her request, and they went to sit by the fire. Before long they were exchanging pleasantries over a large pot of tea and, on Max Conway's part, several slices of cake. He wasn't teasing when he admitted to being hungry, Mary thought, and wished she had offered sandwiches as well.

A silence fell. Mary fiddled with the tray. 'Didn't I hear you playing?' Max Conway volunteered into the void.

'Yes, you did. It was … I was …' Tears welled up. 'I'm sorry,' Mary gulped. 'I had this letter from home and—'

'And it made you yearn to be there,' he finished for her. 'And home is?' She told him. She told him about Lilian and the baby. About her father not being well and having to put in long hours at the workshop in Kester's absence. He heard her out, putting in the occasional question, nodding, entirely sympathetic to her problems and clearly interested. 'I know a way of cheering you up,' he said next.

He rose and went to the piano. Opening the score to *Love's Rhapsody*, he launched into one of the livelier pieces and sang along in a lively tenor. Mopping her damp cheeks, Mary went to join him. Very soon they were working through the songs together. Mary's unhappiness had gone. She was beginning to enjoy herself.

The sprawl of houses, manufactories and tall chimneys had been left behind at last. The train was now chugging steadily through silent winter fields. 'Look Uncle Kester. Cows!' cried the child on the seat opposite Kester.

'Those are bullocks, young Georgie. Cows have to be kept snug in their byre this time of year,' Kester told him.

The little boy started to cough and his mother put her arm around him anxiously. 'There then, Georgie. Where's your kerchief? There then.'

Eventually the fit of coughing subsided. The child fell asleep, his dark lashes fanning his thin cheeks.

'Some good country food and fresh air is what he needs,' Kester said. 'Few weeks and you won't know the lad.'

'George used to say the country was healthier, but you have to live where the work is.' Lisbeth's dark eyes were shadowed in the pale oval of her face. These past weeks had been hard for her, Kester acknowledged.

'Look here, George,' he'd said to his brother on arriving at their terraced home in the smoke-blackened Sheffield street. 'You're going to have to give up this Chartist business. For Lisbeth's sake and the boy's, you must stop.'

George touched his bruised jaw and grimaced. 'It was the police got extra rough,' he said. 'Next time I'll try and avoid the truncheons.'

'Next time it'll be prison.'

'Maybe. That's why I wanted you here to tell you myself.

Should anything befall me, you will look after Lisbeth and young Georgie?'

''Course I will,' Kester said promptly. 'But George, it shouldn't come to that. Your responsibility is to your family, not to the cause. Chartism! Rioting and rough play never solved a thing.'

He broke off as Lisbeth entered the room. George went and hugged his wife. 'That was a grand meal you put on, girl. A regular feast to welcome Kester.'

She smiled up at him. 'Thank you, George. I'm glad you both enjoyed it – empty plates speak for themselves!'

He nodded. 'Georgie in bed?'

'Yes, fast asleep. The excitement of having Uncle Kester home must have worn him out!'

They all laughed. For a week or so George kept to his fireside of an evening. And then came another Chartist meeting, another riot. George was captured. He now faced a six months prison sentence. There was nothing Kester could do but bring Lisbeth and George back to Aston Cross.

'Poor George,' Lisbeth said, speaking softly so as not to disturb the sleeping child. 'Six months in that awful prison.'

'George will survive,' Kester replied. 'But this is his last chance, Lisbeth.'

If anything her face became whiter. 'What do you mean?'

'Next time the Law won't be so lenient. George must give up the cause. I tried to tell him but he wouldn't listen. Rough play never solved anything.'

'I thought you were a sympathiser, Kester. You used to go along to the meetings.'

'I went along for the ride.' Kester rubbed his face hopelessly with his hand. He could hardly admit to Lisbeth that a rowdy Chartist gathering had been preferable to the agony of stopping at home with her by her quiet fireside. And now she was coming to his own fireside. 'True, the cause does evoke my sympathy. The Reform act fuelled a great deal of disappointment. But mob violence and anger isn't the right way of expressing it. No-one, no high-ranking person that is, would give those trouble-makers time of day.'

'So what would you suggest?'

'A spokesman. Someone who can put over an opinion. The toffs have their own speakers, there's no reason why the working man shouldn't as well. And let's not forget the press as well. The written word holds great power. Public sympathy can be roused by what is fed them in the daily newspapers.'

'It's all beyond me,' Lisbeth admitted sadly. 'We had our little home and enough to eat. I never hankered for more. It was George who wanted better.'

'Never mind. It'll work out.' Kester's glance went to the window. 'There's Aston Cross church spire. Better wake the boy, Lisbeth. We're almost there.'

The train drew into the small station, and there was a delay while their effects were retrieved from the goods van. When the train pulled away they were left standing on the windswept platform, surrounded by household goods and baggage. Lisbeth held the whimpering child in her arms.

'Wait there,' Kester said. 'I'll find some transport.'

The short January day was ending as they took the road to Aston Cross in the hired cart, the horse plodding his patient way, the laden cart creaking protestingly. Entering the woods, the darkness deepened. 'Soon be there,' Kester said, keeping his voice cheerful. 'You'll like the cottage. Mary made curtains. It's brightened the place up.'

Nearing the cottage, he was surprised to smell woodsmoke and see the glow of firelight at the window. 'Someone's lit the fire. Must be Lilian's doing. If I know her there'll be food on the shelf too.'

Someone had shut in the chickens for the night too, and fed the pig, Kester noticed as he made a hurried inspection of his home. Bye, but he was glad to be back!

Inside, Lisbeth heated up the food waiting in a brown crock. Soon all three were sitting at the rough-hewn table, tucking in to the simple supper of good beef broth rich with herbs and vegetables, and crusty new bread.

Lisbeth glanced about her. Not country reared, she found the silence of the woodland unnerving. But in here all was cosy and safe with the logs crackling in the grate and the flames reflected in the brasses on the hearth.

''Twas Mary brought those from Beamsters,' said Kester. 'The easy chair too. You'll find us not short of household gear. Mary saw to that.'

Lisbeth put down her spoon. 'Who's Mary?'

'The boss's daughter. She helped me get the cottage to rights.' Kester smiled. 'Odd thing. When I was patching up the old plaster I found a lovespoon in the wall.'

'A ... lovespoon?'

'Yes. It's a carved wooden spoon a lad gives his lass on their betrothal. Be quite old I should imagine. I let Mary have it – well, she was just a youngster. Her face lit up.'

Lisbeth made no comment. Meal over, Kester pulled to his feet. 'You're going out?' Lisbeth said with alarm.

'Must see Tobias. He's a good man, but I'll not rest easy until I've explained the situation. Don't wait up. There's a room above. You and the lad can sleep there. I'll kip down on the settle, no problem.'

Ruffling Georgie's dark hair, he went out into the winter night. Lisbeth took the boy on her lap and listened to Kester's booted feet tramping away through the trees. The silence closed in again.

Mary sat in the empty stalls of the Queen's Theatre in the Haymarket, fascinated by what was happening on the stage. First night was scheduled for April, and they were now well into January. 'It doesn't seem very long to put a show together. Cousin Esme only had the weekend to learn a whole part. Songs as well,' she whispered to Max, who had left the players and come to keep her company.

'Learning the words doesn't seem a problem to actors,' Max told her. 'And the music speaks for itself – or so I hope!'

He pulled a funny face, folded his arms and sat back to watch the proceedings. Mary had already acquainted herself with the plot.

Set in a mountain village near Salzburg, preparations for the summer festival were being made with much dancing and song. Hero Franz is betrothed to heroine Marietta played by Esme. But Marietta has her eye on handsome young forester, Stephan. They fall in love, while Franz is attracted to Marietta's younger sister, Sophie. A musical tangle ensues and eventually sorts out with the two couples happily matched. It was a bright, fast-moving, colourful show, entirely suited to Esme's bubbling personality and to the handsome appeal of leading man, Frederick Mears. The part of Stephan was played by up-and-coming young tenor, Darcy Cavendish. A pretty if somewhat plump soprano played Sophie.

'Must say you look very fetching in that gown,' Max said of a sudden, and Mary dimpled.

'Thank you, kind sir!' The gown was new, a splendid affair of tawny satin, ruched, beaded and painfully tight in the bodice. Standish had laced Mary's stays to gasping point. They had come here directly from the dressmakers and were late, which had put Esme in a bad mood. Added to which Mary had broached the subject of the dressmaker charging more than she should for her services.

'Nonsense! I've used Madame Babette for years and never any trouble. What bunkum you do talk sometimes, Mary!'

The disagreement had not helped Esme's temper at all, and Mary was glad to make her escape to the stalls.

'That's Morgan Rees-Jones, the director of the show.' Max nodded towards a stocky man with a mane of grizzled dark hair and an eloquent Welsh voice which rang out just then across the theatre.

'Not turned up you say? Why ever not, for pity's sake?' Max stood up. 'What is it? What's wrong?'

Morgan Rees-Jones wrung his hands together dramatically. 'Sophie hasn't arrived. We can't proceed without her, can't afford to waste time either.'

Max went forward to the stage. There was a short conference, and Max returned grinning. 'I've told them not to panic. You know the song.'

'I do?'

'Mmm – we sang it the other night, remember?'

'The one with the high e? But I can't always hit the note.'

'Of course you can. Come on.'

He held out his hand and she took it and allowed herself to be led on to the stage.

Esme said, 'Are you sure you can do this, Mary?'

Mary nodded. Suddenly her mouth had gone dry. She wished her stays were not so tight. How would she get her breath to reach that final top note? Rees-Jones sent her a nod. 'Want to give it a try? Piano, please!'

The pianist played the opening phrases and Mary swallowed, tried to fill her lungs in the restricting garments and missed the first notes. 'Sorry,' she quavered. 'Could we start again?'

All eyes were on her. Cast and chorus, watching and waiting. From the stalls Max's dancing black eyes sent every encouragement. The pianist struck up again and this time Mary was ready. Flowing into the music, she forgot the watchful figures around her. She was Sophie, young, pretty – in love for the first time. All the tenderness and yearning of her young heart went into the song. The last high fluting note lingered pure and clear on the spaces of the theatre. There was a silence, and then came a tremendous burst of applause that sent the blood rushing to Mary's cheeks.

'Bravo!' cried Max, standing up still clapping furiously. 'Well done, Mary. What do you say, Morgan?'

Rees-Jones's swarthy face was smiling. 'I say she's won herself the part, Max!'

Mary's heart hammered. Singing on stage was wonderful and exciting. But, she asked herself, is this what I want? Could I spend my life performing? Like my mother?

Six

⚬

Lilian gazed out of the parlour window at the bleak winter land-scape, a hand to her aching back. January now, and the babe supposedly due at Christmastide. Surely she would not have much longer to wait. She yearned to hold her baby in her arms, and how gratifying to be able to see her toes again!

Snow flurried against the glass and Lilian watched it with concern. A white-out was the last thing they needed at present, with the doctor some three miles distant and Widow Goodyear a lengthy walk across the fields in the opposite direction.

Trudging up the lane came a slight figure with a small boy in tow. Lilian stiffened. Kester's new wife and her child, if the gossip was right. The hussy had better not be heading here! Only yesterday Edna Morris from the general stores had remarked how shocking it was, Kester Hayes turning up with that woman, and never a hint he was getting wed.

''Course, they're like that, townsfolk,' she sniffed. 'No scruples at all. Likely she took Kester for a good catch. Her with a child to support as well. Though I'm surprised at Kester falling for it.'

Lilian agreed, yet an old regard for Kester prevented her from voicing it aloud. The least he could have done was bring the new Mrs Hayes to Beamsters to be introduced, she felt. The fact that he had not – not even spoken of the union, come to that – hurt more than she could imagine.

Edna had not been the first to come shouting her opinion, and though Lilian enjoyed the company of her neighbours, the more she heard of Kester's fall from grace, the more she was inclined to believe that there was something in what was being said. Talk had even gone as far as to suggest the couple were not in fact wed. If true, then what was Tobias thinking of, letting Kester get away with living with someone who was not even his wife?

The young woman halted briefly at the entrance to the yard, then came walking on towards the house. Lilian's first instinct was to pretend not to be available, but curiosity got the better of her. Besides, had she not always told her children never to believe gossip, but to make sure and form your own opinion of a person first?

Making her careful way through to the kitchen, Lilian reached the door just as the caller was about to knock.

'Mrs Sutton?' enquired a clear voice. She looked no more than a girl. Her skirt and topcoat were worn but neat and clean, and she had rather fine dark eyes in a pale, oval face. An arresting face, Lilian thought with a stab of pique. Always a plain Jane herself, she had never felt less attractive than now. At his mother's side, the small boy peered up solemnly from under the brim of his hand-knitted scarlet woollen cap.

'My name is Mrs Lisbeth Hayes. I'm Kester's sister-in-law,' the woman said. His *sister-in-law*? Lilian blinked. It got worse! 'I was wondering if you could sell me a dozen eggs?' Lisbeth Hayes went on. 'Our hens have stopped laying, you see. We've called at Widow Goodyear's but hers are the same. It was she sent me on here.'

Eggs, was it? Lilian had eggs to spare, but she was not inclined to sell any in this direction! At that moment the boy started to cough. Lilian took in his thin frame and hollow cheeks and felt her heart melt. After all, the child was innocent. 'Dear me,' she said to him kindly, 'what a nasty cough you have. Would you like a cup of warm milk and honey to make it better?'

'Oh, but we mustn't intrude,' Lisbeth Hayes began, but already Lilian had the door open wide and the child had run in to warm his chilled hands by the kitchen fire.

Very soon the three of them were seated at the table in the big, homely kitchen with its good smells of baking bread and the newly-ironed linen airing put to air over the range. Georgie was sipping his warm milk, and Lilian, against her better judgement, was pouring tea for them both. Everywhere shone. Earlier in the day a spurt of energy had driven her to clean the already spick kitchen from front to back.

'There you are.' She handed Lisbeth a steaming cup and offered a slice of sponge cake. 'My youngest, Violet, made it. Violet's turning out quite the little housewife.'

'I would have loved a daughter, a sister for our Georgie,' Lisbeth said wistfully, and helped herself to cake. 'Thank you. This does look good.'

Lilian gave Georgie some, cutting it into fingers the way she had done for her own children when they were small. 'There now. Eat it up. It will make you grow big and strong like my boy Ned.'

'Fank you,' said Georgie politely.

'Georgie's cough is much better than when we first came,' Lisbeth said. 'Kester got some linctus from Widow Goodyear. Kester has been so supportive. I don't know what we would have done without him. My husband, George – but Kester will have explained what happened.'

'No, not a thing,' Lilian said. 'Though come to think of it, Tobias once mentioned a brother of Kester's. Wasn't he involved with the Chartists or something?'

'That's right. This last time George was heading a group of protesters and things became … difficult.'

'You mean your husband was responsible for the recent riots?'

'Not responsible, exactly. But George was captured, and ...' She sent a warning glance towards her son, who was scoffing cake with apparent concentration, and probably taking in every word that was being said.

'I think,' Lilian suggested quietly, beset with a horrible feeling that she had made a gross misjudgement, 'we could talk more freely if I find Georgie something to keep him occupied.'

Over a second cup of tea Lilian listened with growing concern and self-reproach while Lisbeth poured out her story. Georgie, given a box of toy soldiers to play with, was busily lining them up for battle under the table.

'When George received his sentence there seemed nothing else for it but to do what Kester suggested. I didn't want to leave my home, but I could not have met the rent myself, and Kester was worried about his job here. It seemed the only alternative to come and keep house for him. I suppose there has been gossip. When I go into the village the people are not very friendly.'

Lilian swallowed. She was as guilty as the rest for believing the worst of this brave young woman, to whom she was warming by the minute. 'Dreadful, to have to leave your home and everything you held dear,' she sympathized. 'And Kester's cottage is not the most comfortable. Fine for a man alone, but it has only the basics in furniture. I've plenty of odds and ends here. Is there anything you especially need?'

'Bed linen, if you could spare it. Perhaps curtains for upstairs?'

'No problem at all. I'll send them with Kester, and whatever else I can think off. And don't worry about eggs. As long as our hens keep in lay, you're welcome to some.'

'Thank you,' Lisbeth said gratefully. 'Though you must take care not to overdo it, with the babe due and everything. Kester mentioned you have three daughters. I expect you're hoping for another lad this time to even things up a bit.'

'Quite honestly at this moment I don't mind what I have. I just wish it would happen. Ten days overdue, would you believe!'

'Then it *must* be a lad, to keep you hanging about waiting like this,' Lisbeth said, and they both laughed.

While they sat chatting the snow stopped and a thin winter sun appeared. Lisbeth got up to leave. 'Come, Georgie, we mustn't keep Mrs Sutton any longer. We'll have a nice walk back in the sunshine.'

'But Mam,' Georgie objected. 'The battle's not over yet!'

'You can take the soldiers with you if you like,' Lilian offered. 'They were Ned's. I'm sure he wouldn't mind.'

'Say thank you,' Lisbeth bid the child, on her hands and knees packing the tin figures back into the box. 'Put your coat and hat on.'

'Don't forget the eggs,' Lilian said. 'No, of course I don't want paying for them. The very idea.'

She saw her visitors out and watched them walk away across the yard. At the gate, they paused and waved, then set off down the wintry lane towards the wood.

Soon afterwards Tobias appeared, puffing and blowing and scattering mud all over the pristine floor. His face was red from the raw outdoors and he rubbed his chest in that way he had of late, as if it troubled him. 'Just thought I'd look in on you, my love. Is everything all right?'

'Everything is splendid.' In fact the ache in her back was still there, but observing her husband's anxious expression Lilian said nothing. 'Guess who called just now? Lisbeth Hayes and Georgie. I found her very genuine. Such nonsense, the gossip that's flying about. Her reason for being here is quite legitimate. She told me the whole story. It's been nothing but worry for her since her husband took up with those wretched Chartists. That's why she's here. Nothing indelicate at all.'

Tobias snorted. 'How folk love to tattle! Kester did confide in me,

but I felt it was their business alone. Happen I should have anticipated a problem and been more outgoing. Glad you and Lisbeth
have met up, Lilian. It's handy for you having another woman
around just now. Pity Mary wasn't here.'

'Yes. But it can't be helped.'

'Maybe not. Seems you've had a busy morning, my love. Why
don't you go and rest?'

'I'm perfectly all right, Tobias,' Lilian assured him again.

'Aye. Well then, in that case I'll get back to the workshop. We've
a repair job on. Payment on delivery.'

'That's good. See you later.'

After he had gone, Lilian felt restless. The sun still shone and she
fancied some fresh air. She had sorted out some outgrown boys'
clothes for the chapel poor fund. Some of them would fit Georgie,
the thick cloth coat with the high collar in particular.

Bundling the garments up into a parcel, she put on her warm
cape and bonnet and left the house. It was good to be out in the
sparkling winter cold. The hawthorn in the hedgerow was bare, but
holly berries glowed crimson amid the glossy green leaves. She
stepped out, taking deep lungfuls of air. Over to the east snow-
clouds were banking up. She must not be long.

She had entered the wood when the first pain knifed through
her. She dropped the bundle of clothes, grasped the bough of a
beech for support and breathed deeply. Sweat sprang up on her
brow; she felt it trickle between her shoulder blades. The pain
eased and she straightened. There was no mistaking the signs. It
was the baby. What a fool she was to have come out.

She darted a panicking glance back up the lane. Beamsters was a
long way off. She was closer to Kester's cottage by far. Picking up
the bundle, she walked forward, and was alarmed when another
pain overtook her almost immediately. That was quick. They were
coming too close for comfort.

Abandoning the parcel now, she stumbled on, her eyes fixed on the light from the cottage window shining between the trees. It was snowing again, big flakes, spinning down between the black network of branches overhead.

Next time the contraction was all embracing. She felt her knees buckle and the ground rushed up towards her. There was a roaring in her ears; everything was going dark.

'Help!' she called on a sobbing gasp. 'Help me!'

Vaguely she was aware of pattering feet and a small hand tugged at her sleeve. 'Mrs Sutton?' said a childish but positive voice. 'It's me, Georgie. Have you got a tummy ache? Will I fetch my mam to you?'

'Oh, please,' Lilian bid him, and gave herself up to pain.

Mary took out the letter and read it through again. The baby boy was small but healthy and Lilian had come through her ordeal better than expected. She was home again now and tucked up in bed.

'I am being thoroughly spoiled,' Lilian wrote. 'No-one will let me lift a finger and Widow Goodyear calls every day.

'Until yesterday, that is, when there was another heavy fall of snow and the lane was cut off. However, we are cosy enough here. My little William Henry thrives and I am getting stronger every day. No arrangements made yet for the christening, but rest assured, Mary, you will receive an invitation, which will I hope bring your dear presence to Beamsters and to your family once more.'

Mary bit her lip. The show was scheduled to run throughout the summer season. There was no chance of her getting away, no matter how pressing the occasion. She read on.

'Your father is working hard at keeping the business afloat. The new carriage yard at Much Wenlock has hit Sutton's hard, as you will imagine. Kester is a rock as always. Being a man of the times, he has come up with suggestions for the business which your father is considering.

'I cannot speak too highly of Lisbeth. It would not have been easy for her, having a weakly woman and newborn child to cope with in that tiny cottage all that time, and the doctor insisted I must not be moved. Poor Kester had to sleep in the barn! Georgie was intrigued by the baby and did not want us to leave. I cannot thank Lisbeth enough for what she did. We have become friends ...'

Mary let the page slip through her fingers. She was in the theatre, taking a break between sets. Rehearsals up to now had gone fairly smoothly. Today though, she had stumbled over her lines and received a blistering telling off from Morgan Rees-Jones. Had she but known it, what with novice performers and a great many hiccups, the director was hard put to get the show together in time. Recalling the sharpness of Morgan's tongue, Mary felt the sting of tears.

'Why, Mary. There you are.'

Max was coming towards her, his clothes endearingly crumpled and his shock of hair in customary disarray. 'I've looked everywhere for you. Have you had lunch?'

'Not yet.' Mary struggled to compose herself. 'I was reading through this letter from home again. Everything seems fine, but I can't help feeling a bit worried. The baby's a month old and my mother is still bed-ridden. She was up and about well before this with Violet. Cousin Esme says I'm looking for something to moan about. But I'm not at all.'

'Of course you are not. Perhaps your family are giving your mother a total break to let her get her strength back. You're bound to worry. She is your mother after all.'

Mary bit her lip. Not for the first time was she tempted to blurt out to Max that she was not Lilian's daughter. Common sense stopped her. Max was bound to ask questions, and she did not want to involve Esme if she could help it.

'I suppose you're right,' she said slowly. 'Oh dear, why is everything so impossible? Even the rehearsal went badly. My part in it, anyway.'

Max grinned reassuringly. 'Shouldn't worry, Rees-Jones is just whipping the show into shape, that's all. Wait till the dress rehearsal. Then you'll see him in full flow!'

'Cousin Esme said the dress rehearsal was often a disaster. She said I wasn't to get worked up about it.'

'Quite right. It's a run-through to bring all the problems which have not been anticipated to light. So cheer up. Tell you what, tonight we'll go out somewhere. You choose.'

She brightened. 'That little Hungarian café where they play that wonderful gypsy music and we can get up and dance?'

'The *Troika*? Won't you be danced off your feet after the rehearsal?'

'Not a bit of it. Food's wonderful. Once I've eaten my fill of that gorgeous goulash with spices and herbs I'm ready for anything. And the music really sets your feet tapping.'

'Fine, the *Troika* it is. Now what about lunch? I saw them going round with the trolley.'

'Lumpy cheese sandwich and tea weak as dishwater? I can't wait!' Mary giggled and stuffed the letter back into her pocket. Her worries were forgotten. Tonight she'd wear her midnight-blue silk with the jet embroidery, get Dorcas to dress her hair in that new style with the flowing ringlets. Max would surely be stunned speechless!

'So how did it go?'

Perry sat back in his chair in the secluded corner of their favourite Knightsbridge restaurant and looked at Esme across the table.

'The dress rehearsal? Oh, please, Perry dearest, don't remind me!' Esme rolled her eyes dramatically and affected a shudder. 'The usual plethora of hitches that nobody thought might happen. Trouble is, when things go wrong it gets people so worked up. Including yours truly.'

To everyone's dismay the show, which had been improving steadily and had suddenly, incredibly, reached near perfection, seemed all at once to have developed faults. What with missed cues, fluffed lines and a lead dancer who could not keep in step, Morgan Rees-Jones was practically tearing his hair with frustration.

Something went wrong with the lighting, and topping it all a section of mobile scenery, which had not given a hint of previous trouble, became well and truly stuck.

'Stage hands! Scenery operators! Anyone! *Do* something!' Rees-Jones had roared in anguish.

Recalling his performance, Esme could not help a chuckle. 'They should put Morgan on stage and let someone else do the producing. He's a natural.'

'What about Mary? How did she cope?' Perry asked.

'Oh, Mary's a natural too. Max had primed her well so she took all in her stride. Bit apprehensive of course, but she played the part without any obvious mistakes.'

'That's good.'

'Mmm. She admitted she was glad she'd made the choice of stopping and taking up Morgan's offer. I should think so too. A girl of her talent, stuck away in a country village! Doesn't bear thinking about.'

'You seem pleased about her, Esme. Do I detect a change of attitude towards Mary? I rather thought you were afraid of her stealing your thunder?'

'Dear me, you make me sound quite impossible! But you are right. I'm still as jealous as can be. It's all going to happen to Mary and I'll be pushed into the background. I can just see the headlines. Esme Greer steps down to make way for new star. And this was supposed to be my move up the ladder. Musicals, instead of music hall.'

'But you're still brilliant. You can't help but be.'

'Thank you, Perry.'

'You're welcome. Always the devoted fan. Ah, here's the waiter. Shall we have the roast beef?'

He gave the order, selected wine from the trolley and poured them some. Then he raised his glass in a toast. 'To the show, and to your eternal success.'

'To *Love's Rhapsody*.' She sipped wine. 'Ah, lovely. You know, the challenge of this change of direction is quite something. Musical plays have been a consideration of mine for some time. I couldn't keep on with music hall and my voice is not powerful enough for opera. Mary coming on the scene has given the whole thing a new dimension. It's enjoyable, encouraging the new generation.'

'You sound surprised at yourself.'

'I am.' She stopped. She'd be inhuman not to be proud of her own daughter, but she could hardly admit that to Perry. The talk was getting tricky. A change of topic might be no bad thing.

'How did the visit to your family go?'

'Oh, so-so. Father still disapproves of my political ambitions. Good thing I've a brother to take over the estate when the time comes. Randal's in his element running the farms and riding the land. Thank heaven he was born first, and I don't have to get tied up with inheritance.'

He reached for the carafe of wine and topped up their glasses. 'Not easy when the family are so unaccommodating. I'd have thought my father of all people would have shown more interest in a new political scene.'

Esme had read about the Marquis in the newspaper. He had been airing his views on the current Chartist outbreaks. Surprisingly, his sympathy was with the working class, though he abhorred their method of mob rule.

'Maybe your father can go along with the new political scene providing his own family are not involved.'

'Maybe. But I do need someone on my side. A wife, Esme.'

She sighed. 'Oh, Perry. We've been through all this before. I'm not the right person for you. An actress as a wife? I'd be in the way of your prospects, and that would never do.'

'Rubbish. You'd play the part to perfection. I love you, dammit. And you love me. What's more, we're friends, and that's as good a foundation as any for a successful marriage.' His blue eyes deepened. 'Marry me, Esme? Please?'

She shook her head. 'No, thank you. I told you, I'm not suitable for you.'

'Is it because of Mary? She's your daughter, isn't she?'

There was a petrified silence. Esme's face went white. 'You … you know? Who told you? Not Mary, she wouldn't!'

'Of course she wouldn't. I guessed. The moment I first saw her, actually. The likeness was remarkable.'

'But if you've put two and two together, then others must have as well. Oh, and I thought we had got away with it.'

'And so you have. Don't worry, my love. I'm sure no-one else has given it a thought. It's just me, knowing you so well. So I am not wrong?'

'No.' Esme swallowed hard. 'I should have told you, though some things are best kept secret and I considered this one of them. Giving her up isn't something I'm proud of. I was young. When Tobias found out about Mary he arranged for us to be married. Then I was offered this chance to sing. It was in Paris of all places. I couldn't resist it.

'Oh, I know it sounds selfish and cold-blooded, but it wasn't like that at all. I really suffered for what I did. Missed her, you see. Kept wondering how she was and if she was missing me, even though I knew she would be all right with Tobias. Night after night I cried myself to sleep. In the end I paid a detective to find out how she was. Turned out Tobias had married Lilian and they were bringing up Mary as their own child. It couldn't have been better. She had a comfortable, secure home, nicer by far than I could have given her. Brother and sisters too, in time. Then she found out about me and tracked me down. You know the rest.'

'Yes. My poor love, it can't have been easy. I'm sorry you had to suffer that way. Still, Mary's turned out a fine girl.'

'Hasn't she just. I'm proud of her. She was such a little prude before. It's a treat to see her wearing pretty clothes and enjoying life here in London.'

'Mmm. All this doesn't make a jot of difference to my feelings, y'know. Want you as my wife more than ever. Promise me you'll give it some serious thought, now we've cleared the air, so to speak.'

'Yes, all right, Perry. I promise.'

The meal arrived and conversation ceased. Perry did not bring up the subject again during the evening. But after he had delivered her home and she was enjoying a nightcap, Esme wondered if she should consider his offer. It would mean her giving up what she held most dear – the stage. Then again, there would be compensations. And she did love Perry. Most desperately she did.

First night arrived all too soon. As Mary walked along the corridor to Esme's dressing room she was aware of the theatre gradually coming to life around her. Gone was the dreary stillness and echoing spaces of the empty auditorium. A strange excitement was infiltrating into every dusty nook and cranny backstage. The very air seemed to be taking on a shimmer. Mary drank in the charged atmosphere and felt her pulses pound in response.

A burst of laughter issued from a dressing-room further along the passage. Somewhere, someone was chanting his lines over and over again. Mary could hear Esme's bold soprano fluting up and down the scales. She always did that before a performance. It was what she called getting her voice together.

Mary tapped on Esme's door and entered. The small room was awash with flowers. Perry's bouquet of crimson roses stood on the dressing table. Their rich fragrance met Esme as she came in. Esme broke off from singing and smiled at her. 'Mary? Are you all right?'

'Think so. Apart from rubbery knees and a stomach full of butterflies!'

'I'm the same. Don't worry my love. Everyone has an attack of nerves before a performance. Once you step foot on the stage it will go. I promise.'

Mary hoped Esme was right. At this moment she could not remember a word of her lines. And what if she hit the wrong notes of her song? Her knees trembled at the very thought. She said, shakily, 'Everywhere feels different somehow. You can sense the excitement.'

Esme laughed. 'That's theatre magic. Here, I've something for you. A memento of your very first performance.'

She handed Mary a small box. Inside was a gold pendant in the shape of a shamrock leaf on a slender gold chain.

'Oh, how lovely. Thank you! I'll wear it always.' Mary's eyes shone.

'I'm glad you like it, child. Ah, there's the chorus arriving. Better go and get ready, don't you think?'

Back in the dressing-room she shared with four other members of the cast, a posy of tawny rosebuds was waiting for her. There was a message.

'To my dear Mary. With love and good wishes for her debut. I shall be with you every note of the way. Your best admirer, Max.'

'Oh, Max!' Mary's voice throbbed, and not only with gratitude. The butterflies were there again. Right now she needed all the encouragement she could get. Dear Max, what would she have done without him all these long weeks of singing lessons, elocution training and rehearsals?

After the show, a party was to be held in honour of the opening night. A room had been booked at the Dorchester. All the glittering theatre crowd would be present. Mary's pulse quickened. How she loved a party!

The door opened and Dorcas was there, chatting and chivvying. 'Come along, miss. Time to get into your costume. Oh, look at them roses. Miss Esme's got red ones in her dressing-room. And we know who's sent them, don't we?'

Suddenly Mary's face was white. 'Dorcas, I can't. I can't go on.'

'There now, 'course you can. One foot on that stage and them collywobbles will vanish. Very professional, I heard Mr Morgan say you were, and he's not one for giving praise where it's not due. Them folk out there don't know what a treat they're in for this evening, so there.'

Dressed in her peasant-girl costume of green skirts, white blouse and embroidered bodice, she was no longer ordinary little Mary Sutton from Aston Cross, but Sophie, the beautiful daughter of the shoemaker in the faraway Austrian Alps.

Max's music sang in her head. Fear of failure was now laughable – of course she could do it! She could not wait to get out there and give *Love's Rhapsody* all she had got.

*

She waited in the wings for her cue. It came at last.

'Sophie? Where has that girl got to?'

At once Mary put a winning smile on her face and ran out into the hot brightness of the gas lamps and the colourful alpine set.

'Did you call me, Father? I was picking flowers for the house ...'

The orchestra struck up with the introduction, the chorus came on laughing and chattering and before Mary knew it they were into the first song of the show, a catchy number entitled 'Flowers Bring Happiness'.

It brought the house down. Mary, a little breathless, darted her audience a saucy glance from under long lashes and sang them an extra chorus. She was delighted when some joined in and others hummed along with the melody.

By the time her next turn came up – a song and dance this time – Mary was wholly into her stride. She flirted and laughed, parrying with her handsome partner and with the audience. She tossed her head and swished her skirts. Her feet in their satin slippers twinkled over the floor. Her voice had never been better. Everything was coming together beautifully.

With the glare of the footlights it was impossible to see her audience. Yet she could feel their presence and the vibes of approval were dazzling. This was wonderful. Mary relished every heady moment. She had never felt so at home anywhere.

Towards the end of the first act, she glimpsed a tall figure in the wings. It seemed familiar and she faltered, but recovered herself. Surely it was not Kester? As soon as she had the chance she looked again, but the person had gone.

The curtain fell. Cast and chorus hurried off the stage, anxious to assuage their thirst with cooling sips of water, to get into their next costumes and touch up their sweaty make-up for the next act.

Mary hovered behind. He was there again. It *was* Kester! Kester, come to see her first performance.

'Mary, come on. Only ten minutes to go.' Esme called a warning, and all Mary could do was send Kester a merry wave and scoot.

'Oh, miss, you were marvellous!' cried Dorcas, ready with new gown and powder puff. 'You got the loudest applause of the lot!'

It was the same in the second act. The audience was all eyes for the lovely young soprano with the lively expression and graceful figure. In one night Mary had sung and danced her way into many a heart and somehow, she knew it.

At last the show drew to a close – a total success. An enraptured audience which included the customary music critics and hardened theatre-goers confirmed the fact with a thunderous applause which sent the crystal chandeliers in the roof dancing. The cast took curtain after curtain. Sumptuous bouquets of flowers were presented and Mary bowed and smiled until her face ached.

Coming off the stage between calls, her gaze fell on the tall figure standing in the shadows. In the magical but confusing heat of the moment she had forgotten about Kester. Only when he stepped forward and the light fell across his lean dark face did she come to her senses.

'Kester!' she cried, darting up to embrace him. 'Oh, Kester, you came to my first night. Did you enjoy the show? How was my performance?'

Kester smiled down at her. 'Mary, congratulations. You were a joy to watch. But I'm afraid I've brought grave news. You're needed back home, girl. Your father has been taken badly and Lilian is still far from strong. Alice and Violet can't cope.'

Someone was shouting her name and Mary glanced round at the call-boy in bewilderment. 'They're requesting an encore, miss. Everyone back on stage please.'

'I have to go, Kester,' she said. 'I'm wanted on stage.'

'Mary, if we don't leave now we'll miss the train. You must come. They need you at home.'

She stared at him, appalled, fear and panic making her voice shrill. 'Go with you? But I can't. I can't leave now!'

Seven

༄

'What is it, Kester? Tell me what's happened.'

Mary faced Kester, anxiously clutching the bouquet she had been given. The final call had seemed endless and her smile was forced as her mind fretted on Kester's sudden untoward appearance and the unfortunate news he obviously had to relate. As soon as the curtain had fallen she had hurried offstage. Now people were pushing past them, laughing, chatting jubilantly about the performance, their spirits high in the wake of the encouraging tribute they had just received.

'Couldn't have been better!' was the general cry, and members of the chorus paused to hug Mary and tell her how splendid she had been. Time and again Mary had to break off to acknowledge them. After they had gone she returned her gaze to the tall, sombre figure before her. 'Kester?'

He said, with growing impatience, 'It's Tobias. He's had some sort of seizure. He's bad, Mary.'

'Father? Oh, no!' Mary's cheeks paled under the thick layer of stage make-up. 'When did it happen?'

'Few days ago. He was in the yard, shouting orders to the men as usual. Then he clutched his chest and fell. The doctor's pretty sure it's his heart.'

'He's not lost the use of his limbs?' She remembered a neighbour having a seizure which had left her pitifully disabled. Her father would have hated that.

'He's bedridden – for now. Thinking back, he's not been so good for quite some time. Always rubbing his chest as if it pained him. Bit out of breath. And his colour wasn't good.'

'He isn't ... he will get better?'

'Providing he doesn't have another attack there's every chance, apparently. Widow Goodyear calls in to see him every day and so does the doctor. Problem is the nursing. Lilian's still weakly after the child. She does her best, though she's obviously not up to it.'

'She never said as much in her letters.'

'Well, that's Lilian for you. She wouldn't want to worry you or appear complaining.'

There was a bright burst of laughter and a troupe of dancers pushed by with a waft of perfume and a swish of colourful skirts. One of them was bewailing her sore feet and another exclaimed how hot it was under the lights. 'I thought I was going to melt. I really did!'

'Well done, darling,' a dancer said to Mary in passing. 'You held your audience perfectly. They simply loved you!'

Again Kester had to wait until they had gone. He ran his hand in exasperation over his face. 'Anyway, as I was saying, Lilian is far from strong, and there's the baby to see to, as well as running the house and nursing Tobias. Young Alice has been grand, but she can't be expected to do everything. And Violet's only a child. Besides which Lilian worries about Alice missing school.'

'Was it Lilian sent you?' Since being in London she had grown used to thinking of her stepmother by her first name.

'No. She knows nothing of this. It was your father. I go up each day to see him and give him bits of news of the yard. Carefully censored, I might add. Business has been up and down lately. But that's another issue. I've come because Tobias badly wants you home, Mary. "Tell Mary we need her," his words were. He didn't want you travelling on your own, so he asked me to escort you back.'

'But I can't just drop everything and leave,' Mary said. 'You can see how it is here. Can Father not employ someone to keep house for the time being? If it's a question of money I could send—'

''Tisn't that. They need someone they know. Someone organised who knows the ropes. You, Mary.'

'Kester, I can't just walk out on the show.' Mary's voice shook with emotion. 'I'd come and look after them willingly, but there's the contract. I'm legally bound to see the production out.'

He snorted. 'Surely they can get a replacement? How long is the show expected to run anyway?'

'Depends on the reviews. All summer maybe.'

Someone shouted her name across the echoing stage and a smiling Max appeared. He took in her downcast expression and launched into a bit of confidence boosting.

'Mary, there you are! Marvellous performance, my love! Absolutely marvellous! I was just saying to Rees-Jones. What a blessing we took Mary on. Was she not wonderful?' he asked of Kester. 'There'd be no show without Mary!'

In spite of her dilemma, Mary smiled and coloured up prettily under the extravagant praise. Nodding amicably to Kester, Max went drifting off to join the others.

'You see?' Mary said. 'I'm needed here as well. I can't be in both places at once.'

'Tobias is counting on you, Mary,' Kester repeated in a tone which said clearly what he thought of her arguments. 'I shall delay leaving until the last train. It leaves just before midnight. I've got you a ticket so you won't be delayed. I'll be waiting for you by the entrance to the station. See you later.'

He dropped a kiss on her cheek and went striding away,

descending the steps into the now empty auditorium and heading off up the aisle to the exit. Mary stared after him, panic thundering in her ears. Whatever was she to do now?

'Mary, my sweet!' Esme's fluting voice called out to her. 'There's a first-night celebration going on backstage. They're asking for you.'

'Coming.' Still gripping the elaborate arrangement of hothouse flowers, Mary turned and followed her mother.

In Esme's dressing room they were greeted by a blast of delighted laughter and the popping of champagne being opened. It was hot and stuffy, the air buzzing with excitement. One after another members of the cast and crew fell upon Mary with their congratulations. Morgan Rees-Jones was there, glass in hand, his black eyes glittering with satisfaction and unusual good humour. 'The reviews tomorrow should be interesting,' he was saying to Max. 'I didn't see a single long face amongst the critics, and they were all here.'

'It's a hit! They all loved it! Oh, well done, everybody!' Max couldn't keep the grin from his face.

Someone pushed a tumbler of champagne in Mary's hand. She sipped it thirstily, but the bubbling sweetness did nothing to quench her thirst or sooth her troubled mind. Dazed after the performance during which she had given so much, and then confronted with Kester's news, all she wanted was to go somewhere quiet and get her thoughts in order. She made a huge effort and talked and joked with the rest of the cast, but her heart was not in it.

All at once the room seemed to waver around her and she pushed her way through the crowd to the window. It was open slightly, and she welcomed the cooling draught of air that fanned her hot face. Blackness beyond, lit by a thousand city gaslights and echoing to the clatter of late night traffic. A milk float rumbled by on its way to the station to await the new delivery, empty churns rattling loudly as the cart bounced over the cobblestones of the road.

A church clock started to chime. Mary counted the strokes.... Ten, eleven, twelve. Kester would be aboard the train now, her empty seat beside him. She pictured how it was at home and felt the tears rise in her throat.

'She never turned up, Lisbeth,' Kester said, shrugging off his topcoat and going to sit down heavily in the chair by the cottage fire. 'More or less what I expected, but I still hoped ...'

He shrugged and gratefully accepted the mug of tea Lisbeth handed him. The journey home had been long and tedious. Kester had napped fitfully, waking when the train stopped at every small station to pick up the milk and the mail, plus an astonishing bevy of overnight travellers. He could have done with a few hours in his bed, but he was anxious to get up to Beamsters to see how things were. He watched Lisbeth's quiet face as she bent to turn the rashers that sizzled fragrantly in the big black frying pan over the fire. 'It was Mary's first night, wasn't it? So how was the show?' she asked.

'Oh, very enjoyable in fact – or would have been if I'd been less worried about things at Beamsters. Mary's a natural on the stage. Takes after her m ...' Exhaustion made him careless, and he quickly corrected himself. 'Her cousin.'

Lisbeth looked at him strangely. 'I never could work out that relationship. Esme Greer is Mary's cousin?'

'Something like that. It's a long story. Point is, what's to be done up at the house, given Mary's opted to stop in London? Must say I'm surprised at her. I'd have thought her loyalties lay here, given all Lilian and Tobias have done for her. This is a crisis after all.'

'Maybe she's committed to the show.'

'She said as much. Though I have to wonder how difficult it is to drop out of something like that. There'd be an understudy, and I should imagine there are plenty of young artistes to be called upon to fill in for an absent member of the cast. No. If Mary had wanted to she'd have been here now.' Kester scowled into the fire, his dark face gaunt and shadowed in the flickering light.

'You know,' Lisbeth began carefully. 'Duty apart, if Mary is reluctant to come back, I can understand it in a way. Oh, granted Lilian's the ideal mother with her good works and so on. And yes, she's a fine upstanding person who would never set out wittingly to harm anyone. Don't get me wrong, I like Lilian very much indeed. But for a girl with spirit – and that's how Mary comes across, though I've never met her – I should imagine that life at Beamsters must have been a bit … cloistered.'

'You mean Mary felt smothered. Yes, there's some truth in that. She was always such a merry imp of a girl with her singing and her dancing. Bright too. She was keeping the books for Tobias and she was only a lass.'

'Probably she's better stopping where she is. Not everyone is suited to being a country dweller. I'm not myself. I like the town and people around me. What about Ned? Can't he come back? Then at least there'd be a man about the house to see to the animals and the heavier chores.'

'Ned's serving his apprenticeship. Tobias doesn't want him to miss out on that. No. Tobias wanted Mary. He's going to be hugely disappointed with her decision and I'm not looking forward to telling him. I just hope the news doesn't put him back. The doctor was hopeful of him making a complete recovery – course, he'll have to take things quieter in future.'

They caught each other's gaze and shook their heads. Both knew how impossible that was. 'They'll have to advertise for a housekeeper,'

Kester said. 'It wasn't what Tobias wanted. 'Tisn't the money. He said he didn't like the idea of having a stranger in charge and frankly, I don't blame him. The Suttons have never been a family for employing servants. Lilian was happy to manage her household herself.'

Lisbeth broke a couple of eggs into the pan. Then she said quietly, 'What if I went to help out? Lilian knows me well enough, and we got on fine when she was here.'

Hope leaped inside Kester. 'Think you could cope? It's a big house. Two invalids and a young infant. Won't be easy. And there's Georgie to consider.'

The little boy was outside playing on the swing Kester had rigged up in the apple tree. He was putting on flesh and there was colour in his cheeks now. The cough which had plagued him all winter had gone. Lisbeth glanced at her son through the window and smiled fondly. 'Oh, Georgie won't be a problem. There are horses at Beamsters. You know how much he loves them. Most likely he'll spend all his time in the stables.'

'Aye. So long as he keeps out of mischief!' For the first time in days, Kester's smile reached his eyes. Lisbeth's suggestion seemed the perfect solution, and his weariness had suddenly fled. 'All right. Get your bonnet on. Let's get up there and put the proposition to them. But first let me have this breakfast. My, Lisbeth girl, that bacon doesn't half smell good ...'

When they arrived at the yard, Georgie with a capful of carrots for Brownie the trap pony, the men were gathered around a mud-encrusted tumbrel cart with a broken axle. The owner, a local farmer and a good customer, was in despair.

'Need it immediately, I do. Got to get the last of the mangel-wurzel crop in while this weather holds. The ground's overdue for ploughing as it is.'

'I'm real sorry, Mester Askew,' put in Dan Turvey who was acting as spokesman in Kester's absence. 'We're already up to the eyes in repairs. New axle's a big job. Be next week before we can tackle it.'

Kester thought of the bills outstanding. Already the timber merchant had refused a new delivery until the payment for a previous order was met. Then there was the blacksmith, also asking for his money. Kester said to Lisbeth. 'You go into the house and talk with Lilian. I'll get things sorted here.'

She nodded and left, Georgie in tow. Kester fixed a smile on his face and approached the gathering. 'Morning, Farmer Askew. See you've got problems. Had an argument with a boulder or something, did it?' He addressed the men. 'How about us all putting in an extra couple of hours today? If Chas and myself get this thing to bits, we could fit the new axle and have the cart ready by nightfall, eh?'

Lilian tucked the covers snugly around Tobias and gazed critically down at his sleeping face. He did look better. Widow Goodyear had said as much earlier. Tobias had even expressed his agreement.

Those first weeks after the attack had been worrying indeed. But slowly and steadily her husband had rallied. Now he was able to get up for a few hours each day, and the doctor called only twice a week.

Beyond the window the July afternoon was gloriously blue and gold. The garden blazed with flowers and Tobias's bees were at work amongst the blooms. Josh Millet the wheelwright had volunteered to take over the hives in Tobias's absence. The good man arrived faithfully earlier each morning to tend them.

Everyone had been so caring, Lilian thought. Kester, always a pillar of strength. And Lisbeth volunteering to house-keep for them had been the saving of them all. Even Mary clearly held them in her thoughts, having written regularly and sent many beautiful gifts from London.

Lilian picked up the most recent offering, a delicately pin-tucked and embroidered baby gown and petticoats in finest cotton lawn, which she had brought in to show to Tobias. But her husband had turned away, as he did every time Mary's name was mentioned.

Lilian sighed heavily. Mary's continued absence was doing Tobias no good. If the girl could have spared but a few days from the theatre to visit, she may well have redeemed herself in her father's eyes. But Mary had not, had not even been able to attend the christening.

As if he sensed his mother's thoughts on him the baby woke with a wailing cry. Lilian tiptoed from the room as fast as she was able, a hand to her back which still pained her mercilessly.

Entering the nursery, she went to the cot and gathered little William Henry up in her arms. Because of her illness she had not been able to feed him herself, so at Widow Goodyear's suggestion the baby was being reared on goat's milk and honey. His fury mounted when the bottle he had demanded was not immediately forthcoming. The cries grew louder.

'Hush now. Hush.' Lilian tutted gently into her small son's angry red face and rocked him. He felt heavy in her arms, even though she knew he had not the robust weight of her other children at the same age.

A light running step on the stair announced a second response to the baby's summons. Moments later Lisbeth came in, smoothing her crisp white apron over her slender hips, slightly out of breath.

'All right, all right, Master William Henry my lad! Can't a body get on with the ironing without a certain young man demanding attention all the time?'

Smiling, she took the baby from Lilian and said to her with mock severity, 'And what are you doing away from your bed? A rest every afternoon without fail, the Widow said. Ah, here's Alice with the bottle. Thank you, my pet.'

Lilian made to take the bottle of warmed milk, but Alice handed it promptly to Lisbeth who sat down and offered the feed to the baby. The squawking miraculously stopped.

'Mrs Hayes, I've finished the polishing. Is it all right if I get on with my essay now?' Alice asked, then added hastily, 'It's for a competition at school.'

'Yes of course, Alice. You should have told me. That's far more important than any shiny old furniture!' Lisbeth gave an apologetic little laugh and Alice sent her a shy smile of forgiveness.

'The prize is an anthology of poetry,' the girl said. 'It's one I've wanted for ages. D'you think I stand a chance?'

'Of course you do. I'll keep my fingers crossed anyway.'

'Thank you. Oh, and Violet's turning Brownie out in the bottom field. She wants to know if she can let Georgie ride him there.'

'Yes, that's fine.'

Alice nodded and bustled out with a rustle of well-starched petticoats.

'There are moments lately,' Lilian sighed, 'when I feel distinctly surplus to requirements!'

'Oh, listen to you!' Lisbeth was gently scolding. 'That's not true and well you know it! Let's forget about your afternoon nap for now. Come and sit by me and chat, while William Henry has his feed. Lawks, see how he guzzles! You'd think there was no tomorrow!'

Mollified, Lilian went to sit on the easy chair the other side of the fireplace. There was no fire lit today since the weather was hot, but sticks and coals were laid in readiness and the black grate and brass fender and fire irons gleamed with polish and a good deal of elbow grease.

'He is putting on weight at last, don't you think?' Lilian said, her eyes fixed lovingly on the baby.

'Indeed he is, little soul! See his hands, how dimpled they are. And with a smile like his there'll be some broken hearts in years to come, you mark my words!'

'He started to improve the moment you took over here. I can't tell you how grateful I am. How grateful we all are. You've been a godsend, Lisbeth.'

She coloured up. 'There now, it's a pleasure being here in this lovely house amongst friends. It isn't like work at all.' Lisbeth paused, then said, 'Talking of work, Kester had the men stay late again yesterday. That's every day this week.'

'I see. Is it a big order they're tackling?'

'No. Kester wishes it was so. These are just repair jobs. You know, broken shafts and wheels, things like that. Fiddly and time-consuming, to quote Kester. Not terribly lucrative either, by the time he's paid the men their dues.'

'Oh dear.' Lilian's face fell. 'I suppose the other yard gets the orders for carriages and wagons now.'

'Seems so. Kester has no idea why, for the workmanship is nothing like Suttons. Thing is, the other place is a big modern yard with two workshops on the go. They can honour an order within a couple of weeks if necessary.'

Lilian frowned. 'Don't let's tell Tobias. He'd be so upset, his old customers not staying faithful to the yard and all.'

'Of course we mustn't mention it.' Lisbeth offered the last drop of milk to the baby, then eased him on to her shoulder to wind him. Patting his back gently, she spotted the expensive new baby garments which Lilian had draped over the chair. 'My, just look at the pin-tucking on the robe. And the lace. What a gorgeous thing. Is that from Mary?'

'It is. She must have spent ages choosing it and Tobias wouldn't even give it a glance. He says it's Mary he wants to see, not frills and falderals.'

'Is that right? How awkward men are at times!' Lisbeth kept her voice carefully light. 'I'm sure Mary will come as soon as she can, and then everything will be mended between them.'

'Well, she has promised to visit as soon as she can get away from the theatre.'

'There you are then. How wonderful, having such a talented daughter. You must be so proud of Mary. And two other lovely girls here at home as well. I'm quite envious.'

'Oh well, you're young yet.'

'I suppose so. I'd dearly love a girl of my own. Your Violet is turning out a proper little housewife. Alice tells me she hopes to be a teacher.'

'Mmm. That's been her ambition always.'

'She's a clever girl. Wonder how she'll fare in this competition. Wouldn't it be marvellous if she won?'

Lilian smiled. 'It would indeed.'

'She takes her school work very seriously. She deserves to do well.' Lisbeth paused. 'Had a letter from George this morning.'

'You did?'

'Yes. His release comes through shortly. George thinks it might be best if we make a fresh start. In America.'

'Oh my goodness! Well, America is a land of opportunities, so I'm told. And you have Georgie to consider too. I wish you all the very best of luck, though I shall miss you and Georgie very much. When do you suppose you'll be going?'

'I've no idea yet. But … Lilian, there's something I think you should know. George has written to Kester asking him to go with us.'

*

Mary sat at the piano in the elaborate withdrawing room of the house in the quiet South Kensington square, idly picking out her favourite melodies.

Sunlight blazed beyond the heavy lace curtains of the window, and normally she would have been out there, boating on the river or just having a stroll around the park.

Today she was too tired to bother.

Life on the stage was taking its toll. She never had been one for late nights and sleeping in till ten in the morning. To be honest, Mary felt that her whole existence had been turned upside down.

And oh, what hard work it was, the relentless dancing, singing and acting. Even though your body might ache with fatigue and your throat felt like sandpaper, the show had to go on and every performance must be as brilliant as the last. Not an easy thing to achieve.

Of course, there was still the buzz that performing gave her, but a few days' respite from the theatre would have been very welcome indeed, Mary concluded with faint surprise.

Which brought a shift of thoughts. How were they at Aston Cross? They seemed to be coping remarkably well, thanks to Lisbeth Hayes. Though Lilian's missives, Mary suspected, gave no indication as to the true picture.

What a worry it all was to be sure!

Pain flickered between her eyes. She recognised with alarm the onset of one of the headaches which had plagued her lately.

The door opened to admit Esme. 'Why Mary, I thought you'd be out with Max. Are you feeling all right?'

'Mmm. Bit of a headache. It'll go.'

'You must take one of my migraine powders. We can't have you being off form for tonight's show, can we?'

'I suppose not.'

Esme's green eyes narrowed. 'You don't sound too enthusiastic. Not tiring of the stage already, surely?'

'Not at all. It's just so very demanding. I never realised how much you have to put into every performance.' Mary closed the lid of the piano and turned to Esme with a sigh. 'And I'm concerned about Father.'

'Dear Tobias,' Esme said with quick sympathy. 'Have you had any more news of him?'

'Yes. Lilian says he's much improved. He's able to get up for a few hours now, only to sit in a chair of course, but it's a start. I do wish he'd write to me. It isn't like Father to be churlish. It's because he's angry with me for not returning home with Kester. Actually, you can't blame him. Fine daughter I've turned out!'

Esme reached out and squeezed Mary's hands. 'You're my girl too,' she reminded.

'I know. I didn't mean to sound ungrateful. But I'm so worried about them. Not just Father but Lilian too. Little William Henry is seven months old now, and it still doesn't look as if Lilian has regained her health. I know Lilian. It's not like her to have another woman taking care of the house. I should have gone with Kester that time.'

Outside in the square, a flower seller sang out her wares in a strident cockney voice. Both of them glanced up, listening. The room they sat in was already bright with flowers, and the woman was left to go on by past the window. Her song faded slowly away.

'You can't put the clock back, Mary,' Esme said. 'You did what you thought was right at the time. And they have managed without you at Beamsters, haven't they?'

'Well ... yes. But that's not the point.'

'Mary, if you are having doubts about the stage, then this is the time to change your mind. Now, before Pierre Pascal finds you another contract. Don't make the same mistakes I did. I lived for the stage and missed so much. Seeing you grow up for one thing. It's only now I've found happiness. Take care it doesn't happen to you.'

'Mmm. I'll think about it.'

'That's right. This is a decision only you can make. Now, there's some news I'm longing to tell you.'

Mary stared at her mother. Esme's eyes were bright with excitement and her cheeks glowed. 'It's Perry. He's asked me to marry him and this time I've accepted.'

'Oh, I'm glad,' Mary said with a smile. She was, genuinely. She liked Perry very much. 'I'm pleased for both of you. When is the wedding to be?'

Esme gave a trill of laughter. 'Oh la, don't rush me! I vow you are worse than Perry. He was all for making a date for the autumn. The rush of it. Imagine! My dressmaker would barely have time to stitch together my wedding gown! Now, let me fetch you that remedy for your headache, then I must go and have my rest. Must be fresh for the show tonight ...'

Whether it was the aftermath of the headache or just plain exhaustion, but that evening Mary's performance was the worst ever. Her voice wavered frighteningly out of control on the top notes and twice she missed her cue.

Worry gnawed at her, and for the first time she could not lose herself in the acting. All the while as she mouthed the words and executed the dance routines, she could not get away from the knowledge that she was really only a simple country girl playing at being an actress.

The first act ended to the customary storm of applause, though Mary knew it was not for her. None of her songs had been met with any great enthusiasm and she was not surprised at all. She left the stage with a heart heavy with dejection, her head down and very close to tears. On the way to the dressing room she shared with another girl, she was accosted by Max.

A very different Max, his face frowning, his eyes cold and critical. 'Mary! Whatever's the matter with you tonight? Twice you fluffed your lines and your singing is the worst I've heard. Have you a head cold?'

'No. I ... I'm a bit tired, that's all. I shouldn't have gone on tonight. Maybe the understudy had better take over.'

'Don't talk so ridiculous!' Max snapped. 'Of course you must carry on. You'd never hear Esme wanting to give in.'

'That's not fair. I simply thought it might be best under the circumstances.'

'Oh, grow up, Mary! What a child you are sometimes.'

'I'm not a child. It's a matter of getting used to the work and the late hours, that's all.'

'More a question of professionalism, I would say. Take your cousin, for example. Professional through and through. I forget you're not used to the stage. My own fault entirely. I should have known better than to put my faith in an amateur!'

'I'm s ... sorry,' Mary stammered. 'I didn't mean it. Of course I'll carry—'

'Oh, just get on with it, Mary, for goodness sake.'

Shocked and upset, she watched him go stalking off. Then she went on doggedly to her dressing room to change her costume and refresh her make-up for the next act.

Somehow she managed to get through the performance. She hated every moment of it and could not wait for the final curtain to fall. She was first off the stage. The tears which had threatened all night now welled up with purpose and streamed readily down her cheeks. Her shoulders heaved as she sped past the startled call boy and ran sobbing down the corridor. She could not get away from the front theatre and all it represented fast enough.

With Max's hurtful words still chiming in her ears she burst into

Esme's dressing room. She was so confused and blinded by tears she did not notice that Esme was not alone.

'Oh Mother, he's hateful!' Mary wailed. 'You're right. I've made a dreadful mistake. I've decided to go home!'

Eight

❦

Mary froze, her hands to her face, watching in horror as the man with Esme started to scribble rapidly in his notebook.

A newspaper reporter!

What had she said? What in the world had come over her? 'I … I …' she stammered.

Esme whirled round to face the man. 'My cousin is not herself tonight,' she said, lightly bluffing. 'A migraine, poor dear. We can forget all this.'

A sly smile flicked across the reporter's lips. He was young, eager, clearly out to make a name for himself. 'Cousin, you say? My dear Madame Greer, I distinctly heard the young lady call you something very different. What a scoop! My boss is going to relish this!'

'I really don't think—' Esme began. But the man was already pushing past Mary and slamming out. The pots and jars of make-up on the dressing table rattled in the speed of his exit. Mary's eyes met Esme's fearfully.

'I'm sorry!' she blurted. 'Whatever came over me? He'll put it in the paper. The whole world will know!'

Esme made a small gesture of scorn with her hand. 'Let him publish if he must! Who's bothered? Certainly not me. I'm proud to have you as my daughter. You're beautiful and talented, a daughter any mother would be proud of.'

'But what about Perry? Your marriage. This could be bad press.'

'Not necessarily. Chin up, Mary. We'll cope.'

'It was Max's fault,' Mary went on, angry now, the unfairness of Max's accusations blazing through her. 'All right, so I've not been on form tonight. Didn't hit the top notes very well, and I fluffed my lines a bit. But he shouldn't have gone for me the way he did.'

'True. Everyone has a bad night now and again. I still do myself sometimes. Chances are very few members of the audience will have noticed anything amiss.'

'Think so?'

'Positive. Anyway, what's the odd mistake? You're an artiste, not a machine!'

A smile appeared. 'Suppose so. I'd best go and change for the next act. I feel better now. It'll be all right.'

And it was. The headache which had plagued all day had suddenly cleared and the final act, which contained Mary's best-loved solo, went better than ever before. The show ended to tumultuous applause. When Mary took her bow, the shouts and whistles added to the solid pounding of clapping hands said all. As far as her performance went, she had nothing to fear.

As the applause began to die down, Esme stepped forward and raised her hand for total silence. She smiled charmingly at her audience, embracing them with her sparkling green gaze.

'Thank you. Thank you everyone so much. I should like to make an announcement. This wonderful new operetta of Max Conway's is to be my final performance on stage. When the show closes at the end of the summer I shall be retiring from the theatre – for the very best of reasons. I am to be married.'

The clapping started up again, warm and spontaneous. Esme smiled and gazed about her. Then her hand came up again for quiet. 'Thank you, all of you, for your support in the past. I hope you will continue to support my dear relative, Mary Sutton, who will hopefully be stepping into my shoes.

'Mary?'

She held out her hand to Mary, who stepped forward and took it readily. Together they acknowledged the applause, which went on and on until it seemed to Mary that the very rafters of the auditorium roof must be rocking to the din.

Next day, Max presented Mary with a slender silver chain and locket. 'To say sorry.' His long lean face was repentant. 'I was a wretch. Forgive me?'

'Nothing to forgive.' Mary lifted her hair for Max to fasten the chain round her neck. 'Thank you, darling Max.'

On the surface they were friends again. Yet things were not quite as they had been between them. Mary was guarded. And it was not Max Conway's fiery gleam, but Kester's dark gaze which hovered constantly on the edges of her mind.

There was no big outcry following the reporter's column in *Stage Review*. Sensation, gossip, all was rife amongst the stage crowd. Theatre-goers assumed that someone had it in for Esme Greer and was trying to do her harm. With a following such as hers it did the very opposite, and the news intended to set the sparks flying went out like a snuffed candle.

All through the heat of July and into August, *Love's Rhapsody* continued its run. Engrossed though she was, Aston Cross and her ailing father were never far from Mary's mind. Every morning when Dorcas brought Mary's breakfast in bed, Mary's gaze slid expectantly to the tray for a letter from home.

When it came, in Lilian's hand, the letters spiky with haste, Mary did not think twice.

'Dorcas, please put out my travelling suit and pack my trunk. Tell Standish to waken Cousin Esme. She is to say that my father is worse and I am summoned home. Oh, and I'll need a cab to get me to the station.'

An hour later she was part of the bustle of the great Euston Terminal, boarding the train bound for the north. Esme, looking remarkably trim considering how hastily she had been summoned from her bed, had accompanied her to the station. Both mother and daughter had tears in their eyes as they bid each other goodbye.

'Be sure and give Tobias my fondest love,' Esme said, standing back when the whistle sounded and the guard waved his flag. 'My thoughts will be with you, Mary. All of you. Write and tell me how things are. And don't concern yourself with the show. We'll cope.'

'All right. Explain to Max, will you please? Tell him I'm sorry I didn't see him before I left.'

Slowly the train began to pull away from the platform. Mary watched Esme's elegant figure getting smaller and smaller until she was a mere dot amongst all the other travellers and people waving their farewells. Mary left the window and sat down in her seat. Soon they were gaining speed and London and all it represented was being left behind.

The journey seemed endless. As the train rattled between green meadows and the countryside changed to the harsher landscape of her homeland, Esme prayed she would be on time.

Alighting at Aston Cross, she found Kester waiting with the trap. 'Lilian bid me meet the train. In you get. Is that your luggage? Let's have it in the back.'

He clambered up into the driving seat and clicked his tongue to the horse. Mary waited until they were bowling on through the village, then turned to Kester anxiously. 'My father?'

'Holding on, never fear. Tobias knows you're on your way. You should have seen him smile when Lilian told him you're coming.'

'Really?' That sounded promising. 'But what happened? Had he tried to get up too soon, or what?'

'Not at all. He seemed to be making a good recovery. Then he complained of pains. They sent at once for the doctor, but by the time he appeared Tobias had suffered another attack.'

'Oh dear. How are my ... my mother and others taking it? Is Ned here?'

'Not yet. But they've sent for him. Lilian is coping pretty well. Alice and Violet too. Upset, naturally. Lisbeth's been sleeping over at the house. She's got everything in hand.'

'Mary.' Kester took his gaze off the road and looked into her set, white face. 'Think I should warn you. It's bad. He doesn't look like the Tobias you knew. Bit shocked myself. He was doing so well.' Kester's voice was raw. He clapped the reins across the horse's rump. 'Get on there, Prince! Trot on!'

At the house, Lilian was obviously listening out for the trap. For as soon as the horse was drawn to a blowing, scrunching halt on the gravelled drive, the front door opened and she appeared.

'Mary! Oh, Mary my dear, here at last!'

'Mother!' Mary scrambled down from the trap and embraced Lilian. Shocked at how thin and gaunt her stepmother was, she was momentarily at a loss for words. Then she said, 'I came as soon as I got your letter. How is he?'

'Waiting for you. Come along in.' And to Kester. 'Thank you, Kester. Are you joining us?'

'Not just now. I'll put the horse away and lock up the workshop. No doubt the men will have gone.'

'They knocked off early. I don't think anyone had much heart for work, so I sent them home. Come, Mary.'

It was a very subdued house she entered. In the parlour Mary caught the strained faces of her two sisters and a dark-haired, slender woman who must be Kester's sister-in-law, Lisbeth Hayes.

Lilian divested Mary of her bonnet and pelisse, dumping them unceremoniously on one of the tall carved chairs of the hallway. They went through to the parlour, and Violet jumped up and flung herself tearfully into Mary's arms. 'Oh, Mary. I'm so glad you've come!'

Mary hugged her sister. 'There now, it's good to see you all again. My, how you've shot up, Violet. Hello, Alice,' she bid the girl over Violet's mouse-brown head.

'Hello, Mary,' Alice said coldly. 'You won't know Lisbeth of course. Lisbeth, this is our sister, Mary.'

The young woman greeted Mary quietly. 'What a pity we have to meet in such worrying circumstances. I expect you could do with a cup of tea. I'll go and make one.'

She left the room. Mary peeped into the cradle in the corner where William Henry slumbered soundly. 'He's bonny. Look at those dimples. Like little dents in cream.'

'I know,' Lilian said proudly, then added, 'best go up to Father now, Mary.'

'Of course. I'll just wash my hands. So smutty, train journeys. I'll go to the kitchen, shall I? Be quicker.'

If Lilian's gaunt frame and sickly pallor had come as a shock to Mary, a greater one lay in store upstairs. Cushioned in the big bed by many soft pillows, her father was a shadow of his former self. His face was grey and his hair and beard which had been so thick and vigorous were now wispy and sparse. But his eyes warmed as she bent to kiss him. 'Father, it's me. Mary.'

'Mary, lass.' His voice was faint and she had to bend to hear him. 'Wanted a word.'

Lilian and the nurse in attendance had gone out, closing the door softly behind them. 'Father, about what happened,' she began. Tobias checked her with a slight lift of his hand.

'You're here, that's the main thing. My, but it's good to see you, lass. You always were my lass, know that?'

She nodded, her throat full. 'Father, I must tell you. When I left that time it wasn't … I wasn't running away from you. Nothing like that. I'm sorry to have hurt you.'

'Doesn't matter. I understand.' He licked his dry lips. Seeing a water jug and glass on the bedside table, Mary poured some and let her father sip it. 'Better, thanks. You mustn't fret, Mary. I understood all along, didn't … didn't want to recognise it for what it was. What hurt most was the fact that I'd lost you, like I'd lost Esther all those years ago. Loved her a lot, you know.'

'I do know. And she loved you, still does I'd say. Father, Esme – well, that's the name I know her by – she sent a message. She's never forgotten you. She's sorry for the upset and anguish she caused and she's regretted it time and again. She hopes you have forgiven her.'

'Course I have. Done a lot of thinking, lying here. I've worked out what it must have been like for her. You too. It's a need. Some women, like my Lilian, bless her, are made for home and family. It's their place in life and they are to be commended for it. Others have … have a different vision. Like you and Esther. It's no less worthy. She mustn't … mustn't blame herself.'

He was getting weaker and Mary's heart stabbed. 'Father. Don't talk any more. Have a little rest.'

Feebly his head went from side to side. 'No time. 'Bout the yard, Mary. Business … not been good. If it wasn't for Kester we'd have gone under. Grand lad, Kester. Promise you'll do what's best for everyone. Lilian, Ned and the girls. Little William Henry. Look after them.'

'I will. I promise.'

'Love you very much, child. My own Mary. My dear, beautiful, sunshine girl.'

Mary took his cold, dry hands and held them as he dropped off to sleep. She felt the tears trickle down her cheeks. When his breathing became deep and regular, she gently released her grip of him and tucked the covers around him warmly.

The door opened to admit the nurse. 'Sleeping?' she asked in a soft voice. 'That's good. I'll sit with him now, if you like, miss. Mrs Hayes said to tell you the tea is made.'

'Thank you.' Mary took out her handkerchief and dabbed her eyes. 'Don't think I could face anyone just yet. Might go out to the stable.' She shot another look at Tobias. 'You'll come for me if there's any change.'

'I will,' the woman promised, taking her seat beside her patient.

As Mary went down the well-remembered stairway, she heard William Henry start to wail for his feed and Lisbeth's voice, hushing him. Mary slipped through the deserted kitchen and out. In the stable she found the pony, Brownie, munching his feed of hay.

'Brownie! Oh, dear old Brownie!' Putting her arms around the pony's warm neck, Mary started to weep. She wept for her father who would never be well again. She wept for the long-ago days of her childhood which seemed now so golden. And she wept for the closeness of the few precious moments they had just shared and for opportunities lost. If only she had come sooner. They could have spent time together.

Kester, coming in to tend the animals for the night, found her there. 'Mary? I thought you were with Tobias. Ah, Mary, don't take on so. Come on, there's a brave girl.'

Yet still her tears spilled over helplessly. Tenderly, he took her in his arms and rocked her like a child. She buried her face in his broad shoulder and continued to sob as if her heart would break. 'It's so awful, Kester,' she gulped on yet another sobbing gasp. 'So … hopeless. I can't bear it.'

Eventually the storm of weeping subsided.

Gently Kester cupped her chin with his fingers and raised her face to his. 'My Mary,' he murmured. And suddenly he was kissing her. For one sweet, wild, treacherous moment Mary felt herself yield. She whispered his name in disbelief, her heart thudding furiously. But then a cold horror at her behaviour checked her. She struggled, breaking away, and fled back to the house.

Just before dawn, Tobias Sutton drew his last breath. His family were gathered around him. Pain and grief tore at Mary afresh. It was over. Her father was gone.

'Miss Mary. Could we have a word?'

Mary, crossing the yard with her head down, the business ledgers clasped in her arms, paused and looked up into Dan Turvey's round, be-whiskered face. Behind him were the rest of the men. All looked troubled.

Mary mustered a smile. 'Of course, Dan. What is it?'

'We were wondering how things were going to be, now the Mester's gone. Our jobs, like.'

Dan shuffled his feet uneasily. At the funeral Mary had barely recognised the men, scrubbed and unfamiliar in their dark Sunday suits and too-tight collars. Now, back in working garb, the big double doors to the workshop open, emitting a reassuring whiff of timber and the strong pipe tobacco the men smoked, everything seemed normal again. Enduring, as if no matter what, life would continue as it always had. It struck her with a shock that the men were looking to her for guidance. Her. Not Lilian or even Kester, but her. The Mester was gone but what he represented remained.

She stood very still and thoughtful, the breeze ruffling her skirts of mourning black and blowing a stray tendril of chestnut hair across her pale face.

One by one her eyes acknowledged them. Dan and his son, Alfred, shaft-makers. Wheelwright Josh Millet. Chas Pilkington and his brother Wallace, body-makers supreme who could put a finish like satin on a length of wood. Roland Parks, painter and chamferer, magic in his fingers. Odd-job lad Chips, grown taller and beginning to fill out. Kester had already gone indoors for a meeting called by Lilian.

Mary cleared her throat. 'Oh, I think we can safely say that business at Sutton's Yard will continue as always.' Even as she said the words, she trusted she could honour them.

Dan Turvey doffed his cap. 'Thank 'ee, Miss Mary. That's all we wanted to know. I'd like to add how good it is to see you back and all. Come on, lads. Back to work.'

Nodding agreeably, they went shuffling off into the workshop, and the heartening clamour of hammer and saw followed Mary as she entered the house.

In the curtained and black-draped parlour, the family had gathered together. Lilian sat on the sofa with Ned at her side. Alice and Violet sat at the table, their faces sallow against their sombre gowns of unbecoming black.

Kester stood with his back to the empty grate. He nodded briefly at Mary as she came in with the books. 'Sorry to keep you waiting,' she said. 'I was stopped by the men. They wanted to know about their jobs. I told them business would go as normal. I hope that was right.'

'Of course it is,' said Lilian firmly. 'It was my promise to Tobias. That we would keep the firm going, somehow.'

Mary recalled her own promise to her father and bit her lip. She was tied here now. There was no going back. Already her life in London had taken on a dream-like quality. Unreal, insubstantial almost. Perhaps, after all, this was where she belonged.

'I've looked at the books.' Mary caught Kester's eye and shrugged. 'They don't tell a very encouraging story.'

'True,' Kester said shortly. 'We've been steadily losing business to that other yard. Repair work, plus the odd order for a farm wagon and such, has kept us going till now. I did suggest once we branched out a bit into furniture. Kitchen stuff, dressers, tables, that sort of thing. God knows, the men are skilled enough. Tobias wouldn't hear of it.'

Ned spoke. 'Father was right. Sutton's is a carriage-yard, not a maker of furniture. It'll be all right. I'll give up my apprenticeship and come home.'

His young face was eager, but Mary shook her head. 'Ned, Father would have been appalled to have you pulling out before you've qualified. You're better off to the firm as a fully-fledged craftsman.'

'Mary's right, Ned,' Kester endorsed. 'Another couple of years will see you back here running the show. Until then, we can manage.'

'Of course we can,' said Lilian. 'It is agreed then? We continue as usual?'

'Yes,' Mary said. 'I'll run the office. Kester will have to head the workshop. Dan could be promoted to Kester's job.'

Alice, who had so far held her tongue, now rounded on Mary spitefully. 'Hark at her! Telling everyone what to do! Mary's not been here. She doesn't know what's going on. Kester won't be around much longer. He's going to America with Lisbeth and her husband!'

Shock just about knocked Mary speechless. Kester, leaving? Why had he not mentioned it?

Around her the meeting continued. Lilian was glancing at the books and suggesting they increased their prices. Kester answered her, but for Mary it all passed in a blur. Calling on her limited but invaluable stage experience, she put on a reasonable act of joining in with the talk. Never had she been more glad to see something draw to a close.

Kester left immediately. The family drifted through to the

kitchen, where Lisbeth was brewing tea and buttering scones. Mary followed them, though refreshment was not on her mind. 'None for me, thanks. I have to see Kester a moment.'

She went out into the warm August afternoon and popped her head round the workshop door. 'Kester here?'

'Him's gone down to the forge, Miss Mary,' Chas told her.

She went hurrying off down the road. The forge was situated at Aston Cross just off the green. The ring of the hammer on metal greeted Mary as she approached. She ducked under the low lintel and paused, adjusting her eyes to the dim, smoky pall of the smithy. Opposite, the furnace blazed fiercely. Kester, sweat beading his brow, was at work at the anvil. Seeing Mary, he flung down the hammer and slid what he was making on to the scuffed and scored wooden bench.

'Mary? Something wrong?'

'I should say there is!' Mary stepped closer, her breast heaving, the strong smirch of burnt hoof and hot metal catching at her throat. 'What's this about going to America? Why have you never said?'

'Me never said? You haven't been exactly communicative yourself, have you?'

Hot colour flooded her cheeks. It was true. Since the incident in the stable she had avoided Kester.

'Anyway,' Kester went on, 'I assumed you knew. You've been home two weeks now. I'd have thought someone would have told you. Lilian. Or Lisbeth herself.'

'Lisbeth's run off her feet looking after William Henry and the house. And Mother has other things on her mind.' Mary found she had quickly slipped into addressing Lilian as Mother again. 'Kester, you've no idea what a shock it was. To have it sprung on me like that.'

'I'm sorry.'

'Is that all you can say? You're part of the workforce now. A vital part. All that talk about extending the business and raising prices, and all the time you knew you were leaving?'

'No choice, Mary. My brother George finishes his sentence shortly. He'll never get another job in this country. It was his idea they emigrate. Trouble is, his health. He's not the robust fellow he was. Lisbeth needs some support too.'

'But Sutton's needs you as well.'

'George is my only brother. They're the only family left to me. They must comes first.'

'Of course they must but—'

'Oh?' Kester's face was tight and angry. 'It takes some people a long time to find that out.'

'And what's that supposed to mean? You're talking about me, aren't you, Kester? When I went to London. I had other loyalties then. There was my real mother, remember?'

'Esme Greer! I remember how totally you fell under her spell. It changed you. I hardly recognised you that time at the theatre. All that paint and glitter!'

'It wasn't all fun. London was hard work.'

'But you enjoyed it. The freedom. The glamour.'

'I was never free,' Mary argued hotly. 'You never are, really. Of course I loved London – the outings, the parties, the clothes. Who wouldn't? And Esme was very generous. She's not the shallow creature you make her out to be. She's brave and clever and hard-working. I liked the stage too. It was an experience.'

'But you grew tired of it, didn't you Mary? Like you'll grow tired of being back here once the novelty wears off.'

'That's a vile thing to say. I will stop here. I promised Father. I will stay.'

'Maybe. But will you be content? I doubt it. You'll be like a young horse, raking at the bit, wanting its freedom.'

'There you go again. Freedom! Is that what you hanker for?' Mary's voice throbbed. 'Is that why you've plumped for America? All those wide open spaces. A chance to prove yourself. At what, Kester? Well, you can go! We'll cope without you. I don't care if I never see you ever again!'

She whirled round and left. Kester stared after her. Then he turned back to his work.

The lovespoon he was making had an intricately tooled handle. Once, in his varied career, he had worked for a locksmith. He still had a set of precision tools necessary for fine ironwork. The spoon was done now. Taking up the tongues, Kester dipped it into a wooden pail of water to cool. Steam hissed up, dispersing. Kester picked the spoon out of the water and laid it, wet and glistening, on the anvil. A wry smile tugged at his lips. It was beautiful.

Alighting from the cab in the quiet South Kensington square, Mary turned to attend to her luggage. She was in London for the wedding. She had relaxed her mourning and wore a tailored travelling suit in lavender woollen with a matching pelisse and bonnet.

The green paintwork and brass knocker of the door of number fifteen were as bright as ever, but Mary was amazed at how sooty the October air was after the country. And as for the noise and bustle of the streets!

The door shot open and Esme appeared. She looked radiant and was clearly overjoyed to see Mary. 'Mary my love! Oh, I've so much to tell you. Come along in do.'

Leaving Webster to deal with the cabbie and baggage, Mary followed Esme into the house and was at once struck by its opulence. There was no doubt about it, part of her had missed the luxury of living here. And Esme's taste in furnishing was closer to her own than the solid familiarity of Beamsters.

Dorcas was there, beaming a welcome. 'Dorcas!' Mary said. 'How well you look.'

'Thank you, Miss. Let me take your pelisse and bonnet. You must be exhausted after the journey. You go and sit down and I'll bring the tea tray.'

Mary followed Esme into the parlour. 'Why, you've redecorated,' she cried, glancing round approvingly. 'It's lovely. Cream and gold always looks so elegant.'

'Yes. We shall be living here after we are married. Well, Perry's rooms are no more than bachelor quarters, and I'm fond of my house. We contemplated selling and buying afresh, but there really didn't seem any point. Perry doesn't mind where he lives so long as we are together!'

There was a pause while Dorcas entered bearing a laden tea tray set with hot muffins under a gleaming silver lid and the pretty rosebud tea service. As soon as she had gone, Esme poured the tea and handed Mary hers. 'There. Now we can talk.' She sent Mary a searching look. 'You're thinner. Bit peaky, too. But there, it can't have been easy.'

'No.' Mary bit into a buttered muffin, her favourite.

'Did you ... were you able to make your peace with your father?'

The muffin suddenly tasted like sawdust in her mouth. With some difficulty she swallowed it down. 'Yes, I did. It was so strange. He understood how I felt. He understood perfectly. But oh, Esme, after he died I had such a sense of guilt. It's never quite gone. Everyone was so kind. No-one accused me of not caring or anything. But I cannot rid myself of the notion that if I'd gone sooner, I might have saved Father from pushing himself so hard.'

'I doubt it. Knowing Tobias, he'd have gone his own way whether you were there or not.'

'Think so?' Mary frowned, considering. Lilian had tried to reason with her. Lisbeth too. Somehow their words had not helped. This was different. 'You know, you're probably right. It had never occurred to me.'

'You were too close to it all, that's why. An objective view is often of value. Dear Tobias. I can't believe he's gone. Such a handsome, robust fellow he was. Older than me of course. He would have made such a loyal husband. How was it ... the end? Was it peaceful?'

'Very. And I gave him your message. He was glad to hear from you. He said you must not blame yourself. He said you took the right course for you, and that was best. I think, as he lay poorly all those weeks, he'd worked it out for himself.'

'Ah. Dear Tobias.' There was a poignant silence, broken by the chiming of the ormolu clock on the mantelpiece.

'Now, what of the wedding?' Mary said, more cheerfully. 'How many guests? And Esme, what am I going to wear?'

Esme brightened. 'Hundreds of guests! Don't know where we're bound for our honeymoon, Perry insists on keeping it a secret. Oh, there's no need to panic over your outfit. I've had a word with my dressmaker.'

'Not that dreadful woman who kept diddling you?'

'La, no. I finally caught Madame Babette out. I've a new dressmaker now. She's excellent. Wait till you see the ensemble she's made for you. It's the very latest mode, in dove-grey silk with mauve trim. She took the measurements off one of your old gowns. Might need nipping in a bit, you've lost weight ...'

After the first day or two it was as if she had never been away. It was good to gossip with Dorcas and catch up with old acquaintances. The show had finished its summer season and was about to go on tour – with a different female lead.

Max, Mary discovered to her faint regret, was travelling in Europe so would miss the wedding. 'With a new escort, I might add.' Esme's eyes twinkled. 'Letitia Bartholomew, an heiress and an insipid creature to boot! But there, I never did feel Max was right for you.' She paused, then said innocently, 'How's Kester? You haven't mentioned him at all.'

Mary felt her colour deepen. 'Kester's well enough,' she replied, managing to keep her voice steady. 'He's going away with his brother and family. To America. In fact I was glad of the opportunity to come away. Oh, it wasn't an excuse. I really wanted to come to the wedding and to see everyone again. But it was a relief to get away from home and not have to see Kester leave.'

Kester and the family were due to sail from Portsmouth on the day after the wedding. Mary recalled how awkward their leave-taking had been.

'Take care, Mary.' Kester had looked very serious and distant. 'Any problems with work, Dan is the one to approach.'

'Yes. I know. I ... I hope you find your brother in reasonable health.' She swallowed. Neither felt at ease with the other. 'Safe voyage, Kester.'

On the morning of her departure, she was glad that Chips was driving her to the station and not Kester, who was busy helping Lisbeth pack their belongings. The two girls and Lilian, baby in her arms, stood on the porch to wave her off. 'Goodbye everyone,' Mary called from the trap. 'Mother, don't overdo things, will you?'

'Of course not, Mary.'

'You will come back, Mary?' That was Violet, still far too quiet, still grieving for her father.

'Oh yes. Two weeks, maybe three, and I'll be home again. We shall plan Christmas together. I know it will have to be a quiet one,' she added hastily. 'But it's William Henry's first Christmas and he deserves something special.'

Her sisters brightened at this, and as Mary was driven away they all waved their farewells with moderate good cheer.

'I was hurt at Kester for going off,' she confessed to Esme now in a low voice. 'We need him at the yard. Business is beginning to pick up a bit. The doctor's put in an order for a new trap for his rounds. The men were overjoyed to have their better skills called for at last. If only Kester were there to oversee the work.'

'You think a lot of Kester Hayes, don't you, Mary?' Esme said. 'Love him, perhaps?'

'Yes ... oh, I don't know. I don't know how I feel. It's too complicated. We had this awful row. We both said things we shouldn't have said and didn't mean. Anyway, he's going. So he doesn't much care for me, does he?'

'Maybe he's putting duty before his own feelings.'

'Maybe.' Mary felt her heart ache and went for a determined change of subject. 'Two more wedding gifts arrived earlier. What if we use the dining room to display them all? Dorcas can help me fix up the big table, if you agree.'

'Good idea,' Esme said. 'Thank you, my sweet.'

On the day before the wedding, Mary was helping Esme and Perry to arrange the presents. Other parcels in exciting boxes done up with coloured ribbon had been delivered throughout the course of the day. Esme was sifting through them.

'One from Pierre. My agent that was, Perry. Sweet of him to think of us. Oh, one for you, Mary. La, but it's heavy.'

Mary took the parcel wrapped in stiff brown paper tied with string and looked curiously at the postmark. Aston Cross. The bold handwriting in black ink could only belong to one. Her pulse started to race.

At the other side of the room, Esme and Perry were unwrapping their gifts. 'Oh, see what Pierre has sent,' Esme said. 'A chased silver punch bowl. Oh, Perry, how wonderful.'

'Indeed,' Perry said, a smile in his voice.

With hands that trembled, Mary fumbled with the string and layers of paper on her own parcel. Out came a gleaming lovespoon in forged black iron. She caught her breath, hope and despair mingling impossibly within her. He loved her. He wanted her. And now it was too late.

'Perry dearest. Do tell me where we are bound for our honeymoon? Secrets are my passion, but I have to let Robson know where I shall be,' came Esme's plea from across the room. 'A whole six weeks – where?'

'Wheedler! I wanted to surprise you. But if you insist. We're off on a tour of Italy. Venice, Rome, Florence … there's nowhere like Italy for romance. We shall be sailing from Portsmouth. On the day after the wedding.'

Nine

‘I’ve never been on a boat before,’ said Lisbeth, her brown eyes half-fearful. ‘Just hope we don’t have a rough crossing.’

She had spent all day packing and scrubbing out the cottage. Kester and Georgie had just manhandled the travelling trunk containing their belongings down the narrow stair. Wearily Lisbeth flexed her aching arms and cast a critical glance around the now spotless but bare little living kitchen. Only the breakfast things to pack away, and that could not be done until morning.

Georgie said boastfully, ‘I don’t care how rough the sea is. I can’t wait to get to America. Will there be horses there like Brownie, Uncle Kester?’

‘Sure to be, bigger and faster than old Brownie, I reckon.’ Kester ruffled the boy’s head and reached for his coat.

‘You’re never going out?’ Lisbeth said with exasperation. ‘There’s still some outside work needs doing – and you don’t want to be late to bed. Early start tomorrow.’

‘I must say goodbye to Lilian. Had a farewell drink with the men earlier. This is different. Lilian has been good to me. I owe her a few words in private.’

‘Can I come, Uncle Kester?’ Georgie clamoured.

‘Not now, young fellow. Stay here and help your mam. Fetch a bit of kindling in for the morning, eh?’

Kester sent Lisbeth a nod and left the cottage.

There was a touch of autumn in the air and Kester strode briskly along the woodland path, his booted feet stirring the woodsmoky whiff of damp earth and rotting beechmast. Above him the leaves were on the turn and hung in great gold and crimson bracts on the bough, waiting for the first frosts of winter to nip them off.

Kester wondered what Mary had thought when she had received the lovespoon. There had been no word from her. He wished, how he wished he had patched up the quarrel between them before she had left for London. Told her how he felt about her, instead of allowing the days to trot by with her doing her utmost to avoid him, only speaking during their working hours together, and then in a manner so aloof and cold they might have been strangers. Proud, was Mary – but then so was he.

He reached the edge of the wood and turned on to the lane to the village. Evening shadows were long-drawn across the fields. Ahead, lamplight from the windows of Beamsters spilled out into the gathering dusk.

Something caught at Kester's throat. He'd miss it all, by heck he would. The carriage-yard. His workmates. The Suttons. Beamsters was the nearest he had ever come to calling home.

Lilian was standing on the front porch, as if in wait for him. 'Kester, is that you?' she called as he opened the yard gate and went to join her.

'Aye, it is. Mustn't stop long, else there'll be Lisbeth to reckon with.' Kester followed Lilian in and through to the kitchen. There was the lingering smell of the good meat and vegetable pie they had eaten for supper, though the pots were washed and everything tidied away. It was very quiet.

'Girls not in?' Kester asked, sitting down at the big table and accepting the cup of tea that Lilian poured him. She was looking better, he thought with relief. More her old self. Amazing, how resilient women were.

'No. They've gone to a bible meeting at the chapel. The minister's driving them back.' Lilian sat down with her own tea. 'I'm glad you've called. A letter arrived earlier. From a Charles Rossiter. I wondered if you knew of him.'

Kester frowned. 'Rossiter? Don't think so. What does he want?'

'He says he's interested in buying a business premises and wants to know if this one might be coming up for sale. It's a very polite letter. I'll fetch it.'

The missive was written in neat brown script and, as Lilian had said, explained that the sender was looking for a business investment locally, largely to give him an interest. It was signed, Your obedient servant, Charles Rossiter.

'Sounds a bit lonely,' Lilian said.

Kester snorted. 'Don't be fooled by all that. My advice is to play wary. I thought you agreed not to sell?'

'I did, and I'll stick by my word. Mary would be horrified if she knew about this.'

'Then write to the fellow, tell him no. Have you heard from Mary since she went to London?'

Lilian shook her head. 'No. Didn't really expect to. Well, she'll be busy with the wedding preparations, knowing Mary.'

'She didn't … didn't mention me at all before she left?'

'Not that I recall.' Lilian paused, then said gently, 'You think a great deal of her, don't you, Kester? Love her, perhaps. Does she know?'

Again Kester thought of the lovespoon. He pictured Mary getting it out of the wrapping, fingering the intricate metalwork with its secret message. 'Aye, she knows. What a mess this has turned out. Timing all wrong. For the yard, and on a more personal level. For two pins I'd have backed out of this scheme to emigrate. But it wouldn't be right. There's George, his poor health and so on. Someone has to see the three of them safely to their destination and set up with somewhere to live.'

'Of course they do. Family comes first, Kester. Mary knows that. And as for the carriage business … well, we shall just have to do our best until Ned has finished his apprenticeship. When do you sail?'

'Day after tomorrow. Managed to get a passage on the Star of Portsmouth. She's a handy vessel, makes pretty short work of the voyage, so I'm told. We're leaving for Portsmouth first thing in the morning. It's a full day's journey by rail.'

'And your brother? He's got his release?'

'Oh yes. George is meeting us off the train. I've booked us in at a boarding house overnight.'

'You're a good man, Kester. I'm only sorry it's turned out so impossible for you and Mary. Tobias thought a lot of you and so do I. It would have been gratifying if things had turned out differently. But there it is.'

'Aye well.' He drained his cup and stood up. 'Better get off. Goodbye, Lilian. Thank you for all you've done in the past. I shall write. Any problems with the yard that Mary or the men can't deal with, be sure and refer to me.'

'I will. Goodbye, Kester. Safe voyage, and God be with you all. Tell Lisbeth my thoughts are with her.'

Kester saw Lilian's eyes fill up with tears. Giving her a gentle smile, he bent to kiss her cheek and left, striding out of the house and across the drive, soon to be swallowed up by the dusk.

'What a wonderful day it's been!' Mary said to Esme as they snatched a much-needed respite from the heat and clamour of the ballroom of the Hyde Park Hotel. 'The church, the flowers, the wedding luncheon! And now the dancing! I swear I've been waltzed off my feet!'

They sat at a small table in one of the alcoves, toes still tapping to a lively rendering of a popular waltz by the ensemble of musicians, despite Mary's words to the contrary.

The wedding ceremony had been held locally at Brompton Parish Church, its rather austere interior brightened by bounteous arrangements of out-of-season roses in gold and white, and by the richly-attired assembly of guests.

In cheerful defiance of superstition which declared green unlucky, Esme wore a gown of rustling watered silk in her favourite emerald, embroidered all over with glistening diamanté and the tiny seed pearls that were all the rage. Perry, distinguished and undeniably handsome in top hat and tails, made his vows in a strong, clear voice, and looked well pleased as he escorted his radiant new bride from the church.

One of the new-fangled photographers had been engaged. Bride, groom and guests had to pose for ages on the steps, while the man fretted and fussed under a black cloth draped over the curious rectangular wooden construction on a tripod, which he called a camera obscura.

'A wonderful day,' echoed Esme, flicking open her laced-edged fan and wafting her flushed, smiling face. 'And to think it has been captured forever on daguerreotype. To think I shall be able to conjure up today whenever I want, just by looking at the pictures. I shall send you one, Mary.'

'Oh, lovely. A group picture with Dorcas on would be best. She looked so pretty in her new gown with her hair dressed in ringlets, instead of scraped up under that wretched cap. Dear Dorcas. I shall miss her sorely when I go back.'

Esme trilled a laugh. 'I vow the girl feels exactly the same about you. Most grieved she was, when she heard you were no longer going to be living with us.'

'Well, we got on splendidly together.'

'Take her back to Aston Cross with you if you want,' Esme said in a sudden fit of generosity. 'It's no hardship for me to engage another maid for ourselves, and an extra pair of hands would likely be welcome at Beamsters.'

'It would indeed.' Mary said. 'But hadn't I better ask Dorcas first? I don't think she's ever been out of London in all her life. She's a city girl. She may not want to move out to the country.'

The fluttering fan stilled. 'My dear Mary,' Esme said with mock reproof. 'How often do I have to remind you? One does not consult servants as to their preferences. One tells them. My guess is that Dorcas will be as delighted to join you as you are to have her. She always was more your maid than mine. Let's consider the matter settled, shall we?'

'Of course. Thank you, Cousin Esme.'

'You weren't thinking of departing immediately, I hope. Stay on a few days, enjoy yourself.'

'Don't tempt me, please.'

'Now would I do that?' Esme broke off to chat with a passer by. 'Why Angeline, how adorable you look in blue ...'

Mary sighed to herself. In truth there was nothing she would like more than to lengthen her stay here. She liked being back in the hurly-burly of the city. It had been wonderful these past days, meeting up with old friends and learning all the latest gossip. She felt at the heart of things here in London. Aston Cross, the slow pace of country life, was worlds apart.

Around her, the bright chatter and laughter of the wedding guests, the music, the heady perfumes of the ladies and the warm scent from the multiple arrangements of hothouse flowers, all seemed to recede into the distance. Mary gazed down at her mauve silk skirts with the elegantly flounced hemline, beneath which peeped the pointed toes of her dancing slippers of soft white kid. There would be no dancing for her back north, not for a long, long time.

The future stretched ahead bleakly. Nothing but problems and hard graft. The nitty gritty of everyday chores was surely poor exchange for the thrills and glamour of the stage. Mary thought of the long hours closeted in the dusty little office next to the workshop, battling to keep the struggling yard from closure.

Responsibilities. All those people – not only her immediate family, but the men and their wives and families too – dependent upon her. Good people who loved her. People she would never, ever let down. But oh, what a weight it was to bear. No father to help her any more. No Kester.

'You are coming to Portsmouth on the morrow to wave us off?' Esme asked Mary brightly, the other guest having gone to join her party. 'Our boat does not sail until late afternoon. You have plenty of time to get there. The carriage is at your disposal. Mind you have Dorcas chaperon you.'

The musicians were striking up again, a merry galliard, pulling the couples out on to the floor. Mary saw Perry and some handsome young blade threading purposefully through the throng to claim them.

Portsmouth. Kester too was sailing tomorrow, but on the morning tide. It seemed like fate. If she could somehow get to see him, talk to him.

'We'll be there,' Mary replied.

It was a grey dawn, a cold wind whipping in from the open sea, the air full of the mewling of sea-birds and the shouts of porters as they laboured on the busy wharf. The healthy whiff of rope and tar overlaid the oily reek of murky harbour water.

'This is ours, I reckon.' Kester brought his family to a stop by the landing stage and with a grunt of relief lowered the heavy trunk to the ground. Straightening, he glanced about him. Other people were waiting to board the ship, their faces red and nipped with the early morning chill.

High above the dockside, the side of the *SS Star of Portsmouth* reared black-painted and sheer.

'Isn't she huge?' Georgie marvelled from his perch on his father's shoulders. 'Look at her chimneys. Look at them! There's smoke coming out of them both.'

'Funnels,' George put him right. 'There's stokers down below, lad, heaping coals into the furnaces to get up enough steam to sail. Not long now, and we'll be aboard.'

His free arm went round Lisbeth in a hug. Observing them together, Kester felt his chest tighten. Always he had envied George his wife and child, the warm closeness that enfolded the three of them, but never so much as now. Not for the first time he wondered if they actually required his presence on this voyage.

True, the man who had met the steam-train yesterday was barely recognisable as his brother George. The long months of privation, the poor food and frequent bouts of ill health, had taken their toll. George's sturdy, upright figure was now wasted and slightly stooped. His thick black hair was thinning and frosted with grey. But the fire was still there in his dark eyes – blazing now not for the cause for which he had sacrificed so much, but for his ambitions for their future.

America would be good for George, Kester had thought as he listened to the brief, excited exchanges. All that space and opportunity. This country was too small to contain a man like him. Yet where did that leave Kester?

In the event George had come over with a violent attack of coughing and Lisbeth had cried out in alarm. Resolutely Kester had shouldered the travelling trunk and led the way out of the smoke and bustle of the crowded railroad terminal. Of course they needed him.

This morning it was Kester who collected the passage tickets from the Immigration Office at the harbour. Kester who chivvied the little family along the busy wharfside with its sailing ships, steamers and tug boats to where the SS *Star of Portsmouth* was docked.

'Looks like they're opening up the gangway at last,' George wheezed, the cold briny air catching at his lungs. 'Come on, we're moving.'

Hefting up the trunk once more, Kester fell in with the others, shuffling along the narrow gangway on to the deck of the ship. Steerage accommodation for immigrant travellers was way down in the bowels of the boat. Notoriously dark, stifling and cramped, having planked bunks arranged in tiers on either side of a narrow walkway, Kester had paid extra and booked cabins for them. Though by no means the best available, these at least afforded them privacy during the twelve-day voyage.

'When you've sorted out your bunks,' Kester said to Lisbeth, 'come back up on to the top deck. We can watch the boat leaving harbour from there.'

They were here now, the four of them. Georgie, his cheeks scarlet with excitement, demanded to be boosted up again for a better view. This time it was Kester who obliged, wincing as the weight of the child descended on the tender, travel-sore flesh of his shoulders.

Quite a throng had gathered on the quayside, families mostly, here to wave their loved ones off to a new life across the ocean. The slim figure in the stylish lavender gown and pelisse stood out amongst the dull greys and browns of the commonplace homespun of the rest of the onlookers.

Kester's heart skipped a beat. It wasn't. It couldn't be.

There was another young woman with her, small and quick, dressed in the neat dark blue of a maid in service. The pair were swiftly working their way along the quayside, darting in and out of the groups of people, their eyes anxiously scanning the row of passengers lining the decks of the ship.

'Look, it's Mary!' screeched Georgie, pointing. 'Mam, Father. Uncle Kester. It's Mary. She's come to wave us off. Mary, we're here! Ma ... ry!'

Kester stood frozen, his face registering sheer disbelief. Lisbeth clutched his arm. 'It *is* Mary, Kester. She's waving, she must want to speak to you. Go on, you've still got time. They haven't finished loading up yet.'

A lot of activity was going on below on the landing stage. A couple of late-comers were being hustled aboard. Two porters clattered to and fro with handcarts loaded with last-minute supplies. Mary and Dorcas, breathless, their hair tugged by the wind, their full skirts billowing, had reached the foot of the gangway.

Mary cupped her hands to her mouth and hollered. 'Kester! Kes ... ter!' She waved frantically and Kester, spurred suddenly into action, transferred Georgie to his father's shoulders and ran. Feet slithering on the slippery wet boards of the upper deck, Kester headed for the steep flight of steps to the lower deck, gasping apologies as people stepped aside to avoid him.

Gaining the gangway at last, a burly sea-man in white oilskins, wearing the peaked cap of officialdom, stood with arms outstretched, blocking his path. 'Sorry sir, you can't disembark now.'

But Kester was desperate. 'Won't be long. Have to see someone. It's urgent.'

He pushed past the man, covered the gangway in a few bounds and Mary flew into his arms.

'Kester, oh Kester!' she gasped. 'I thought we'd missed you. We got held up in the traffic. I thought we'd never make it in time.'

'Well, you managed it,' he said, hugging her so fiercely that she pleaded laughingly for mercy.

'The lovespoon. It's beautiful! I'll treasure it always. Kester, do you have to go?'

As if in answer the ship's hooter blared loudly and urgently.

'Kester,' she began again, and was silenced as his lips came down on hers in a lingering, salty kiss.

He broke away. 'Listen Mary. I have to see this through. George, Lisbeth and the boy, they need me. You've got to understand. I've no choice but to go with them.'

'But I need you as well,' Mary said, her blue eyes swimming. 'We all need you back at Beamsters. I thought we'd cope without you, but I know now we can't and ... oh, Kester, I love you so much. Please don't go.'

'It won't be forever. A year, two maybe. Then I'll be home again. We can be together, and I won't have my brother's well-being to worry about any more. We'll be free to get on with our lives.'

At that moment the sea-man in charge shouted for the all clear. 'Come along sir, aboard this minute if you please!'

'I'll write,' Kester said wildly, his voice raw and choked. 'Wait for me, Mary. Soon as I can, I'll be back.'

'Promise?'

'I promise. Love you, Mary.'

He kissed her again and gently pushed her from him. Then he turned and ran back up the gangway. Seconds later it lifted and the hooter blared again. It was the most desolate sound Kester had ever heard. With dragging steps he made his way back to his waiting family. Mutely Lisbeth took his hands in hers, sympathy in her eyes.

'Isn't Mary coming with us?' piped up Georgie.

'No lad, it's not possible,' his father told him.

'Why isn't it? I like Mary. Why can't she come to America with us?'

'Georgie, that's enough,' Lisbeth said, then went on to explain patiently that a passage had to booked on a boat, and none had been obtained for Mary.

Kester heard none of it. He stood wooden-faced by the rails, watching Mary bravely waving, her slight, lavender-clad figure getting smaller and smaller as the ship ploughed a smooth path through the harbour waters, heading for the open sea. Carrying him away.

'I'll tell you this, Miss Mary,' Dorcas said, deftly unpacking the metal-banded leather travelling chest in Mary's bedroom at Beamsters. 'Here's me thinking we were off to the back of beyond, nothing but cows and silly sheep for company. Yet it ain't like that at all. There's the workshop, men hammering and singing fit to burst. And the village, everyone nodding to us as friendly as can be. And your ma couldn't be more pleasant.

'I get on a treat with Miss Alice and Miss Violet. Not to mention little William Henry. Oh, the way he smiles up at you. Fair softens your heart, it does. 'Tisn't like work being here. It's more a pleasure!'

Adding the final garment to the neat pile on the bed, Dorcas slammed down the lid of the chest and turned to Mary with a grin that almost split her face.

'I'm glad you're not disappointed, Dorcas,' Mary said repressively. Whilst relieved to hear that the maidservant was happy with her change of direction, she did not wholly share Dorcas's enthusiasm at being here. At this moment Mary did not want to be shackled to a house and business, spending all day and every day in an office trying to make the impossible rows of figures balance. She wanted to be with Kester, facing whatever hardships life might toss at them in that vast, exciting new world across the ocean, but facing it together!

Guilt gnawed at Mary and she turned away, lest Dorcas guessed her thoughts. Last evening when they had arrived, Lilian had been pitifully pleased to have her back, had greeted her with a warmth and affection that was totally genuine. Mary, tired, dispirited, more than a little nauseous after the journey – she never had been good at rail travel – was only too happy to give in to the motherly administrations.

A good meal awaited, a hot brick put in her bed to air and warm it. The old house with its homely aroma of beeswax and fresh-baked bread had felt welcoming.

Home. But at a price.

She said to Dorcas, 'Well, I shall leave you now. No doubt you and Mother can sort out the household and nursery duties between you. Time I went out to the yard.'

Mary had dressed carefully for her first official day in charge; dove-grey gown, white lace collar and cuffs, her hair piled up in a glossy brown coronet on the top of her head. Her cheeks were pale, her eyes shadowed. She felt older than her years.

Downstairs, Alice and Violet were putting on their bonnets and topcoats for school. 'This must be your final year at dame school, Alice,' Mary said, thinking how grown up her sister was looking. 'You'll be leaving at the end of term.'

Alice shook her head. 'Didn't Mother tell you? I'm stopping on as a student teacher. It's what I've always wanted.'

'Oh. I see. Well, that's splendid.'

'When I leave school, I'm stopping at home to help Mother,' Violet put in. 'Or else I might marry Chips. Chips wants to be a shaft maker like Dan Turvey. He doesn't want to work anywhere else but Suttons. That suits me a treat. I'll never have to leave Aston Cross, ever.'

Lilian had come through to the hallway at the end of this declaration, a basket containing the girls' lunch of cold meat pasties and apples on her arm. 'Such plans! I only hope Chips is aware of what you've got in mind!' Smiling, she handed over the lunch basket. 'There's the school bell going. Better scoot, the pair of you, or you'll be late. That will never do for a schoolmistress-in-the-making, Alice!'

The girls hurried off, and Mary made her way across to the workshop. During her absence the men had begun work on the latest order, the new trap for the doctor. Set up on trestles, the bodywork of the trap was already taking shape. Seeing the satin-smooth finish of the woodwork and the careful joints, Mary's spirits lifted.

'That's looking well,' she said with delight. 'It's going to be a four-wheeled vehicle then, not two like his old one.'

'Aye,' Chas Pilkington nodded. 'The doctor, he wanted something sturdier this time. Two-wheelers are fine for summer driving. But in winter, you need something more substantial to get you through the mud.'

''Course,' added Dan Turvey with a wry smile. 'He'll need a bigger horse to pull it. Wonder if the doctor's thought of that?'

'Oh, I'm sure the fact hasn't escaped him,' Mary said, beginning to feel more at ease. 'He'll probably trade the pony in for a cob.'

Chips spoke. 'Don't think so, Miss Mary. Doctor Brownley called at the Widow's only yesterday.' Chips still lived at Widow Goodyear's and helped with the holding. 'I was taking in the logs for the fire, so I couldn't help but overhear what was said. He wants a governess cart for his little lasses and their mam. He's keeping the pony on for that because it's good and quiet, like. He wants us to make the cart for him.'

Mary's heart leaped. 'Another order, Chips? Are you sure?'

'Yes, I heard clear as anything. The doctor's dropping in later to see you about it.'

'Chas,' Mary said to the man. 'Are the plans for governess carts still on the shelf?'

'As far as I know, Miss Mary. Kester left everything to hand. If there's more you need to know, any extras like a basket seat for the youngest, give me a shout and I'll be right over.'

'Thank you, Chas. I'll do that.'

Encouraged, Mary went on into the office, sat down at the desk and soon became engrossed in the paperwork.

At around mid-morning there was a light tap on the door and Lilian entered with a tray of tea and shortbread.

'Just what I need,' Mary said, rubbing tired eyes. 'But you haven't brought a cup for yourself.'

'Dorcas is making one for us. What a blessing that girl is going to be. Such a hard worker, and so good with the baby.'

'Yes. Esme thought you'd appreciate the extra help.' Mary poured herself some tea, then looked up to find Lilian hovering in the doorway.

She said, hesitantly, 'Mary, Kester came to see me before he left.'

'Oh?'

'He confided how he felt about you. And you about him, apparently. I wanted to say how sorry I am that it hasn't worked out for you both.'

'It hasn't *not* worked out,' Mary said, sharper than she intended. She swallowed and added, more rationally, 'He's gone to America to help his brother, that is all. He'll be back. I spoke to him just before he sailed.'

'You did?'

'Yes. Dorcas and I travelled to Portsmouth to wave Esme and Perry off. Kester was sailing the same day. He told me he'd be back as soon as he could. He wants to see George and Lisbeth settled first.'

Lilian looked dubious. 'I can't help thinking of Widow Goodyear. Her man left for America to seek his fortune and never returned.'

'I thought she was widowed as a young woman. She's always been known as Widow Goodyear.'

'That's just a title that befits her line of work. She's never been married.'

'I see.' Mary shrugged. 'Kester's not like that. He'll be back. Two years at the outside. He promised.'

'And I'm sure he meant it. But just remember. America's a vast country with huge prospects, especially for a man like Kester. He might start up a business of his own. A carriage-yard like this one, or a smithy. Anything. A business is not easy to leave.'

About to retort she would go to him, Mary bit it back. Upsetting Lilian would do no good at all.

'Another thing,' Lilian went on. 'Kester's always been a bit of a rover. Never stopped long in one place. A man like that generally finds it hard to settle down. I don't want to dash your hopes, Mary love,' Lilian added gently. 'I'm just pointing out the facts, that is all.'

She went out, leaving Mary staring after her, the tea cooling at her elbow. Lilian was wrong. Kester would never let her down. Would he?

Eventually Mary drank her tea, then picked up her pen and carried on with her work.

It was getting on for midday when the clatter of hooves heralded a caller. Thinking it might be the doctor about the governess cart, Mary rose and went outside.

It wasn't the doctor at all. Riding into the yard came a total stranger on a breedy chestnut gelding. Spying Mary, he doffed his cap, revealing a head of well-groomed but receding light-brown hair. 'Good morning,' he bid her briskly. 'Am I addressing Miss Sutton?'

'That is correct,' Mary replied. 'And you are, sir?'

'Charles Rossiter ma'am, at your service.'

He dismounted, a dapper gentleman, perhaps in his early forties, dressed in quality riding togs and high boots of best black leather well polished. Mary did not miss the swift glance he threw around the house and workshop, as if assessing the place, and she experienced a stab of alarm. However, his face when he turned back to her was nothing if not honest, and his grey-brown eyes held a shrewd kindliness that put her immediately in mind of her father.

He said, 'I wonder if I might have a word with the owner? I wrote to Mrs Sutton recently. Don't know if she mentioned it?'

'No, not a thing.'

'Ah. Fact is I'm looking to purchase a business. This looks a likely prospect. It's been my occupation, y'know. I've bought up firms that are – shall we say, no longer making their way – and set them right again.'

Mary bridled. 'You have come to the wrong place, sir. Suttons is not a failing concern, nor is it for sale.'

'Ah. That is not what I have heard.'

'Then you are misinformed, Mr Rossiter.' Mary lifted her chin and met his gaze squarely. 'I think you had better leave. We are in mourning here at Beamsters.'

'Yes, so I heard. My condolences, ma'am. Not an easy time, I know. I am recently out of mourning myself. My wife, y'know. Agnes has been gone now these twelve months. House is still quiet without her. Work helps.'

There was no doubting the sincerity of his words and Mary was not unsympathetic. But she steeled herself. 'I'm sorry for your loss, but I'm afraid I cannot help you,' she said firmly. 'As you can see, this is not the situation you supposed. This is a thriving yard. It is also a family concern, and likely to remain so. There is nothing for you here. Good-day, Mr Rossiter.'

He looked about to say more, then clearly thought the better of it. Sketching a bow, he bid her a polite goodbye, remounted his horse and rode out of the yard. Mary stood frowning, listening to the hoofbeats trotting away down the lane.

Deep in thought, Mary made her way towards the house, vaguely aware that the sawing and hammering from the workshop behind her had ceased. The men were downing tools for their midday repast. From the open nursery window of the house came the angry wail of William Henry, awake and demanding his feed.

'All right, young mister. I'm coming,' chirped Dorcas's Cockney tones. 'My, what a racket! The sooner we get you on to beef stew and dumplings the better! Come on then, that's my big boy.'

The wailing miraculously stopped. About to enter the kitchen where Lilian could be heard setting the table for a cold luncheon, Mary had second thoughts. 'Mother, I'm going to get a breath of fresh air,' she called. 'Won't be very long.'

Without waiting for a reply she walked on. Round the corner of the house, down the path and out of the side gate on to the lane. Ahead lay the village and the red-brick chapel where her father was buried. Mary set off through the misty October air.

A blackbird was singing in the churchyard. There was nobody else about. The heavy oak doors to the chapel stood open and inviting, but Mary walked on past.

Reaching Tobias's grave, she stopped. There was no stone as yet and the mound was bare of grass. Her father had not been a man much for flowers, but someone – most likely Lilian – had arranged some tawny chrysanthemums from Beamsters' garden.

She stood staring down at her father's final resting place, remembering the long years Tobias had put into the carriage-yard. It had been more than a job of work to him; it was a way of life. She had been right to send the fellow packing.

Mary gnawed uncertainly on her lip. She had nothing against her caller. His manner had been wholly respectful and he had not prevaricated when she had asked him to leave. That said, she could not shake off the feeling that they had not seen the last of Charles Rossiter.

And where was Kester when she needed him? Off to America with his brother and Lisbeth. Mary wondered about Lisbeth. Had she some sort of hold over Kester? Before, Mary had taken the rumours over the two of them lightly. Now it was different.

'Oh, Kester,' she muttered, angry suddenly and doubting. 'What am I supposed to do?'

Ten

༄

'My dearest Kester,' Mary wrote. 'I was happy and relieved to receive your letters all together in a bundle. We worried how you fared these long months, and no word from you. Glad to hear that you have arrived safely in America and are all well after the voyage.

'I was surprised and not a little alarmed initially to see the address on your most recent missive, which I opened first. However, reading through the letters in order, all was revealed to me. What a stroke of luck to have met with Mr Aaron Croft on the boat, and for him to have pointed you in the direction of Wisconsin, instead of settling in New York as you had planned. I see you travelled across country in a wagon drawn by two oxen. What a wearying journey it must have been, and so slow. No wonder your letters took so long to get here. The American countryside sounds so different from home it is hard to imagine. Vast, those wide plains and towering mountains with deep gorges to have to traverse. How terrifying to have come across a tribe of Red Indians. What tales young Georgie will have to tell his children one day.'

Mary looked up from the escritoire in her bedroom, where she had retired to write her letter. Penning lines of a more personal nature proved impossible in the office with all the interruptions. Either one of the men came in for advice over something, or else it was Lilian with one of the many tea trays she deemed necessary to sustain Mary in her working day.

It was Saturday afternoon. The weekly accounts were done, the figures entered in the ledger – showing a pleasing profit, even after the men's wages and payment for a delivery of timber had been deducted – and her desk tidied for the start of a new week. Mellow September light filtered through the lace curtains at the window. Mary realised with a start that almost twelve months had passed since she had taken over the business. Long, gruelling months, in which she had tried not to worry over the lack of communication from Kester and put all her energies into work.

It had paid off. Absently Mary rubbed the nape of her neck, a habit she had acquired of late. She took up her pen, dipped it in the ink horn and continued to write.

'Sutton's Yard is now on an even keel, and it's all thanks to you, Kester. During a slack week, Chips took it into his head to fashion a three-legged kitchen stool from off-cuts of wood, as you once suggested. When the doctor brought his wife to view the new trap he had requisitioned, she bought the stool and ordered five more, plus a deal-wood table to go with them. Her friends in the Methodist Circuit admired the set greatly and wanted the same. We now have a line in kitchen furniture and cannot make enough of it. Of course, the older men will stick with their carriage making, but Chips and Dan Turvey's Alfred are into cabinet work with a vengeance.

'Assuming you have received my earlier letters telling you that Dorcas is now resident here during Esme and Perry's lengthy honeymoon, I am pleased to say how well she has settled at Beamsters. Lilian (who sends her deepest love) wonders how we shall manage without Dorcas when she returns to London early next year. She is so patient with little William Henry, walking now, chatting away and into everything. It is hard to believe that he will be two years old come January. Alice is enjoying her job of work as student teacher at Aston Cross school. Violet leaves next summer and will stay home to help Mother. Ned is enjoying his apprenticeship and is full of new ideas. He comes home for Christmas, which will be nice.

'Scanning these lines, Kester, I give the impression that things here have been straightforward. Must confess it is not the case. It's been hard, bearing the weight of the firm all alone. Other than Chas Pilkington (and I have to guard my words lest they get repeated in the workshop) there is no one here with whom I can relate. I shall be glad when you return, and can share the burden of the yard with me.'

The clatter of hooves on the yard brought Mary's head up. She rose and went to the window, lifting the lace curtains to peer out. Below, Charles Rossiter was handing his horse to Chips. With a sigh towards her unfinished letter, Mary tidied a few straying curls from her forehead, shook the creases from her dark-blue working skirt and went down to greet the caller.

By now Dorcas had shown Charles into the front parlour. He stood with his back to the fire, and met Mary with a smile.

'Mary my dear. How very efficient you look in your blue and cream. It suits you. Was just passing and thought I'd drop in to see how you all fared.'

'We are well, thank you, sir. And yourself?'

'Fine, fine. The men are hard at it, I see. I was admiring the brougham in the barn. Like it very much indeed. Roland was priming it ready to start painting come Monday. What colour will it be?'

'Black with yellow trim. It's made to a standard design of my father's. We've turned out a great many of them and we've never, ever had a complaint. This one is for the silversmith at Hereford.'

'Ah. And the new line? The kitchen furniture?'

'I took another order for a six-drawer Welsh dresser and table and Windsor chairs only this morning. That's the third this month.'

'My goodness me, if this continues you'll need to open up an extra workshop. You've done well, Mary. What a blessing you took the plunge and went ahead with the furniture venture.'

'What a blessing the bank backed us! They almost didn't. Not their usual policy to do business with a woman, I was informed. Pompous creature! I had to use all my powers of persuasion.'

'There you are then. Proves that even a bank manager isn't averse to a pretty face. I've heard reports you drive a hard bargain when it comes to buying in materials.'

Mary dimpled. 'Really?'

'Really. Fine job you're doing here, Mary. A fine job.'

She mocked a curtsey. 'Thank you, sir. Will you take some refreshment? Some of my mother's ginger wine? Or will I ring for Dorcas to bring us some tea?'

'Let us sample the wine. We can toast your success then, Mary.'

The weeks leading up to Christmas went by so swiftly Mary wondered where the time went. Letters came from Wisconsin more regularly now that Kester was settled and building a house for them – a house of pine logs hewn from the forest, of all things. They had started their own smithy, Kester wrote. As the area was largely agricultural, he was concentrating on ploughshares, chains and other farm implements, as well as general repairs which was George's side of things. So far, business was steady.

At Beamsters, preparations were going ahead for the festive season. Lilian, out of mourning now and much improved in health, was stitching herself a gown of mulberry woollen to wear on Christmas Day. Violet had made her own dress, a pretty creation with a ruffle at the neck and cuffs in a pink sateen. Lilian had thrown up her hands in horror and declared the fabric too thin for winter, and wouldn't Violet catch her death.

Alice told her mother to stop fussing. 'If Violet's happy to shiver, then so be it. I shan't bother with anything new, Mother. My brown check will do perfectly well. It's warm and I feel comfortable in it.'

'Comfort is everything,' declared Mary, sitting with her feet on the fender and relishing the heat from the fire on her frozen toes. Sleet slithered down the window and the wind moaned menacingly in the chimney. 'That stove in the office is useless. Next winter, I vow there will be changes.'

'Your dress, Mary,' Violet prompted. 'What will you wear?'

'My tawny. Might need new cuffs and collar. In white lawn, I think.' Mary glanced at Dorcas, sitting in the family circle around the hearth, stitching a rip in William Henry's short frock. 'What about you, Dorcas?'

Dorcas looked up. 'Don't know I'm sure, Miss Mary. I've never needed anything special before. At Miss Esme's – I mean, Lady Sayle's – house in Kensington, the mistress was generally working over Christmastide. We servants had a pork dinner and a pudding, and that were that.'

Lilian said, 'We must make up for it while you are with us at Beamsters. Christmas is a time of celebration, and this year we shall be quite merry, what with Ned coming home, and Charles Rossiter invited. Widow Goodyear too and Chips – a handsome fellow he's turned out. Roland Marks always spends the day with us too, having no family of his own. And we mustn't forget that nice young schoolmaster lodging with the widow.' Lilian sent a sideways glance at Alice, who blushed. 'With such a gathering, Dorcas, a new gown is a must.'

'Well, ma'am.' Dorcas lowered her sewing to her lap. 'Drab colours are the way of servants. I've always hankered for something cheerful. Crimson, or a cherry red. And a petticoat with real lace on it. I'd dearly love a lace petticoat.'

'I'll make you one myself,' Violet cried. 'Full skirted, with two layers of lace. I'll do the dress as well. We'll go to the market on Thursday and buy the stuff. Won't take long to make up if you help with the cutting out.'

'Oh, miss!' Dorcas's eyes shone.

'Dear me,' said Lilian, smiling. 'What a good thing I'm well in hand with the cake and the puddings. There'll be no time for last minute baking, with all this sewing going on!'

Ned arrived with the snow on Christmas Eve.

'Hello everyone,' he cried, stamping the snow from his boots on the mat and dumping down his large canvas bag, which bulged with mysterious and exciting-looking parcels. He shed his snow-speckled topcoat, which was promptly whisked away by Alice and hung on the clothes airer over the hearth to dry out. 'Thanks, Alice. Here, give us a kiss. You too, Violet. My, you've shot up.'

'Me! Me!' shouted William Henry from his playpen in the corner. Ned strode over to the toddler, lifted him out and tossed him up high. 'What a ton weight! Young William Henry, you'll break my back! There.' He delivered the child a smacking kiss and put him back again amongst his toys.

'What a journey I've had. The roads are well nigh impassable already. Mother, come here. Aye, but it's grand to be home.'

'Ned, my own dear boy. How you've grown!'

Broadened too, and with his side whiskers and bushy beard Ned had a strong look of his father about him. Lilian embraced her son warmly and drew him close to the fire. The kitchen was ablaze with light and smelled of good things to eat; ham shank with cloves, spiced pudding and new baked bread. The big old table was set for supper and the kettle sang on the hob.

Holly and trailing ivy festooned the ceiling beams and through the open door the bannisters could be seen similarly draped with greenery bright with berries. A fir tree in the corner of the hall glistened with glass baubles, a beribboned candle on every spiky bough.

Perched on the topmost rung of a stepladder, tying a bunch of mistletoe to the centre beam, was Mary.

'Mary.' Laughingly Ned escaped his mother's arms and strode into the hall. 'Here, let me do that.'

'It's done now. Trust a man to turn up when the work's over.' Mary came down the ladder with a flash of white petticoats, to be seized by the waist by Ned and bounced unceremoniously to the floor.

'There.' He kissed her cheek, then held her from him, appraising her. 'Bit frayed around the edges, I warrant. They've been working you too hard. Have to make up for it these next days, eh?'

'I'm fine,' Mary insisted. 'Ned. You haven't greeted Dorcas.'

He looked at Dorcas's slight figure in her grey gown and all-enveloping white pinafore. 'Hello Dorcas. You've survived life in the country, then?'

'I have, Master Ned,' replied Dorcas, gravely. 'And never been happier.'

Silence. They held each other's gaze. The clock on the wall ticked away steadily and logs crackled in the grate.

Then, 'Supper,' called Lilian, and the moment was broken. Everyone gathered round the laden table, chairs scraping on the stone flags of the floor. From his playpen, William Henry started to bawl.

'I'm coming, my fine man.' Dorcas swooped the child up, sat him in his high chair next to her and tied his bib around his neck. Someone placed a plate of finely chopped meat and vegetables on the tray in front of him. Dorcas handed him a small silver spoon.

The sobbing stopped. Lilian at the head of the table murmured Grace, and the first family meal of the holiday began.

Late that night, alone in her bedroom, Mary took out her gift from Kester. Earlier in the week a large crated parcel had arrived full of carefully wrapped gifts from America, some were from Lisbeth, George and Georgie. Kester had remembered every one of them too. There was a box of biscuits called cookies, and another of little chocolate-coloured sweet cakes called brownies.

Mary had fully intended opening her present with the rest of the family after Christmas lunch was eaten and they were all gathered around the tree. Then she had changed her mind and brought the parcel upstairs with her.

It was small and square. Carefully she unwrapped the red paper patterned with tiny fir trees. Inside was a solid jeweller's box. Her heart was thumping wildly. A ring. He'd sent her a ring to seal their promise.

It wasn't a ring. A pendant lay on the soft bed of velvet. A single pearl, threaded on a fine gold chain.

There was a prettily embossed card with a message in Kester's bold hand. 'To my Dear Mary wishing her a Very Happy Christmas. With all my love, Kester.'

Nothing more. Not even a few scrawled kisses. The words might have been aimed at any member of the family. Alice, Violet. Lilian even.

Mary's throat felt full and heavy. Picking the pendant up, the gold flashing in the light from the lamp on the bedside table, she held it in her palm. It was a lovely thing. Just not ... not what she expected.

She drew a deep, shuddering breath. Was Kester having second thoughts about them? Had he found someone else?

Unbidden, Lisbeth's smooth Madonna-like face swam up from the brink of Mary's memory. He had loved Lisbeth once, he'd as good as admitted it. Maybe that love was not as dead as he thought.

A dark, aching weariness crept over Mary. Unconsciously she rubbed the nape of her neck under the heavy mane of hair, trying to ease the knot of tiredness and tension that had subtly tightened. The tears which threatened now fell freely.

Foolish, she chided herself, brushing them away. It's Christmas. A poignant time, bringing out the yearning that all the rest of the year you keep in check. On the other side of the world Kester was likely thinking similar thoughts of her.

She had sent him a daguerreotype portrait of herself, mounted in a wallet of brown Moroccan leather. She had gone specially to the new studio at Market Drayton to have the picture taken, posing breath-held while the photographer stood under his black draped camera obscura box – much like at Esme and Perry's wedding. The resulting picture did not resemble her one bit. The stiff curls and expression, the stiff poise too, 'As if your stays were killing you,' Alice remarked, not without some truth.

Mary wrote on her card, 'To my own Darling Kester from his Sweetheart, Mary Sutton.' She felt silly now. What an overdone sentiment to have sent Kester of all people.

The family had chipped in with the other gifts. A tin of the mint humbugs Georgie loved. Hand-knitted woolly scarves and gloves to guard against the fierce unrelenting cold of the Wisconsin winter.

Placing the pendant around her neck, Mary crossed to the window and gazed out into the night. The snow had stopped and the countryside was tranquil under its new white blanket. High above, stars gleamed silently in the blackness.

'I love you, Kester,' she murmured across the hundreds of miles of land and ocean. Shivering suddenly in her thin cotton shift, she clambered into the muffling warmth of her bed, her cold toes seeking the hot brick wrapped in a piece of flannel that Dorcas had put there earlier.

She was asleep in seconds. She awoke to the clamour of church bells and someone, Ned probably, going out to see to the animals. Not long afterwards her bedroom door opened and Dorcas appeared bearing hot chocolate on a tray. 'Happy Christmas, Miss Mary,' she said perkily.

Mary stretched, flung back the covers and swung her feet to the floor. 'Happy Christmas, Dorcas,' she bid the maid.

They all turned out for chapel, ploughing through the deep, soft snow of the lane, William Henry perched red-cheeked and beaming on Ned's shoulders.

Mary sang The Holly Berry, Lilian's favourite carol as a solo. The congregation joined in heartily with the other hymns and shivered patiently through the sermon.

The Suttons arrived back at Beamsters to the mouth-watering aroma of the goose sizzling in the range. Ned stirred the banked-up fires into life, piled on logs and poured himself a secret tot of Malt, sneaked in when his mother wasn't looking. Though Lilian had relaxed many of her ideals of late, in some matters her rigid upbringing held fast. Alcohol was the curse of the devil. In no way would she wittingly have anything more potent than her own ginger brew across her doorstep.

Chatter and laughter issued from the kitchen where the womenfolk stirred and basted and clattered the pots and pans for the feast of the year, aprons over their Christmas finery. Mary was in the dining room, setting the big polished table. Lilian, having confessed to waking in the night worried that the snow would put paid to their guests, was visibly relieved when the party arrived, red-faced from the tramp across snowy fields, well muffled up against the cold, and bearing gifts.

The day flew by with food, merriment and present giving. If

Mary's thoughts were many miles away, she was careful not to show it. As the afternoon deepened into dusk, they all gathered in the front parlour to sing carols and play games. John Black the young schoolmaster, who gave every appearance of being stolid and straight-laced, astounded everyone by proving a past master at mime and had them all in tucks of laughter with his anecdotes. Mary sang to her own piano accompaniment and Alice recited a poem. Then Roland took up his fiddle and the floor was cleared for dancing.

It was a merry gathering and Charles Rossiter, emboldened by what everyone took to be ginger wine but was actually Ned's secret malt, hurried the ladies off for kisses under the mistletoe.

'Happy Christmas, Mary my dear,' he murmured, and brought his lips down firmly upon hers. Mary waited for the fire that had blazed through her veins at Kester's kiss, but it did not come. Smiling at her, his mature and handsome face inscrutable, Charles handed her back to Ned with whom she had been dancing and went to claim Lilian.

Over in the corner, sipping a cooling glass of lemonade, Alice watched them. She looked almost pretty tonight. The russet tones of her dress suited her and Mary had put her hair in rags so that it curled in ringlets around her face. But seeing her mother giggling and flustered as a girl, she remembered Father, dead now these two years. And it struck her with an insight unusual for her rather insular nature how lonesome her mother must be.

She'd seen Charles kiss Mary too, seen his expression as he released her with obvious reluctance.

'He's too old for you, our Mary,' Alice hissed later, having watched him waltz Mary closely in his arms.

Before Mary could reply, John Black appeared and made Alice a formal bow. 'May I have the honour? It's a jig. I like jigs, don't you?'

Alice was swept away, looking so bemused that Mary had to smile. Dorcas and Ned spent a fair amount of time jigging round in each other's arms too, she observed. Dorcas looked very fetching in her cherry red gown, displaying a glimpse of white lace on her new petticoat as she twirled and bobbed to the music. Chips was showing Violet the steps, pretending to limp when she accidentally trod on his toe.

Standing aside by the glittering tree, fanning her hot cheeks with the silk fan exquisitely hand-painted in Italy that had been Esme's Christmas gift, Mary's thoughts strayed to Kester. How she wished he was here with her. Perhaps next year. She fingered the pearl pendant round her neck and tried to ignore the small insistent voice that told her, disturbingly, that Kester might not be coming back at all.

'Mary! My dear child. Let me look at you.'

Mary removed herself from Esme's effusive, perfumed embrace and allowed herself to be closely scrutinised.

Home at last after an extended honeymoon, which had taken them travelling not just in Italy, as was their original intent, but the whole of Europe, Esme and Perry were paying Mary a visit. Since Mary, apparently, was too busy to go to them.

They had booked in at the Hillcrest, an exclusive country hotel outside Much Wenlock, where all the best people stayed. The hotel had the ambience of casual luxury that Esme loved and which Mary, she thought, could do with a sampling.

'You're too wan by far,' she said, settling Mary down in the lounge of their suite. 'What's happened to your sparkle? And Mary, what in the world have you done to your hair?'

'It's more suitable for work in a bun,' Mary replied. 'It falls over my eyes otherwise when I'm writing. I'm pale from being indoors a lot. You wouldn't believe the hours I put in at my desk.'

Esme pulled a little face. 'Looking at you, my love, I would believe anything.'

There was the question of a meeting to be arranged with Lilian. Esme left off contemplating that for now and gave her attention to her daughter.

Esme looked ravishing in her travelling outfit from Paris of twilled brown poplin, flounced and looped, the lace at the neck of the underblouse cascading in creamy ruffles over the bodice. Mary, by contrast, was a bumpkin in her blue silk gown which had once been the height of fashion and was now sadly dated. There was a mark on the skirt which Mary tried to hide with her reticule. Dear me, thought Esme, we shall have to take the girl in hand.

Perry, dashing as ever in plain grey frock-coat over tailored trousers, came into the room and greeted Mary with warm affection. Then he took up his top hat and silver-topped cane and excused himself, saying he was going out to see the sights and would be back in time for luncheon.

'Now,' said Esme, settling herself comfortably back amongst the embroidered cushions of the sofa and pouring the tea which had arrived at her elbow. 'Tell me all.'

After which Esme delivered Mary to the attentions of Standish – still po-faced and silent, but with the same magic in her fingers as always. With her hair tongued into becoming curls, her cheeks lightly rouged and her waist nipped in to swooning point, Mary was buttoned into one of Esme's more youthful gowns of flocked yellow muslin. Standish then stood back and looked a question at her mistress.

'*Much* better,' Esme said. 'You can throw that blue thing out, Standish. 'Tis only fit for the ragbag. Keep the gown, Mary, it looks far better on you than me.'

Perry arrived back then, and they went down to the hotel dining room to lunch on grilled trout with buttered new potatoes and tiny garden peas.

'Fine countryside you have here,' Perry said across the table. 'Not at its best in February, of course. Must be grand in summer. Preferable to abroad, mayhap. That blistering heat.'

'Which reminds me,' Esme put in. 'I brought you some lengths of cloth from Rome, Mary. For your sisters and Lilian too. The colours are quite splendid.'

'Thank you,' Mary said. 'Lilian sends an invite to spend Sunday with us at Beamsters. You may find it, well, different from what you are used to ...' Her voice trailed.

'We'd be charmed to accept,' said Perry firmly. 'Isn't that so, my love?'

'Indeed.' Esme smiled encouragement to her daughter that inwardly she did not feel. 'What shall we do this afternoon? You are not running back to that dreary office of yours. The place won't fall apart without you for one day. Let us take the carriage to Shrewsbury. Wonderful shops there for browsing. We can buy something for the baby. You shall help me choose, Mary. A rattle.'

Mary burst out laughing. 'Cousin Esme. William Henry is no longer a babe in a crib. He's running about and talking.'

'Really? How they do grow. A wooden train then. Shall we ring for our cloaks and bonnets? No mention yet of Kester. You can tell me about his adventures in America as we go.'

In fact the day spent at Beamsters went off better than Esme could have hoped. Things were faintly strained at first, apprehension on both sides, but Lilian's natural hospitality soon overcame any awkwardness and Esme, with her radiant charm and knack of making whoever she set eyes upon feeling special, quickly won the hearts of Alice and Violet. William Henry was bounced on her lap and sang to, much to his delight.

Perry demanded a tour of the workshop.

'Bigger concern than I expected,' he commented as Mary proudly showed him round. He ran his hands over the smooth raw timber of the frame of a carriage set up on trestles. 'Like the shape of this ... brougham, is it going to be?'

'Yes. One of our specialities.'

'Wouldn't mind stating an order. D'you do four horse vehicles?'

'Not as a rule. There isn't the demand here.'

'Would be in the City. If I rustle up some orders from my colleagues – cash on delivery, of course – would you be able to meet the numbers?'

'Perry.' Mary met Perry's shrewd but kindly hazel gaze and smiled. 'I never say no to an order.'

'Quite right too. Ah, is that a kitchen dresser over there? Not bad, not bad at all. Craftsman made. D'you do cottage furniture? Settles, chests and the like?'

'I don't see why not. Why?'

'Friend of mine's looking to update the housing on his rural estate. He says the only furniture available falls to bits the minute it's put to use. He's a Hereford man. Just over the border from here.'

'You'd best refer him to me and I'll give him a quote. Want to see the office now, where the real work is done?'

Perry grinned and bent to drop a kiss on her cheek. 'Mary, you are incorrigible. Yes, I would very much like to see your bolt hole.'

In the house, Dorcas had packed her belongings ready to return home with her rightful mistress. She presented a woebegone face and barely responded to Esme's questions on her life at Beamsters.

'My, what a grump you have become,' Esme burst out with exasperation. 'I can hardly get two words from you. Is this what living in the country does?'

Dorcas began to weep. 'Oh, Miss Esme. I mean, Your ladyship.'

'Never mind all that. Plain ma'am will do.'

'Yes ma'am. I love it here so much I don't want to leave. Not that I wasn't happy at number fifteen. And me Cockney born as well.'

'Is that what's bothering you? Dorcas, if you prefer to remain here and the lady of the house has no objection, then you are free to choose.' Esme paused, contemplative. 'Lot of work here for one small person, I'd have thought. More than at my Kensington house.'

'It's true ma'am.' Dorcas bobbed a curtsey. 'But I don't mind at all. The Suttons, they're like a family to me.'

'It wouldn't have anything to do with the son.' Esme posed her head astutely. 'Ned, was he called?'

Telltale colour flooded Dorcas's cheeks. 'Well, Ned has written to me twice since Christmas. He's still apprenticed and doesn't have much time. But he wants to know if I'd walk out with him on my day off. He's only at Much Wenlock.'

'Well well. Far be it from me to stand in your way, Dorcas. Want me to have a word with the mistress?'

'Oh ma'am, would you?' Her thin face lit up.

Esme smiled. 'Leave it to me, Dorcas.'

Lilian had invited Charles for the evening meal. The two men got on splendidly. As the meal progressed, Esme, seated next to Charles, watched the interchange between those present with interest.

'Your stepmother is a little in love with that Charles Rossiter,' she confided afterwards to Mary. 'Lilian doesn't know it herself yet, but I bet I'm right.'

Mary stared at her. 'But she loved Tobias greatly. I wouldn't have thought there'd be anyone else for her, ever.'

'Stuff and nonsense. Lilian's young yet. You can't expect her to live the rest of her life mourning a memory. Tell you this though. Charles isn't altogether interested. He's got his eye on you. Don't forget to write me, Mary my love. Let me know how things are progressing.'

A letter arrived from Kester.

Taking a hasty look as she ate her breakfast porridge, Mary saw that he started off with a demand to know what was going on between her and Charles Rossiter.

'Your last two letters have been full of him. He's driven you into town on more than one occasion and even bought you afternoon tea. Isn't he the fellow who once wanted to buy the business? I told Lilian to send him packing. Pity she didn't take my advice.'

Mary smiled to herself. Kester, jealous. Perhaps now he'd come home where he belonged.

'Mary, have you finished breakfast? There's a fellow in the yard wants to speak with you. Bit upper-crust.' Alice stood in the outer doorway, dressed for school. 'I was on my way out. Shall I show him into the office?'

'Oh, no, I'm coming. Sounds like someone Perry mentioned.' Hastily Mary stuffed the unread letter in her pocket and stood up. 'Thank you, Alice. My regards to John!'

Alice threw a withering look and departed; she never could take being teased. Chuckling, Mary smoothed down her skirts and went out to greet the potential customer.

He was with her all day. When he left, Mary had an order to furnish ten cottages and a large farmhouse. How she was going to meet the demand she had no idea, but meet it she would!

The long cold winter had released its grip and spring had come in, gloriously blue and golden. After tea, instead of returning to the office to put in another hour's work, Mary threw her shawl across her shoulders and went out through the side gate. Her steps took her down the lane frothy with hawthorn flowers and into the wood.

Reaching Kester's cottage, she opened the gate and entered the garden. Weeds had claimed it. The orchard trees were full of blossom and the perfume drifted, sweet, evocative. Memories of Kester were everywhere. The gate he had mended, the new pigsty, empty now.

Mary went to sit on the swing Kester had hung for Georgie from one of the apple trees. Setting it in motion, she took out the letter and read from where she had left off earlier.

'It's a great life here, Mary. A great place to be. The smithy has doubled in size. I've taken on another smith and two apprentices. If business continues like this I'll soon have made my fortune.

'George's health has not improved. He can only put in a few hours a day at the smithy. I know you will understand that I cannot leave yet and come home.'

Mary's heart sank. She stopped the swing and sat staring into the distance. Then she gave her head a little shake and read on. Kester's final paragraph blazed out at her.

'I miss you, Mary. Why don't you come out to me? We can be married here in Wisconsin, no problem.'

Eleven

Clear winter sunlight lit the office and beyond the window, the cobbles of the yard and the smooth bare branches of the beeches at the entrance sparkled with frost. It was the sort of day Mary loved, and with a sigh of regret she dragged her gaze from the glittering outdoors and back to the first column of accounts in this, her new ledger for the start of yet another year in business.

January 1856. Come July she would be twenty one.

Twenty one!

That morning, as she put up her hair in front of her dressing table mirror, she had peered at her face closely. She looked jaded. And decidedly older than her years.

Well, she *was* jaded and she felt old. She felt that all her youth and laughter had been swallowed up by hard graft and responsibility. She also knew that given the same circumstances over again, she would have chosen exactly the same route.

Mary drew her chair a little closer to the gleaming black wood-burning stove in the corner which now rendered the previously bleak little office comfortably warm. The stove was a recent innovation, replacing the one her grandfather had installed several decades ago. It was also her one concession to her own comfort and still only put in at the insistence of Lilian.

'Child, the hours you spend out there it's a necessity,' Lilian had said. 'You know how long and hard the winter can be in these parts. Small wonder you haven't frozen to your chair before now!'

Mary's lips twitched wryly. Her stepmother had not been far wrong. This was the first winter her fingers and toes had not itched and burned with fiery chilblains and she had not had to huddle in her thickest woollen shawl over the books, while the former rusted old stove huffed out more smoke than heat.

Picking up her pen, Mary dipped into the standish of ink and began to record the month's figures. The five hundred pounds in the debit column blazed out at her, and she bit her lip. She had not wanted to take on a loan, not even a private one from Charles Rossiter, who had proved a friend indeed. But it had been her only way forward. The furniture venture had taken off and suddenly a second workshop had become essential.

From outside came the hammering of the workmen putting the roofing slates on the new building and store. It stood next to the existing one; a stout stone-built construction of which her father, Mary thought, would have been justly proud. By spring Alfred Turvey and Chips would be installed, and the original premises would revert back to being purely a carriage-making area. Much to the relief of the men, who had thought the new-fangled deal-wood dressers and tables a wounding slight on their craftsmanship.

A light tap on the outer door heralded Dorcas with the tea tray. 'Brrr,' she said, placing the tray on the shabby old desk. 'I swear it never got as cold as this in London. Foggier, yes.'

'I remember,' Mary said, smiling and reaching for the teapot. 'Ugh! You could actually taste those pea-soupers! Warm yourself by the stove for a bit, Dorcas. Want some tea?'

'Lawks, I wouldn't say no. What with the washing and the Monday bake, I haven't stopped all morning. I swear I could drink the river dry!'

Mary poured tea into the spare cup that generally adorned the tray in the event of a visiting client, and handed it to Dorcas.

'How's William Henry?' she asked, settling back with her own drink. 'I heard him coughing in the night.'

'Three times I got up to him, poor little lamb,' Dorcas replied, taking a grateful sip of tea. 'When William Henry falls for one of his head colds he doesn't do it by halves. The mistress is calling on Widow Goodyear on the way back from town, for some of her blackcurrant linctus. Works better than that foul stuff the doctor brews up. Tastes better too.'

'True. Was there … was there anything for me in the midday post?'

'No, just a letter for the mistress.' Dorcas looked at Mary shrewdly over her teacup. 'It's Kester isn't it, Miss Mary?'

'Well—'

'I know you. You've been on pins all week. Shouldn't worry too much. I'll allow it's been a while since you've had word from him, but I expect he's like yourself. Tied up with his work. From what you've said, that smithying business he's building up is going from strength to strength, and wasn't he felling trees for timber to extend that log cabin they're living in?'

'That was back in the autumn.'

'There you are then. Knowing him that homestead will be a mansion by now! Chances are your Kester's been so run off his feet he doesn't even notice the time passing.'

Mary made no reply. Ever since last spring, when she had written to Kester turning down his request for her to go out to him to Wisconsin and get married – the most difficult letter she had ever had to pen – she had been aware of a distinct cooling off on Kester's part.

Faint, but there all the same.

'Kester didn't take kindly to my refusing to leave all this and go out there to him,' she said in a low voice. 'He was offended, Dorcas.'

'A course he wasn't,' Dorcas cried. 'Kester Hayes strikes me as being a man of the world. He'll understand your obligations to your ma and to the carriage-yard. He will!'

'Maybe.' Mary smiled wanly. 'He'll also be of the opinion that he comes second to it all. Not strictly true, though I can understand the reasoning.'

Not *strictly* true, though his assumption that she could just drop everything and go rushing off to him had sparked a small flame of resentment. *He* was the one who had upped and left. He was the one who had promised to return, 'as soon as he had got things sorted.' Well, 'things' seemed very much sorted at Wisconsin, so where was Kester?

'Oh, why did he have to go sailing off to America?' she just blurted out. 'Why couldn't he have stayed here and helped me build up Sutton's?'

'You know why, Miss Mary love. He did what he felt he had to do.'

'But Kester was settled here. Good at his job and liked and respected by the men. We'd be married by now, living at the cottage and happy. Life would have been straightforward.'

'Life ain't never straightforward,' said Dorcas in the Cockney voice that was as broad as ever despite her years away from her native city. 'Look at me and my Ned. Ages us have got to wait afore we can marry. Sometimes Ned and me—'

'Go on.'

Dorcas blushed. 'Well, we play this game. Silly really. We pretend Ned's got a little holding like the widow's, and him and me's all set up cosy together. Ned working on the land and seeing to the animals, me doing the house and the dairy.'

Mary blinked in surprise. 'A farmer? Ned?'

'He likes the land. Ned says he's always had a hankering to have his own acres. He told his father as much once. Seems the Mester nigh on hit the roof.'

'I should think he did,' Mary said spiritedly. 'Though looking back, Ned always was good with the animals. Milking and gathering eggs were never a chore to him. Well well, Ned, a farmer! Don't know about you though, Dorcas. A townswoman, tied to a muddy farmyard and animals?'

'Wouldn't bother me. I'd have Ned and maybe his childer. For me, that would be everything.'

Her gentle logic brought a lump to Mary's throat. 'Oh, Dorcas, you make it sound so right.'

''Tis right,' Dorcas said stoutly. 'Though I'm sure the mistress doesn't think so. The mistress doesn't think I'm good enough for Ned.'

Mary snorted. 'Listen to you! Mother thinks you're heaven sent. She can't praise you enough.'

'As a housemaid, yes. A future daughter-in-law's different. I'll allow the Suttons are not ones to give themselves airs and graces, but the mistress does have a point. Her son, marrying an orphanage girl?'

'It's what you are that matters, not who you are.'

'Maybe, but there's limits. Ned stands to inherit all this one day, remember.'

'Yes,' Mary said, and wondered not for the first time what she was doing sacrificing her happiness for a firm that was not hers, and never would be.

Kester shivered in the slicing cold of the snow-swept Wisconsin valley and let himself into the cosy warmth of the cabin.

'George. You're up then. How are you feeling?'

'Better, I guess.' George flung down his pen, rose from the big scrubbed table where he had been wrestling with the accounts and went to the fire. Office duties never were his line. George was more a man to work with his hands. But Kester knew how desperately his brother wanted to pull his weight in the business, and felt it politic to let him struggle on.

'Damn and blast this chest of mine!' George muttered wheezily, chucking more logs on the fire that already blazed fit to roast an ox in the vast stone fireplace. Over the flames a cauldron of stew rich with beef and root vegetables simmered fragrantly. Of the lady of the house there was no sign, though Kester knew that Lisbeth would not be far away.

'Won't be sorry when spring comes,' George continued. 'Bit of sunshine, and I'll be back in the forge where I belong.'

'Sure you will,' Kester said, holding his hands to the blaze. 'It was a mistake coming out here so soon. I realised that on the boat over. It was too much after all you'd been through. Then that long trail by wagon, and having to get the cabin up once we'd staked our claim on the land.' He shook his head in self reproof. 'Crazy! Should have waited, taken you back to Aston Cross and let you get your strength back.'

'Get away. You did what seemed right at the time and I appreciate it. D'you pick up that iron for the forge?'

'Yep. Took the horse and wagon at first light. Be a good thing when they get the railroad built, save all this journeying by road for supplies.'

George nodded towards the window where the heavy wooden shutters had been fastened back for the day. 'Better fetch a double load next time,' he said. 'There's another new customer, by the look of it.'

Outside, on the wide square yard which had been swept clear of snow, two sturdy dray-horses were being let out of the shafts of a farm wagon. Black columns of smoke belched from the chimney of the forge – a stout building three times the size of the one at Aston Cross – where the man they had taken on as farrier was fettling the new iron shoes for the horses.

'Grand, eh? To think it's our own patch,' George went on. 'We'd never have managed it back home. We'd have been slogging for someone else for the rest of our lives.'

'True. Not sorry you came, then?'

'What do you think? It's a grand country, this. Big. Free. You've got space to breathe. Look at the lad, how well and strong he's growing. Look how he's fitted in here, like a duck to water. Lisbeth too.'

'What's that about me?' said Lisbeth, bustling into the room with a laden basket of laundry to be ironed. She had put on a little weight and there was new colour in her cheeks. In her full-skirted mulberry woollen gown and crisp white pinafore she looked a typical New World matron and Kester threw her a grin of affection.

'Just commenting on how well you've all settled in,' he said.

Putting down the laundry basket on the dresser that took up the whole of one wall, Lisbeth picked up a long-handled ladle and went to sample the stew. She added more salt and an extra pinch of herbs, then she turned and met George's eye. 'Shall we tell him?'

George nodded. 'Go on then.'

'Kester, it's glad news.' Lisbeth blushed prettily. 'I'm with child. Come June, there'll be a new little brother or sister for Georgie. Isn't it wonderful? Just when I thought I'd never have any more.'

A welter of various emotions surged through Kester. Gladness for them both, of course. Fear, for Lisbeth was in her early thirties and Willow Creek was pretty isolated as yet. No proper doctor, no trained midwife or resident nurse. Not even a skilled herbwoman like Widow Goodyear back home – what a different world that seemed, and how achingly far away.

But above all he felt an echo of that earlier envy he had tried hard to quench. They were a family, a unit. And he was an outsider. All right, he had done his bit to help. Now he felt out of it. Was it always going to be like this?

'Well, say something,' George said.

Kester went and kissed Lisbeth on the cheek. 'I'm very happy for you. Fresh start, new life – couldn't be better. Just have a care, that's all. No more lifting rucks of firewood and heavy buckets.' He paused, then forcing a note of joviality he was far from feeling, he said, 'We'll be short on accommodation. Happen it's time I moved on. Come spring, you'll be wanting my room for Georgie anyway.'

Currently the boy slept on a truckle bed in his parents' bedchamber. They had planned to build an extra room as soon as the weather improved. Now it looked as if they needed a nursery as well.

'Listen to you!' Lisbeth said. 'And the babe not due for months yet. This is your home as much as ours, Kester. Always will be. Unless—' She paused, uncertainty clouding her wide brown eyes. 'Mary hasn't changed her mind?'

'About coming out here?' Kester's swarthy face tightened. 'No. Wasn't even a consideration. Well, there's the carriage-yard. Ned won't be taking over for a good while yet. And there's Lilian. Mary takes her responsibilities seriously.'

'But she loves you,' Lisbeth said. 'She'll want to be with you, whether it's here or back in the old country. Kester, if you want to return—'

'No!' George put a silencing arm around his wife and sent Kester a look of raw appeal. 'The lass has waited this long. Another few months won't make any difference. Give it until the end of summer, Kester. The babe will be born by then and thriving, please God. And Hayes Smithy will be better established. I'll be fitter, more able to cope.'

Kester rubbed his chin thoughtfully with his hand. He had been contemplating a journey home come June. There was much he wanted to say to Mary that could not be put into a letter – he never had been good at penning. But as George said, a few more months were neither here nor there.

'All right,' he said. 'I'll leave it till the fall.'

'There you are, Mary,' Charles Rossiter said from the big wide doorway of the stable block. 'I've been looking for you.'

'I was giving Brownie his apple.'

Mary patted the old pony's neck and came out of the stall to join Charles. It was raining, a light drizzle, and the man's greatcoat and greying brown hair were misted with droplets. Already the damp April evening was thickening to dusk. The hens had gone to roost early and from the barn came the plaintive lowing of the house-cow wanting her calf.

'Shall we go into the house.' Charles offered his arm. 'Want a word. It concerns the future.'

He seemed ill at ease and as Mary was escorted across the yard her heart began to thump alarmingly. The loan; he wanted it repaid. Charles had a finger in many pies. At his own insistence he had supplied the sum interest-free. Plainly he wished now to invest in a more lucrative project.

In the parlour, Lilian was seated on the brown plush sofa in front of a crackling fire. She glanced up edgily as they entered and started at once to fuss. 'Mary. Your gown is quite damp. You should have put on your cape.'

'It's nothing, just drizzle,' Mary said.

Charles, having shed his greatcoat in the hall, went and stood in his accustomed place with his back to the fire.

He said to Lilian, 'I've told Mary we wanted a little chat.' And to Mary. 'Come and sit down, m'dear. You look a bit chilled.'

His voice was too hearty and Mary's alarm grew. Struggling for calm, she seated herself beside Lilian and gazed expectantly from one to the other. Charles flung a glance at Lilian as if for support, took a breath and blurted, 'Fact is Lilian and I have grown mighty fond of each other over the past months. I've asked her to marry me and she's accepted.'

'Oh!' gasped Mary.

A wave of embarrassed colour swept over Lilian's normally pale cheeks. 'It's been a while since Tobias passed on, Mary love. And Charles and I … well, we feel at ease together.'

Mary's mind was whirling. All thoughts of loans and business propositions had fled, to be replaced by another, more raw emotion. She said, a bit awkwardly, 'This is wonderful news. Couldn't be better. Congratulations – I'm really pleased.'

She meant it, every word. She was altogether happy for her step-mother and for Charles. But oh, Mary cried silently and passionately, why couldn't her own path be equally as smooth? Why wasn't Kester here now, rejoicing with her? Why, added that small voice that could not be ignored, couldn't they be forming their own wedding plans too?

With a huge effort Mary smiled brilliantly into the two anxious faces before her. 'Wonderful,' she repeated. 'I wish you both every happiness.'

Lilian gave a glad little laugh and embraced Mary. 'There now, Mary love.' They kissed and hugged, and Charles looked on benev-olently and with obvious relief.

At that moment there was a tap on the door and Dorcas appeared. 'I'm sorry for intruding, ma'am, but young William Henry refuses to go to sleep without his goodnight kiss. I've told him his mama will be up shortly, but the young sir insists.'

A loud wailing from the upper regions of the house gave substance to Dorcas's words. Lilian sprang to her feet, skirts rustling. 'My poor lamb, in all the confusion I quite forgot. Charles, Mary, do excuse me. Coming, my precious.'

She swept out. Dorcas followed, closing the door gently behind them. Mary made a wry face. 'Little tyke! He's getting spoilt.' She rose and went across the brown and green patterned carpet to Charles and took his big warm hands in hers. 'Charles. When you came seeking me out, I was worried it might be the loan. I thought you wanted it repaid.'

'What? My dear girl, that such a thing should ever have entered your head!' He squeezed her hands affectionately and then released her. 'You *are* glad for us?'

'I am.'

'Not fretting I might be trying to take your dear father's place? Truly?'

'Truly.'

Some of the concern left the man's face. He said, 'You know, I never thought after my dear late wife passed on, that I'd ever contemplate marrying again. But the wound heals. The scar doesn't and you wouldn't want it to, but life travels on, as they say.'

'Yes.'

'Right from the start I took to Lilian,' Charles blundered on, magnanimous in his gratitude that Mary had taken things so well. 'She's a grand woman. Level-headed, kindly. The sort any man would be proud to call his wife.'

'I'm sure,' Mary said, feeling her own anguish and loneliness rising again in her throat. Firmly she swallowed it down. 'Have you decided upon a date yet?'

'Rather sooner than later, we thought. Well, we're neither of us spring chickens. Doesn't seem any point in dragging out the engagement.'

'This year, then. Er, have you told Alice?'

His eyes twinkled. 'Not yet. Thought as the eldest it was your due to know first.'

Mary blushed and cast down her eyes in confusion. 'Charles, I … there's something—'

'Don't bother about that, m'dear. Lilian has taken me into her confidence, though only very recently, I hasten to add. Makes no difference to me what your background is. Why should it? All families have their secrets and you've proved a first-class daughter to Lilian in every way. If the world looks upon you as the child of Lilian and Tobias, then so be it.'

Mary lifted her head and pecked a kiss on Charles's be-whiskered cheek. 'Bless you, Charles. I can't think of a nicer stepfather. And what a good thing for little William Henry. Oh, this calls for a celebration.'

'A nip of my best port? I've brought some with me.'

'Mother never drinks port.'

'Today she does. Today she'll drink her port with the rest of us. And come the weekend, I'm treating you all to luncheon at that hotel that Esme and Perry rated so highly.'

'The Hillcrest?'

'The very one. Are you in agreement?'

'Oh, indeed I am.'

Lilian's step could be heard on the stair. Smiling broadly, Charles went to the china cabinet and began to take out the best crystal tumblers in readiness.

Arrangements went ahead for the wedding. Midsummer was decided upon. It left precious little space for preparations, but as Charles said it was second time round for both of them, so a quiet gathering would suffice. In the end they plumped for a ceremony in Lilian's beloved chapel, followed by a reception at Beamsters.

'Thirty guests at the last count!' said Dorcas, in a panic at being in charge of the wedding breakfast. 'How many fowl and what weight round of beef do I order for thirty? Are Miss Esme – I mean, Lord and Lady Sayle invited?'

'Yes,' said Mary. 'Of course they are.'

'Game pie as well, then.' The maid wrung her hands together in growing dismay. 'Lord Perry does so love his game pie, and you have to get the balance of herbs just right or it tastes all wrong. Then there's the cake. How in heaven's name am I supposed to make it in time? A good plum cake needs at least six months to mature. It does!'

'Just ask Mother, Dorcas,' said Violet soothingly from the table where she was cutting out her gown. Violet had insisted on making it herself, even though Charles had insisted they attended the best seamstress Ludlow could offer for the making of the wedding finery.

'Ask the mistress to make her own bridal feast?' Dorcas repeated, scandalised. 'The very idea!'

Alice looked up from penning one of her many lists. 'Mary. Have you told Kester?'

'No, not yet. No time, to be honest. I've scarcely had a minute to eat a meal, let alone write letters. What with the equipment for the new workshop needing chasing, and then having to go into Ludlow to the accountant – these yearly audits are a perfect pain, and they come round so quickly – I don't know whether I'm on my head or my heels.'

'Kester must be told,' Alice said, primly.

'Must get word off to Kester,' Mary said later to her stepmother. 'Alice keeps on at me, but I've so much else to say to him as well. I need time to put it all down.'

She sounded wistful and Lilian looked up sharply from the hymn list she was compiling. 'It's been a while since you heard from America. There's nothing wrong, is there, Mary?'

'Not as such. It's all so … so unsatisfactory. Here's you and Charles, on the verge of getting wed, and I don't even know for sure if Kester's coming back to me. Sometimes I think he'll never come back. He's had a change of heart and doesn't know how to tell me.'

'Oh, Mary my dear.' Lilian abandoned the wedding hymns and came to Mary's side. 'You must never doubt him. A man of Kester's ilk does not go back on his word. Nor will his feelings for you die. If anything, they will deepen. Make time to write him, Mary. Send him your love. Mine too. Tell him how joyful I am to be given this second chance of happiness. I'm very fond of Kester, you know.'

'I do know. I'll write at the weekend. Promise.'

But Saturday brought a multiple order for kitchen stools from a furniture wholesaler in Ludlow, and Mary was at her desk late, working out the best deal for both sides. When Sunday came, she yawned through the minister's sermon – a particularly conscience-smiting one based on attention to others – and after a vast lunch, sheer weariness overcame her and she dozed off to sleep.

Monday and the start of yet another hectic week was upon her before she knew it, and the letter still had not been written.

'Our Mary's worked off her feet,' Alice said to John in the school playground. It was noon. Wet April had given way to sunny May and the children were making the most of it, eating their bread, onion and hard cheese, whatever their mothers could spare, sitting on the school wall in the sunshine.

'Working hard seems to be a feature of the Sutton females.' John sent Alice an appraising look. 'You don't exactly shirk yourself.'

Alice allowed herself a small smile. She had taken to wearing spectacles for her short sight. The round frames and wire rims which did little for many, rather served to enhance Alice's sharp features and drew attention to her intelligent hazel eyes. Violet, with her flair for fashion, had made up Alice's school skirt in a fine grey linen and pin-tucked the front of her white cotton blouse. The outfit, though plain, gave Alice's angular figure a certain dash.

'It's the wedding,' Alice said. 'There's such a lot to do. Even a small gathering has to be properly organised.'

'Yes.' John's eyes twinkled. 'When it's our turn, remind me to whisk you off somewhere to get the knot tied. Saves all this fuss and bother.'

Alice sent him a look of reproof, but she was laughing. 'I haven't said yes yet.'

'You will,' John said. 'You can't resist my charms. And think what a future we shall have. We'll invest in a big house and turn it into a school. With your English skills and my science, we cannot go wrong.'

'Meantime, there's Mother's wedding to arrange.'

'Quite. Well, if I can be of assistance—'

'You can,' Alice said. 'You can drive her to Chapel. Violet wants to decorate the carriage with ribbons and posies of flowers. Should look quite fetching. The guest list has risen to forty – and I bet Mary hasn't written yet to Kester.'

'Might be as well to drop him a line yourself.'

'I will,' Alice said. 'I'll do it tonight. Save Mary the bother.'

The letter when she started was not easy to compose. Alice was not one for gossip and frivolity and she had to summon up all her resources to make the missive bright and chatty.

'Dear Kester,' she wrote. 'You will be surprised to be hearing from me, Alice, instead of Mary. I know that communication has been somewhat haphazard between you and Mary of late, due to your being so occupied with your Forge and Mary so wrapped up in the home firm.

'So I thought I would let you know how events are progressing here. Such an exciting time, Kester, and such bustle' – Alice rather liked that bit, it sounded light-hearted, quite girlish in fact – 'what with plans for the wedding going ahead at such a pace. As you would expect, Mr Rossiter has been exceptionally thoughtful and generous. He insists upon funding the wedding breakfast himself and has enlisted the services of a professional dressmaker for us all. Mother has chosen lilac silk for her gown. Mary is to wear cream brocade and Violet and myself as Maids of Honour are in harebell blue. Very grand we shall all look too.

'It would be lovely if you (and your brother and Lisbeth and young Georgie, of course) could be present and enjoy the celebrations with us, Kester. Though I know it is nigh impossible, with so many miles of land and ocean between us. I expect you are a hardened New Englander now. I do admire the pioneer spirit and often wonder whether John might be interested in emigrating and starting his own schoolhouse in your New World.

'Has Mary told you about John? He is from Hereford and teaches at the same school as myself. We have much in common and have been walking out for some time now. Once we get the wedding over with I might sound him out regarding my thoughts on the matter of pastures new. Mother will always have Violet close by, for Violet has vowed never to leave Aston Cross ever. Isn't that so like her?'

Alice chewed the end of her pen for a few moments, dipped again into the ink and added a few sentences about herself and how she was enjoying being a pupil teacher. She mentioned Ned and Dorcas in passing, wished Kester and family well and signed herself, 'Respectfully yours, Alice Sutton.'

'Phew!'

With some relief, Alice folded the letter into an envelope, wrote the address in her neat hand and left it on the desk to be posted later.

'Penny for them, my love?'

Esme turned where she sat on the pretty French sofa to smile with amused affection at her husband as he entered the room.

'Ah, home at last, Perry. You and your politics. I vow they are taking you over.'

'Not quite,' Perry said, coming to sit beside her.

'Well, that's a relief! In fact before you came in I was musing on Mary and Kester. No doubt Mary will have told him about the wedding, and how happy Lilian is. Might be just what's needed to give Kester the necessary nudge. It's disgraceful, the way he's keeping my girl dangling.'

Perry laughed. 'Esme, since becoming a married lady you have got to be quite the matchmaker.'

'Haven't. This is Mary. I don't like to think of her stuck in the country, working in that stuffy office.'

'But she loves it. She's proud of her achievement, and justly so. Sutton's would have gone under, but for Mary.'

'Yes, yes.' Esme flapped her lace-edged fan at him dismissively. 'Seems a shameful waste of talent to me. Good voice, good dancer, good looking. If she cannot be married to Kester – and it looks as if this is the case – she'd be better making a career on the stage. She'll grow old and spinsterish, pouring over those accounts day after day.'

'Her choice,' Perry said. 'Shame Kester can't be here for the wedding, though.'

'That Kester!' Esme's green eyes flashed. 'If only I could talk with him. Confront him. Point out that his place is at Mary's side, not pioneering on the other side of the world. I'd tell him! I'd be my most dramatic self!'

Perry mocked a little grimace. 'Poor fellow!'

'Not at all. Kester Hayes is too single minded for his own good. All very well being noble and so on. What about my Mary? She's pining her heart out for him.'

'If you say so, my love,' Perry said. 'Now, about the arrangements for the dinner party in aid of the Liberal movement ...'

With the pincers Kester picked up the length of white-hot plough chains and flung them with a hiss into a barrel of cold water to cool. Steam billowed, clearing. Kester took up a grubby kerchief and mopped his sweating brow. Bye, but it was hot. No happy medium in this country. It was either cold enough to freeze your clothes on to your back or too sweltering to think straight. Working in the smithy was fine in winter, but come summer he could think of better places.

Kester grinned ruefully. Four in the morning he started, to get the bulk of the smelting done before the sun got too high.

Shutting the doors on the glowing heart of the furnace, Kester left the baking heat of the forge and went down to the lake. First he cast a satisfied glance back at the new extension to the cabin which doubled their living space. Then he cupped his hands into the rippling water and drank deeply, before splashing some coolingly over his hot face and torso.

'Uncle Kester! Hey, Uncle Kester!'

Georgie came sprinting out of the cabin – a very different Georgie, taller, filled out, sun-browned. He was waving a fistful of mail.

'Post for you, Uncle Kester. Ma says there's one from the old country!'

'That'll be from Mary.' Eagerly Kester took the bundle and ruffled Georgie's dark head. 'Thanks, lad.'

'There's Mark and Jimmie. I'm away to school now. Uncle Kester. When I get back, will you take me riding? I can saddle Rocky myself.'

'Aye, right-o.' Kester was studying the handwriting on the envelope from England. It was not Mary's and he felt a prickling of unease.

'Can we go to the canyon?'

'Aye. Wherever. There's the school bell. You'd best get along, lad.'

''Bye Uncle Kester.'

Georgie had not reached his waiting schoolmates before Kester had ripped open the envelope.

It was from Alice.

Rapidly Kester ran his eye over the page. His heart started to thud uncomfortably and his breath came in painful gasps. A wedding? Mary, getting wed and never told him? There had to be some mistake.

He read the letter again, but again the words blazed up at him.

'Mary is to wear cream brocade ...'

Mary, stitching her bridal dress and never even breathing a word of it to him. And as for that two-timing Charles Rossiter!

Sheer all-consuming rage boiled up within Kester and burst out of his mouth in a roar. He crumpled the pages up in his fist, rammed the other post – mostly smithy business – into his pocket and set off at a race of knots for the house.

Lisbeth was at the kitchen table, kneading dough for bread. She looked up in alarm as Kester barged in.

'Kester? What's wrong?'

'It's Mary,' he choked. 'You can tell George to quit worrying about coping alone. Mary's found someone else. I won't be going back, Lisbeth. Looks like I'm here for good.'

Twelve

∽

'**O**h my!' cried Violet as the wedding guests all gathered on the front porch of Beamsters to wave the glad couple off. 'Doesn't Mother look fetching in her going-away suit? Don't they make a handsome couple?'

'They do indeed,' Mary said, smiling.

Alice, her arm through John Black's, edged them both along a little, the better to see the happy pair. 'I'm pleased for Mother. It was a lovely wedding, wasn't it, John?'

John, running his free hand inside his stiffly-starched collar to ease the discomfort, murmured an agreement. 'Lucky with the weather. Midsummer doesn't always turn up trumps, but today's been glorious.'

'I vow I don't know when I've enjoyed myself so much.' Esme, in russet, emeralds sparkling at her ears and throat, trilled a little laugh. 'It's all been so pleasant. The chapel, the villagers, the reception. This lovely old house. There's a sense of belonging in the country you never get in town.'

Perry smiled down at his wife with affection. 'What a change of heart. Would you have us say our vows again and hold the ceremony from here?'

'It's really of no consequence.' Esme patted his arm with a

gloved hand and slid him a coquettish look under long lashes. 'So long as the groom is the same.'

'Flattered ma'am, I'm sure,' her husband returned agreeably.

'There they go,' said Ned. At his side Dorcas dabbed away a tear.

''Bye,' they all shouted . 'Good luck!'

Charles circled the brougham around the pebbled forecourt, flourished his whip manfully and sent the horses scuttering away down the drive. Beside him in the passenger seat, Lilian clung on to her feathered hat – a great concession on her part, since she had never been known to wear anything more lavish than a poke bonnet – and twisted round to smile and wave to them all. Reaching the gates, they turned out on to the lane and were gone from sight.

They were heading for the railway station, and thence to Brighton. It transpired that Lilian had once visited the resort years ago when she had been in London caring for an invalid aunt, and had confessed to being much impressed by the place. As a surprise, Charles had booked lodging in Melbourne Streets, just off the promenade, for a whole fortnight.

'I do wish the mistress and Mr Rossiter all the very best,' said Dorcas rather belatedly. Everyone laughed, and they all trooped back into the house, the menfolk to their cigars and their port, the ladies to partake of a good strong cup of tea.

After the main body of guests had departed the family, together with Esme and Perry and John Black, gathered together in the parlour. The evening was warm, no call for a fire and the arrangement of yellow roses in the empty grate filled the room with their sweetness.

'La, how gratifying to take the weight off one's feet,' Esme said, plumping down on a well-worn brown-plush sofa.

From upstairs came the furious wail of William Henry, left in the hands of his sisters for the duration and already missing his mama.

'Listen to the lad,' Dorcas said, coming in with the supper. 'I've sung to him, told him a story, begged and threatened. But will he go off to sleep? No!'

'The little cherub,' cooed Esme, besotted.

'That's a misnomer, your ladyship,' said Ned with a grin. 'My small brother is spoilt. Too many women fussing over him, in my opinion. I only hope Charles will sort him out, before Mother has a brat on her hands.'

Esme pouted. 'True, it never does to over-indulge a child. But William Henry is such a charmer. And please, let us drop the formalities. Out of Town we are happy and honoured to be treated as the family friends we hope we are and addressed by our first names. Is that not so, Perry?'

'Indeed it is,' agreed Perry beside her. He accepted the coffee Dorcas handed round, but refused a roast ham and chutney sandwich on the grounds that if he swallowed another morsel he would burst the buttons of his new waistcoat!

Dorcas giggled and set the plate down at Ned's elbow, knowing he could do justice to food however full his stomach. She then went up to the nursery and William Henry.

Mary, sitting apart on a low chair near the window embrasure, had not missed the swiftly loving glance Dorcas had exchanged with Ned. Opposite on another sofa, Alice sat ramrod straight beside John Black. Mary suspected her sister's stays were killing her, Alice having put on a little weight lately. Her face had filled out too, softening her sharp features and making her almost pretty.

Or maybe love was the cause. Certainly her attitude towards John was telling, and for an instant Mary's smile slipped. Everyone was pairing off. Even Violet, young as she was, appeared to have given her affections to Chips. She, Mary, had no-one.

And after Kester, not the trustworthy man she had supposed,

Mary was not prepared to risk her heart again. Why, he had not even sent Mother a wedding acknowledgement. The gall of it.

Lilian returned from Brighton as mistress of Elmwood, a large double fronted house built of good red brick that Charles had bought for them. Elmwood was in Ludlow and had every modern contrivance, from gas lighting upstairs as well as down to proper indoor water closets. The kitchen was what every housewife dreamed of and the living rooms were lofty and light. Servants had been well accommodated at the top of the house and there was a small room off the hallway which Charles intended for a study. Lilian proudly displayed her sewing room, south facing and bright, a great improvement on having to make do with a spare bedroom as in the past.

Mary, taken on a tour of the property, came very close to envying her stepmother her new home. 'Oh my,' she said, shown the bathroom and taking in the shining white porcelain bath with gleaming brass taps that gushed cold and hot water simply by turning them on. No more breaking the ice on the water jug of a frosty winter morning, no more running up and down the stairs with pitchers of hot water for baths. 'After Beamsters, this must be pure luxury.'

'Oh, of course I'm delighted, though I never thought ill of Beamsters,' Lilian said, flushed and eager as a girl. She had caught the sun and the sea breezes had whipped some colour into her normally pale cheeks. 'Come downstairs again. You must be gasping for tea. Fancy me having a full time cook and housemaid! I said it wasn't necessary, but Charles insisted. Did I mention he has taken William Henry riding? I thought he was a bit young, but Charles begged to differ.'

They went down the stairway which smelled of new paint and the wool carpet patterned in red and blue, Lilian still chatting away, Mary making careful responses.

Of course, Lilian's taste in furnishing still veered to the practical with a great deal of dark brown paint and brown curtains. Privately Mary preferred the pale colours and delicate furniture in the French style of Esme's London home, though she was tactful enough not to say it.

Suddenly finding herself mistress of Beamsters was turning out a mixed blessing. Mary loved her old home but was not blind to its drawbacks. No matter how much polishing and dusting it received, the wear and tear of decades of family life was all too evident and Mary wished she could wave a magic wand and have it refurbished like this one. 'I shan't be sorry when Ned finishes his apprentice-ship and comes home,' she confided as they reached the tiled hallway. 'The house needs attention, and I don't feel qualified to have it done on his behalf. Anyway, I'm too busy in the office. Dorcas sends her regards, by the way.'

'Dear Dorcas. Is she well? I expect she misses William Henry.'

'She does, and yes, she is in good health.'

Dorcas had been torn between accompanying Lilian to Elmwood and remaining at Beamsters with Mary. But loyalty to her first mistress burned fiercely, and despite impassioned pleas from William Henry, in the end Dorcas stayed put.

'I do miss her,' Lilian said, leading the way into the drawing room and ringing the bell for tea. 'I think Ned had much to do with Dorcas's decision not to leave,' she finished, gesturing to the new horsehair sofa for them both to be seated.

Mary stared at her, startled. 'You knew?'

'Suspected,' laughed Lilian. 'I'm not blind, you know. I noticed the sparks between them. I was quite hurt when Dorcas said nothing.'

'She thought you wouldn't approve, Mother. She feels she isn't good enough for Ned.'

'What nonsense. Dorcas will make Ned an excellent wife. Dear me, doesn't life move on? John Black has asked for Alice's hand.

They've got plans to set up school together. And I always thought Alice would be the one to remain at home.'

'Instead of me, you mean.' Mary's voice was bleak and Lilian squeezed her hand. 'Mary. I meant nothing of the sort. Your day will come.'

Mary shook her head. 'No, I don't think so,' she said stonily.

'Mary—'

Lilian was interrupted by the slam of a door somewhere in the nether regions of the house and Charles's booming voice, accompanied by William Henry's excited patter. A moment later they burst into the room, bringing with them the good outdoor smells of fresh air and horses.

Lilian smiled at her husband. 'Charles. We have a visitor.'

'So I see. No, don't get up, m'dear. I've already told Agnes to put an extra cup out.' Charles bent to kiss his wife and turned to Mary. 'Mary, grand to see you.'

'And you, Charles.'

Lilian held out her arms to her little son. 'There, my precious. Time for your afternoon nap, I think.'

William Henry stuck like glue to Charles. 'Don't want to. Want to ride Cobby.'

'Listen to the lad.' Charles ruffled the small boy's dark hair. 'Not yet three and already a confirmed jockey! Cobby's done enough for one day, young Will. Having to carry a great lad like you on his back has quite worn him out. Do as your mama tells you and have a rest, and maybe tomorrow we'll go out again.'

William Henry stood his ground, a small defiant figure, then saw that his new papa was not going to give in and went obediently to his mother.

'There's my boy,' Lilian said.

The maid came in with the tea and Mary offered to do the honours while Lilian saw to the boy.

'How's business?' Charles enquired when they were alone.

'Satisfactory, according to the accountant.'

'Big relief, eh? You know when everything is going well, but it's good to see it in black and white. Ned's a lucky fellow.'

'I think Ned is more taken with Dorcas than his inheritance at present. They spent a lot of time walking out together when he was over for the wedding.'

Lilian came back into the room on the end of this. 'Dear me, was that quite proper?'

Charles and Mary laughed. 'They were only visiting Widow Goodyear, Mother. She's looking her age, I fear.'

'Hard work, a farmstead, even with Chips doing the heavy stuff.' Charles picked up the newspaper. 'See there's a new Conway musical out in the West End. *Summer Secret.*'

Mary brightened. Max Conway's fame had spread. This was his fourth show, the previous ones all well received by the critics. 'Oh, is there? I'd love to see it.'

'What's stopping you?' Charles peered at her over the paper. 'Get yourself down to the City for a few days. Stop with Esme and Perry. I'll stand in for you at the yard, no problem.'

'Oh Charles, would you?'

'Mind you have Dorcas accompany you,' Lilian put in.

'I'll do it.' Mary stiffened her spine. 'Now, while Alice is home and the school is still closed for the summer. I'll write to Esme the minute I get home.'

She thanked Charles for his offer and allowed Lilian to refill her cup, well pleased.

Reply came from Esme by return. Yes, she and Perry would be delighted to receive Mary. Perry had booked tickets for the performance and they would expect Mary and her maid on the twelfth.

It was August now and sun-baked, and as the train rushed through the parched countryside Dorcas studied her young mistress. Mary looked too solemn, she felt. London might be hot and airless, but the change would do her good. It struck her that it had been a long time since she had heard Mary humming a song in that way she had. Unhappy, that's what. And all because of that Kester!

'Miss, I was wondering how Mrs Lisbeth and young Georgie were making out lately,' Dorcas broached. 'You've not had word?'

Mary's face tightened. 'No, Dorcas. I haven't. I expect Lisbeth is too busy to write.'

'And ... Mr Kester?'

'You know the answer to that. Stop dropping hints, Dorcas. Please.' Mary pursed her lips and fixed her gaze firmly on the passing scenery. Dorcas sighed. It was no good, Miss Mary's hurt went too deep. She wondered if her ladyship could help and decided to approach her if the opportunity arose.

It came sooner than Dorcas could have hoped. The Sayles, it turned out, were in the process of moving to a bigger house in Richmond, 15 Nightingale Square being rather small for entertaining.

'You should have said.' Mary looked in dismay at the half-packed boxes and cases littering the top landing. 'I would never have imposed upon you had I known.'

'Mary, you are never an imposition.' Esme linked her arm in her daughter's. 'I might borrow Dorcas for the day. What if Perry takes you off to see the sights, and Dorcas lends a hand here? She always was a clever packer and she can put me in touch with news as well. You know how insatiably nosy I am.'

'Your ladyship,' Dorcas said next day, disposing a bundle of neatly-folded linen into a box. 'It's Miss Mary, ma'am. She's so unhappy it hurts me to see her. She don't sing no more and rarely laughs. Pining for Mr Kester, she is, and won't admit it. Won't even talk about it. I did wonder if there was anything your ladyship could do, if you please.'

Esme looked thoughtful and the maid held her breath. Normally, Dorcas knew, she would have been frosted for taking liberties, but this was different. This was her ladyship's dear girl, and Dorcas had no doubt that something would be done.

'Thank you for mentioning it, Dorcas,' Esme said. 'If you wouldn't mind starting on the second-best linen, I shall go and get ready for tonight. Perry's booked a box. Some music and dancing might be the very thing to cheer Mary up, don't you know.'

Held at the Shaftesbury Theatre, *Summer Secret* was a truly splendid show. The performance was beyond words and when the music sang from Mary's lips all the way home in the carriage, Esme's heart gave a little flip of hope.

There had been no opportunity so far to convey her worries over Mary to Perry, but that night, curled warmly in his arms in their big, comfortable bed, she told him what Dorcas had said.

'Thought Mary looked a bit down in the mouth,' Perry commented. 'Do I detect a scheme brewing, my love?'

'I'd like to tell Kester exactly what I think of him.'

Perry groaned. 'Poor fellow. Good thing there's a fair drop of water between him and you, otherwise the fur would be flying.'

'It would indeed.'

'You know,' Perry said, suddenly serious. 'Mary's a grown woman. Can't interfere too much, Esme, no matter how good the intentions.'

'You mean I should leave it?'

'Didn't say that. Just issuing a warning, that's all.' He yawned widely and a moment later was asleep.

Esme lay wakeful. At length, hearing the church clock chime

three, she rose quietly, pulled on her peignoir and tiptoed down-stairs. In the parlour she sat down at her escritoire, took up pen and writing paper and began to sketch a letter.

Kester swung down from his horse in the yard and surveyed the crimson and gold of the surrounding forested slopes without a glimmer of pleasure. At one time the fall held him entranced. Not any more. Rather it reminded of the coming winter, snow, ice and hardship. Shrugging, he led the horse into the stall and untacked and rubbed the animal down. Throwing him a wedge of hay, he made for the house. Now four times the size it had been, Hayes Lodge, as their home was called, was an imposing timber building with steep roofs, tall stone chimney stacks and a verandah which caught the evening sun. Kester entered this way, picking up the letter he found waiting for him on the hall table and taking it through to the kitchen.

Lisbeth sat at the hearth, rocking her small daughter in her cradle. Lilian Mary, named at some heartache to Kester, had been born prematurely and for a while her tiny life had hung in the balance. Now the child, dubbed May by her father, was thriving and Lisbeth's happiness knew no bounds.

'Hello Kester. Did you manage to sort out the binder for them?' Lisbeth said.

'Aye. Cogs were jammed, that's all. For a farmer Jake Wells has got a lot to learn. Oh, don't look at me like that. I know he's young and inexperienced, but this was obvious, I'd have thought. Dragging me all the way out there for nothing!'

Today's batch of bread steamed fragrantly on the big central table and Kester, about to cut himself a slice, saw the Sayles seal on the letter in his hand and instead ripped it open.

What, he thought, could Esme have found to write to him about?

'For shame, Kester,' Lisbeth continued. 'You're becoming quite the old grump. Even Georgie complains he can't get a smile out of you these days.'

Her light voice rambled on, gently chiding. Kester, his eyes scanning the closely written lines on the page, heard none of it.

'I find myself truly nonplussed by your attitude, Kester,' Esme had written. 'Not being at your place at Mary's side for her stepmother's marriage to Charles Rossiter was bad enough, though I grant the distance you had to travel may explain it. But not even to acknowledge the event was inexcusable. I dread to think what Lilian must have thought, she who was always so quick to speak up for you.'

Lilian, married to Rossiter? But surely the bride had been his Mary? Alice had said as much in her letter. Or had she? The missive had gone straight on the back of the fire and Kester frowned trying to remember the precise words. Perhaps Alice had not made the facts clear.

A small seed of hope burst within him. He turned to Lisbeth, his face working soundlessly. Lisbeth broke off her admonishments. 'What is it, Kester? Not bad news?'

'Far from it,' Kester said, at last finding his voice. 'Lisbeth, I've been every kinda fool. It's from Lady Sayle, y'know, Esme Greer that was. She's given me the ticking off of my life and I deserve every word. If I've lost Mary, it's through my own pig-headedness. Here, you'd better read it.'

Having read the letter, Lisbeth pulled to her feet. 'You must go to her immediately, Kester. George will cope on his own and we can always hire a manager if need be. I'll pack your things.'

October mist hung low over the woods and Mary turned from the window with a sigh. How melancholy the autumn could be. Another visit to London might be no bad thing. But for her ties here, she wouldn't mind making her home there permanently. She'd have a pretty house like the one in Nightingale Square and visit the galleries and the theatre, and never, never tot up a row of figures in a ledger ever again!

Ned was here for the week, ostensibly to get himself in touch with the carriage and furniture business, in reality spending his time with Dorcas.

The hasty patter of feet brought Mary's head up and the door burst open to admit her maid. 'Oh Miss Mary, what do you think? Oh, mam, I couldn't believe it when I clapped eyes on him!'

Behind Dorcas a tall figure dressed with an American dash, a dark-grey waisted frock-coat with a high colour, was hanging up his top hat on the hall peg. At his feet was a big iron-bound travelling chest.

Mary stared, her heart thudding, her hands flying to her face.

'Kester!' she gasped.

'Hello Mary, love,' Kester said.

Much later they sat by the crackling fire, side by side, Mary gazing up at Kester as if her eyes would never get enough of the feast. A hasty family reunion had been summoned and Dorcas had done them proud, producing roast crown of lamb and an apple pie that melted in the mouth, to which the menfolk did full justice. Lilian wept over her – belated – wedding gift of a double-wedding-ring quilt in the best American tradition, and wept again when Kester apologised for what he called his slip of judgement.

'Oh, please say no more, dearest Kester,' Lilian said. 'Just to have you sitting here with us again is enough.'

Alice, mortified to think she had a part in the chapter of errors, kept biting her lip and appealing to John for support. In vain did Mary impress upon her that it didn't matter and events had turned out all right in the end. Alice said that such laxity was unforgivable, and in a schoolteacher too.

'I agree,' Kester said. 'For two pins I'd give you the thrashing you deserve, but John's a younger man than me and hardy, so maybe I won't risk it.'

Everyone laughed and the atmosphere lightened. Nothing mattered any more but that they were all gathered together as a family again, content and united. Well, not quite all. Esme and Perry had yet to be informed.

'I'm looking forward to that,' Mary said. 'Esme can have her dressmaker sew my wedding gown. Oh, Kester, I'm so happy I could cry!'

'Why women always snivel when they're happy I'll never fathom,' Ned said.

Mary sobered. 'Kester, I've just had a thought. Where shall we live? Not the cottage. I've rented it out to the new joiner – well, he's got a wife and babe and—'

'Mary. I'm a man of means now. I can afford to build you a house. Either we stay here and start up a business of our own – goodness knows what, but nothing's impossible now I've got you back. Or we can go to America.'

'Oh, no!' Lilian's sodden kerchief went again to her eyes. 'You've only just got here. Don't take Mary away, Kester.'

Ned cleared his throat. 'If I might put in a word?'

All eyes turned on him, stocky, red-cheeked, be-whiskered, the image of his dead father, Tobias. At his side Dorcas went suddenly still and pensive.

'You mightn't like what I'm going to say, Mother. On the other hand, you may agree that it's for the best. I don't want the business and I don't want Beamsters. Mary's put more into the place than I could ever do. It's her right that she inherits. Besides, the yard's not for me. I want to farm and Dorcas—' he raised her hand to his lips and kissed it '—is willing to toil alongside me.'

'Farm?' Lilian said. 'You, a farmer? But we have no land – at least, not enough to support you.'

Ned grinned. 'I'm leasing Widow Goodyear's holding, Mother – with your blessing, that is. The widow's through with farming. She's moving in with cousins at Ludlow. Chips is stopping on at the farm for the time being.'

'That's very sensible,' Violet put in gravely. 'Chips can teach you the ropes and still carry on working here for Mary and Kester. We'll be getting married when we're older, you know. We are not leaving Aston Cross, not for anything.'

'That's right, you tell them exactly how things stand,' Ned told his sister affectionately. He addressed his mother. 'Well, Mother, what do you say to having a farmer in the family?'

Eyes slid to Lilian. She glanced at Charles, who gave her a wink of support and encouragement. 'Well,' Lilian said. 'If Kester is agreeable to taking on the business, and Mary too of course, then who am I to object? Personally I can't think of anyone more appropriate. And I always told your father you were more into animals than woodwork, our Ned.'

They all started to talk at once and Dorcas clutched Ned's hand as if she would never let him go. Kester said to Mary, 'Sutton & Hayes. Sounds good, eh? Always was fond of this old house, though I dare say you'd prefer something more modern?'

'It really doesn't matter,' Mary said breathlessly. And it was true. She'd live in a cave, just so long as it was with Kester, and such love and joy surged up inside her she wanted the moment to last forever.

Now the guests had gone, the other young people had retired for the night and they were alone together. Kester put his arm around Mary. 'We'll update this house if you like. And we'll expand the business.'

'Oh?' Mary said. 'Doing what?'

'Sideline in wooden charms?' He pulled a funny face. 'Like lovespoons?'

'What a splendid idea,' Mary said, laughing. And then the laughter stopped as he kissed her, whilst outside a new moon rose over the tattered copses of the wood, bathing the house and yards and workshops with silvery light, brilliant, full of promise.